W9-BOF-604

Edited by Jack Dann & Gardner Dozois

FUTURE SPORTS

EDITED BY
JACK DANN & GARDNER DOZOIS

ACE BOOKS, NEW YORK

This is a work of fiction. Names, characters, places, and incidents either are the product of the author's imagination or are used fictitiously, and any resemblance to actual persons, living or dead, business establishments, events, or locales is entirely coincidental.

FUTURE SPORTS

An Ace Book / published by arrangement with
Jack Dann

PRINTING HISTORY
Ace mass-market edition / July 2002

Copyright © 2002 by Jack Dann.
Cover art by Ben Gibson.

Visit our website at
www.penguinputnam.com
Check out the ACE Science Fiction & Fantasy newsletter!

ISBN: 0-441-00961-1

ACE®
Ace Books are published by The Berkley Publishing Group, a division of Penguin Putnam Inc.,
375 Hudson Street, New York, New York 10014.
ACE and the "A" design
are trademarks belonging to Penguin Putnam Inc.

PRINTED IN THE UNITED STATES OF AMERICA

10 9 8 7 6 5 4 3 2 1

CONTENTS

PREFACE

Sports of one sort or another go back into distant prehistory, and have probably been around ever since something at least vaguely recognizable as a human being came down from the trees to walk on the open savanna (and perhaps before! Jump-tag from branch to branch was probably a favorite sport for our chittering insectivore ancestors). Certainly games resembling checkers or chess go back into ancient Egypt and Sumer, and there's evidence for dice games stretching back into the Neolithic—and, although they leave fewer traces for archaeologists to dig up, I'm willing to bet that chase-and-fight games reminiscent of soccer or football have a heritage going back into the Ice Age as well, wherever there was an open field, good summer weather, and some restless hormone-drenched young hunters with time on their hands.

And probably sports will remain an important part of human existence for hundreds or even thousands of years to come. As long as we *remain* recognizably human, as we understand the term (brains floating in vats or disembodied computer-simulations made of data and pixels are probably *not* going to want to go out in the backyard and kick a ball around), sports will be part of our lives—whether they're high-tech variants of the familiar sports we see today on television, or yet-to-be-invented sports suited for life in space, or in zero-gee environments, or on other worlds.

So open up the pages of this book and let some of science fiction's most expert dreamers take you into the sporting worlds of the future, where you will find baseball being played on the low-gravity diamonds of Mars, football players genetically engineered for superhuman speed and strength, basketball players who download their playing skills from computer chips, Sumo wrestlers who clash minds instead of bodies, cyborg zombie boxers of immense stamina and strength, tests of strength and skill that pit humans against aliens, spaceship races across a course as big as the solar system, gameworlds created by science where the stake is life itself. . . .

No matter how much the details change, though, with sports, even future sports, one thing will always remain the same: There will be winners. And losers. And those who are willing to risk it all for a chance to be better than anyone else can be. . . .

Enjoy.

THE WIND
FROM THE SUN

Arthur C. Clarke

Arthur C. Clarke is perhaps the most famous modern science-fiction writer in the world, seriously rivaled for that title only by the late Isaac Asimov and Robert A. Heinlein. Clarke is probably most widely known for his work on Stanley Kubrick's film 2001: A Space Odyssey, *but is also renowned as a novelist, short-story writer, and as a writer of nonfiction, usually on technological subjects such as spaceflight. He has won three Nebula Awards, three Hugo Awards, the British Science Fiction Award, the John W. Campbell Memorial Award, and a Grandmaster Nebula for Life Achievement. His best-known books include the novels* Childhood's End, The City and the Stars, The Deep Range, Rendezvous with Rama, A Fall of Moondust, 2001: A Space Odyssey, 2010: Odyssey Two, 2061: Odyssey Three, Songs of Distant Earth, *and* The Fountains of Paradise, *and the collections* The Nine Billion Names of God, Tales of Ten Worlds, *and* The Sentinel. *He has also written many nonfiction books on scientific topics, the best known of which are probably* Profiles of the Future *and* The Wind from the Sun, *and is generally considered to be the man who first came up with the idea of the communications satellite. His most recent books are the novel* 3001: The Final Odyssey, *the nonfiction collection* Greetings, Carbon-Based Bipeds: Collected Works 1944–1998, *the fiction collection* Collected Short Stories, *and a novel written in collaboration with Stephen Baxter,* The Light of Other Days. *Most of Clarke's best-known books will be*

*coming back into print, appropriately enough, in 2001.
Born in Somerset, England, Clarke now lives in Sri Lanka,
and was recently knighted.*

*Here, in one of the best known of all Future Sports sto-
ries, he gives the ancient sport of sailboat racing a whole
new dimension. . . .*

The enormous disc of sail strained at its rigging, already
filled with the wind that blew between the worlds. In three
minutes the race would begin, yet now John Merton felt
more relaxed, more at peace, than at any time for the past
year. Whatever happened when the Commodore gave the
starting signal, whether *Diana* carried him to victory or defeat, he had achieved his ambition. After a lifetime spent
designing ships for others, now he would sail his own.

"T minus two minutes," said the cabin radio. "Please
confirm your readiness."

One by one, the other skippers answered. Merton recognized all the voices—some tense, some calm—for they
were the voices of his friends and rivals. On the four in-
habited worlds, there were scarcely twenty men who could
sail a sun yacht; and they were all there, on the starting line
or aboard the escort vessels, orbiting twenty-two thousand
miles above the equator.

"Number One—*Gossamer*—ready to go."

"Number Two—*Santa Maria*—all O.K."

"Number Three—*Sunbeam*—O.K."

"Number Four—*Woomera*—all systems GO."

Merton smiled at that last echo from the early, primitive
days of astronautics. But it had become part of the tradition
of space; and there were times when a man needed to
evoke the shades of those who had gone before him to the
stars.

"Number Five—*Lebedev*—we're ready."

"Number Six—*Arachne*—O.K."

Now it was his turn, at the end of the line; strange to think that the words he was speaking in this tiny cabin were being heard by at least five billion people.

"Number Seven—*Diana*—ready to start."

"One through Seven acknowledged," answered that impersonal voice from the judge's launch. "Now T minus one minute."

Merton scarcely heard it. For the last time, he was checking the tension in the rigging. The needles of all the dynamometers were steady; the immense sail was taut, its mirror surface sparkling and glittering gloriously in the sun.

To Merton, floating weightless at the periscope, it seemed to fill the sky. As well it might—for out there were fifty million square feet of sail, linked to his capsule by almost a hundred miles of rigging. All the canvas of all the tea clippers that had once raced like clouds across the China seas, sewn into one gigantic sheet, could not match the single sail that *Diana* had spread beneath the sun. Yet it was little more substantial than a soap bubble; that two square miles of aluminized plastic were only a few millionths of an inch thick.

"T minus ten seconds. All recording cameras ON."

Something so huge, yet so frail, was hard for the mind to grasp. And it was harder still to realize that this fragile mirror could tow him free of Earth merely by the power of the sunlight it would trap.

". . . five, four, three, two, one, CUT!"

Seven knife blades sliced through seven thin lines tethering the yachts to the mother ships that had assembled and serviced them. Until this moment, all had been circling Earth together in a rigidly held formation, but now the yachts would begin to disperse, like dandelion seeds drifting before the breeze. And the winner would be the one that first drifted past the Moon.

Aboard *Diana*, nothing seemed to be happening. But

Merton knew better. Though his body could feel no thrust, the instrument board told him that he was now accelerating at almost one thousandth of a gravity. For a rocket, that figure would have been ludicrous—but this was the first time any solar yacht had ever attained it. *Diana*'s design was sound; the vast sail was living up to his calculations. At this rate, two circuits of the Earth would build up his speed to escape velocity, and then he could head out for the Moon, with the full force of the Sun behind him.

The full force of the Sun . . . He smiled wryly, remembering all his attempts to explain solar sailing to those lecture audiences back on Earth. That had been the only way he could raise money, in those early days. He might be Chief Designer of Cosmodyne Corporation, with a whole string of successful spaceships to his credit, but his firm had not been exactly enthusiastic about his hobby.

"Hold your hands out to the Sun," he'd said. "What do you feel? Heat, of course. But there's pressure as well—though you've never noticed it, because it's so tiny. Over the area of your hands, it comes to only about a millionth of an ounce.

"But out in space, even a pressure as small as that can be important, for it's acting all the time, hour after hour, day after day. Unlike rocket fuel, it's free and unlimited. If we want to, we can use it. We can build sails to catch the radiation blowing from the Sun."

At that point, he would pull out a few square yards of sail material and toss it toward the audience. The silvery film would coil and twist like smoke, then drift slowly to the ceiling in the hot-air currents.

"You can see how light it is," he'd continue. "A square mile weighs only a ton, and can collect five pounds of radiation pressure. So it will start moving—and we can let it tow us along, if we attach rigging to it.

"Of course, its acceleration will be tiny—about a thousandth of a g. That doesn't seem much, but let's see what it means.

"It means that in the first second, we'll move about a fifth of an inch. I suppose a healthy snail could do better than that. But after a minute, we've covered sixty feet, and will be doing just over a mile an hour. That's not bad, for something driven by pure sunlight! After an hour, we're forty miles from our starting point, and will be moving at eighty miles an hour. Please remember that in space there's no friction; so once you start anything moving, it will keep going forever. You'll be surprised when I tell you what our thousandth-of-a-g sailboat will be doing at the end of a day's run: *almost two thousand miles an hour!* If it starts from orbit—as it has to, of course—it can reach escape velocity in a couple of days. And all without burning a single drop of fuel!"

Well, he'd convinced them, and in the end he'd even convinced Cosmodyne. Over the last twenty years, a new sport had come into being. It had been called the sport of billionaires, and that was true. But it was beginning to pay for itself in terms of publicity and TV coverage. The prestige of four continents and two worlds was riding on this race, and it had the biggest audience in history.

Diana had made a good start; time to take a look at the opposition. Moving very gently—though there were shock absorbers between the control capsule and the delicate rigging, he was determined to run no risks—Merton stationed himself at the periscope.

There they were, looking like strange silver flowers planted in the dark fields of space. The nearest, South America's *Santa Maria,* was only fifty miles away; it bore a close resemblance to a boy's kite, but a kite more than a mile on a side. Farther away, the University of Astrograd's *Lebedev* looked like a Maltese cross; the sails that formed the four arms could apparently be tilted for steering purposes. In contrast, the Federation of Australasia's

Woomera was a simple parachute, four miles in circumference. General Spacecraft's *Arachne,* as its name suggested, looked like a spiderweb, and had been built on the same principles, by robot shuttles spiraling out from a central point. Eurospace Corporation's *Gossamer* was an identical design, on a slightly smaller scale. And the Republic of Mars's *Sunbeam* was a flat ring, with a half-mile-wide hole in the center, spinning slowly, so that centrifugal force gave it stiffness. That was an old idea, but no one had ever made it work; and Merton was fairly sure that the colonials would be in trouble when they started to turn.

That would not be for another six hours, when the yachts had moved along the first quarter of their slow and stately twenty-four-hour orbit. Here at the beginning of the race, they were all heading directly away from the Sun—running, as it were, before the solar wind. One had to make the most of this lap, before the boats swung around to the other side of Earth and then started to head back into the Sun.

Time, Merton told himself, for the first check, while he had no navigational worries. With the periscope, he made a careful examination of the sail, concentrating on the points where the rigging was attached to it. The shroud lines—narrow bands of unsilvered plastic film—would have been completely invisible had they not been coated with fluorescent paint. Now they were taut lines of colored light, dwindling away for hundreds of yards toward that gigantic sail. Each had its own electric windlass, not much bigger than a game fisherman's reel. The little windlasses were continually turning, playing lines in or out as the autopilot kept the sail trimmed at the correct angle to the Sun.

The play of sunlight on the great flexible mirror was beautiful to watch. The sail was undulating in slow, stately oscillations, sending multiple images of the Sun marching across it, until they faded away at its edges. Such leisurely vibrations were to be expected in this vast and flimsy structure. They were usually quite harmless, but Merton watched them carefully. Sometimes they could build up to the catastrophic undulations known as the "wriggles," which could tear a sail to pieces.

When he was satisfied that everything was shipshape, he swept the periscope around the sky, rechecking the positions of his rivals. It was as he had hoped: the weeding-out process had begun as the less efficient boats fell astern. But the real test would come when they passed into the shadow of Earth. Then, maneuverability would count as much as speed.

It seemed a strange thing to do, what with the race having just started, but he thought it might be a good idea to get some sleep. The two-man crews on the other boats could take it in turns, but Merton had no one to relieve him. He must rely on his own physical resources, like that other solitary seaman, Joshua Slocum, in his tiny *Spray*. The American skipper had sailed *Spray* single-handed around the world; he could never have dreamed that, two centuries later, a man would be sailing single-handed from Earth to Moon—inspired, at least partly, by his example.

Merton snapped the elastic bands of the cabin seat around his waist and legs, then placed the electrodes of the sleep inducer on his forehead. He set the timer for three hours and relaxed. Very gently, hypnotically, the electronic pulses throbbed in the frontal lobes of his brain. Colored spirals of light expanded beneath his closed eyelids, widening outward to infinity. Then nothing. . . .

The brazen clamor of the alarm dragged him back from his dreamless sleep. He was instantly awake, his eyes scanning the instrument panel. Only two hours had passed—but above the accelerometer, a red light was flashing. Thrust was falling; *Diana* was losing power.

Merton's first thought was that something had happened to the sail; perhaps the antispin devices had failed, and the rigging had become twisted. Swiftly, he checked the meters that showed the tension of the shroud lines. Strange—on one side of the sail they were reading normally, but on the other the pull was dropping slowly, even as he watched.

In sudden understanding, Merton grabbed the periscope, switched to wide-angle vision, and started to scan the edge of the sail. Yes—there was the trouble, and it could have only one cause.

A huge, sharp-edged shadow had begun to slide across the gleaming silver of the sail. Darkness was falling upon *Diana,* as if a cloud had passed between her and the Sun. And in the dark, robbed of the rays that drove her, she would lose all thrust and drift helplessly through space.

But, of course, there were no clouds here, more than twenty thousand miles above the Earth. If there was a shadow, it must be made by man.

Merton grinned as he swung the periscope toward the Sun, switching in the filters that would allow him to look full into its blazing face without being blinded.

"Maneuver 4a," he muttered to himself. "We'll see who can play best at *that* game."

It looked as if a giant planet was crossing the face of the Sun; a great black disc had bitten deep into its edge. Twenty miles astern, *Gossamer* was trying to arrange an artificial eclipse, specially for *Diana*'s benefit.

The maneuver was a perfectly legitimate one. Back in the days of ocean racing, skippers had often tried to rob each other of the wind. With any luck, you could leave your rival becalmed, with his sails collapsing around him—and be well ahead before he could undo the damage.

Merton had no intention of being caught so easily. There was plenty of time to take evasive action; things happened very slowly when you were running a solar sail-boat. It would be at least twenty minutes before *Gossamer* could slide completely across the face of the Sun and leave him in darkness.

Diana's tiny computer—the size of a matchbox, but the equivalent of a thousand human mathematicians—considered the problem for a full second and then flashed the answer. He'd have to open control panels three and four, until the sail had developed an extra twenty degrees of tilt; then the radiation pressure would blow him out of *Gossamer*'s dangerous shadow, back into the full blast of the Sun. It was a pity to interfere with the autopilot, which had been carefully programmed to give the fastest possible run—but that, after all, was why he was here. This was what made solar yachting a sport, rather than a battle between computers.

Out went control lines one and six, slowly undulating like sleepy snakes as they momentarily lost their tension. Two miles away, the triangular panels began to open lazily, spilling sunlight through the sail. Yet, for a long time, nothing seemed to happen. It was hard to grow accustomed to this slow-motion world, where it took minutes for the effects of any action to become visible to the eye. Then Merton saw that the sail was indeed tipping toward the Sun—and that *Gossamer*'s shadow was sliding harmlessly away, its cone of darkness lost in the deeper night of space.

Long before the shadow had vanished, and the disc of the Sun had cleared again, he reversed the tilt and brought *Diana* back on course. Her new momentum would carry her clear of the danger; no need to overdo it, and upset his calculations by sidestepping too far. That was another rule that was hard to learn: the very moment you had started something happening in space, it was already time to think about stopping it.

He reset the alarm, ready for the next natural or man-made emergency. Perhaps *Gossamer*, or one of the other contestants, would try the same trick again. Meanwhile, it was time to eat, though he did not feel particularly hungry. One used little physical energy in space, and it was easy to forget about food. Easy—and dangerous; for when an emergency arose, you might not have the reserves needed to deal with it.

He broke open the first of the meal packets, and inspected it without enthusiasm. The name on the label—SPACETASTIES—was enough to put him off. And he had grave doubts about the promise printed underneath: "Guaranteed crumbless." It had been said that crumbs were a greater danger to space vehicles than meteorites; they could drift into the most unlikely places, causing short circuits, blocking vital jets, and getting into instruments that were supposed to be hermetically sealed.

Still, the liverwurst went down pleasantly enough; so did the chocolate and the pineapple puree. The plastic coffee bulb was warming on the electric heater when the outside world broke in upon his solitude, as the radio operator on the Commodore's launch routed a call to him.

"Dr. Merton? If you can spare the time, Jeremy Blair would like a few words with you." Blair was one of the more responsible news commentators, and Merton had been on his program many times. He could refuse to be interviewed, of course, but he liked Blair, and at the moment he could certainly not claim to be too busy. "I'll take it," he answered.

"Hello, Dr. Merton," said the commentator immediately. "Glad you can spare a few minutes. And congratulations—you seem to be ahead of the field."

"Too early in the game to be sure of *that*," Merton answered cautiously.

"Tell me, Doctor, why did you decide to sail *Diana* by yourself? Just because it's never been done before?"

"Well, isn't that a good reason? But it wasn't the only one, of course." He paused, choosing his words carefully. "You know how critically the performance of a sun yacht depends on its mass. A second man, with all his supplies, would mean another five hundred pounds. That could easily be the difference between winning and losing."

"And you're quite certain that you can handle *Diana* alone?"

"Reasonably sure, thanks to the automatic controls I've designed. My main job is to supervise and make decisions."

"But—two square miles of sail! It just doesn't seem possible for one man to cope with all that."

Merton laughed. "Why not? Those two square miles produce a maximum pull of just ten pounds. I can exert more force with my little finger."

"Well, thank you, Doctor. And good luck. I'll be calling you again."

As the commentator signed off, Merton felt a little ashamed of himself. For his answer had been only part of the truth; and he was sure that Blair was shrewd enough to know it.

There was just one reason why he was here, alone in space. For almost forty years he had worked with teams of hundreds or even thousands of men, helping to design the most complex vehicles that the world had ever seen. For the last twenty years he had led one of those teams, and watched his creations go soaring to the stars. (Sometimes . . . There *were* failures, which he could never forget, even though the fault had not been his.) He was famous, with a successful career behind him. Yet he had never done anything by himself; always he had been one of an army.

This was his last chance to try for individual achievement, and he would share it with no one. There would be no more solar yachting for at least five years, as the period of the Quiet Sun ended and the cycle of bad weather began, with radiation storms bursting through the solar system. When it was safe again for these frail, unshielded craft to venture aloft, he would be too old. If, indeed, he was not too old already . . .

He dropped the empty food containers into the waste disposal and turned once more to the periscope. At first he could find only five of the other yachts; there was no sign of *Woomera*. It took him several minutes to locate her—a dim, star-eclipsing phantom, neatly caught in the shadow of *Lebedev*. He could imagine the frantic efforts the Australasians were making to extricate themselves, and wondered how they had fallen into the trap. It suggested that *Lebedev* was unusually maneuverable. She would bear watching, though she was too far away to menace *Diana* at the moment.

Now the Earth had almost vanished; it had waned to a narrow, brilliant bow of light that was moving steadily toward the Sun. Dimly outlined within that burning bow was the night side of the planet, with the phosphorescent gleams of great cities showing here and there through gaps in the clouds. The disc of darkness had already blanked out a huge section of the Milky Way. In a few minutes, it would start to encroach upon the Sun.

The light was fading; a purple, twilight hue—the glow of many sunsets, thousands of miles below—was falling across the sail as *Diana* slipped silently into the shadow of Earth. The Sun plummeted below that invisible horizon; within minutes, it was night.

Merton looked back along the orbit he had traced, now a quarter of the way around the world. One by one he saw the brilliant stars of the other yachts wink out, as they joined him in the brief night. It would be an hour before the Sun emerged from that enormous black shield, and through all that time they would be completely helpless, coasting without power.

He switched on the external spotlight, and started to search the now-darkened sail with its beam. Already the thousands of acres of film were beginning to wrinkle and become flaccid. The shroud lines were slackening, and must be wound in lest they become entangled. But all this was expected; everything was going as planned.

Fifty miles astern, *Arachne* and *Santa Maria* were not

so lucky. Merton learned of their troubles when the radio burst into life on the emergency circuit.

"Number Two and Number Six, this is Control. You are on a collision course; your orbits will intersect in sixty-five minutes! Do you require assistance?"

There was a long pause while the two skippers digested this bad news. Merton wondered who was to blame. Perhaps one yacht had been trying to shadow the other, and had not completed the maneuver before they were both caught in darkness. Now there was nothing that either could do. They were slowly but inexorably converging, unable to change course by a fraction of a degree.

Yet—sixty-five minutes! That would just bring them out into sunlight again, as they emerged from the shadow of the Earth. They had a slim chance, if their sails could snatch enough power to avoid a crash. There must be some frantic calculations going on aboard *Arachne* and *Santa Maria.*

Arachne answered first. Her reply was just what Merton had expected.

"Number Six calling Control. We don't need assistance, thank you. We'll work this out for ourselves."

I wonder, thought Merton; but at least it will be interesting to watch. The first real drama of the race was approaching, exactly above the line of midnight on the sleeping Earth.

For the next hour, Merton's own sail kept him too busy to worry about *Arachne* and *Santa Maria.* It was hard to keep a good watch on that fifty million square feet of dim plastic out there in the darkness, illuminated only by his narrow spotlight and the rays of the still-distant Moon. From now on, for almost half his orbit around the Earth, he must keep the whole of this immense area edge-on to the Sun. During the next twelve or fourteen hours, the sail would be a useless encumbrance; for he would be heading *into* the Sun, and its rays could only drive him backward along his orbit. It was a pity that he could not furl the sail completely, until he was ready to use it again; but no one had yet found a practical way of doing this.

Far below, there was the first hint of dawn along the edge of the Earth. In ten minutes the Sun would emerge from its eclipse. The coasting yachts would come to life again as the blast of radiation struck their sails. That would be the moment of crisis for *Arachne* and *Santa Maria*—and, indeed, for all of them.

Merton swung the periscope until he found the two dark shadows drifting against the stars. They were very close together—perhaps less than three miles apart. They might, he decided, just be able to make it. . . .

Dawn flashed like an explosion along the rim of Earth as the Sun rose out of the Pacific. The sail and shroud lines glowed a brief crimson, then gold, then blazed with the pure white light of day. The needles of the dynamometers began to lift from their zeros—but only just. *Diana* was still almost completely weightless, for with the sail pointing toward the Sun, her acceleration was now only a few millionths of a gravity.

But *Arachne* and *Santa Maria* were crowding on all the sail that they could manage, in their desperate attempt to keep apart. Now, while there was less than two miles between them, their glittering plastic clouds were unfurling and expanding with agonizing slowness as they felt the first delicate push of the Sun's rays. Almost every TV screen on Earth would be mirroring this protracted drama; and even now, at this last minute, it was possible to tell what the outcome would be.

The two skippers were stubborn men. Either could have cut his sail and fallen back to give the other a chance; but neither would do so. Too much prestige, too many millions, too many reputations were at stake. And so, silently

and softly as snowflakes falling on a winter night, *Arachne*
and *Santa Maria* collided.

The square kite crawled almost imperceptibly into the
circular spiderweb. The long ribbons of the shroud lines
twisted and tangled together with dreamlike slowness.
Even aboard *Diana,* Merton, busy with his own rigging,
could scarcely tear his eyes away from this silent, long-
drawn-out disaster.

For more than ten minutes the billowing, shining
clouds continued to merge into one inextricable mass.
Then the crew capsules tore loose and went their sepa-
rate ways, missing each other by hundreds of yards. With
a flare of rockets, the safety launches hurried to pick
them up.

That leaves five of us, thought Merton. He felt sorry for
the skippers who had so thoroughly eliminated each other,
only a few hours after the start of the race, but they were
young men and would have another chance.

Within minutes, the five had dropped to four. From the
beginning, Merton had had doubts about the slowly rotat-
ing *Sunbeam;* now he saw them justified.

The Martian ship had failed to tack properly. Her spin
had given her too much stability. Her great ring of a sail
was turning to face the Sun, instead of being edge-on to it.
She was being blown back along her course at almost her
maximum acceleration.

That was about the most maddening thing that could
happen to a skipper—even worse than a collision, for he
could blame only himself. But no one would feel much
sympathy for the frustrated colonials, as they dwindled
slowly astern. They had made too many brash boasts before the race, and what had happened to them was poetic
justice.

Yet it would not do to write off *Sunbeam* completely;
with almost half a million miles still to go, she might yet
pull ahead. Indeed, if there were a few more casualties, she

might be the only one to complete the race. It had happened before.

The next twelve hours were uneventful, as the Earth waxed in the sky from new to full. There was little to do while the fleet drifted around the unpowered half of its orbit, but Merton did not find the time hanging heavily on his hands. He caught a few hours of sleep, ate two meals, wrote his log, and became involved in several more radio interviews. Sometimes, though rarely, he talked to the other skippers, exchanging greetings and friendly taunts. But most of the time he was content to float in weightless relaxation, beyond all the cares of Earth, happier than he had been for many years. He was—as far as any man could be in space—master of his own fate, sailing the ship upon which he had lavished so much skill, so much love, that it had become part of his very being.

The next casualty came when they were passing the line between Earth and Sun, and were just beginning the powered half of the orbit. Aboard *Diana*, Merton saw the great sail stiffen as it tilted to catch the rays that drove it. The acceleration began to climb up from the microgravities, though it would be hours yet before it would reach its maximum value.

It would never reach it for *Gossamer*. The moment when power came on again was always critical, and she failed to survive it.

Blair's radio commentary, which Merton had left running at low volume, alerted him with the news: "Hello, *Gossamer* has the wriggles!" He hurried to the periscope, but at first could see nothing wrong with the great circular disc of *Gossamer*'s sail. It was difficult to study it because it was almost edge-on to him and so appeared as a thin ellipse; but presently he saw that it was twisting back and forth in slow, irresistible oscillations. Unless the crew could damp out these waves, by properly timed but gentle tugs on the shroud lines, the sail would tear itself to pieces.

They did their best, and after twenty minutes it seemed that they had succeeded. Then, somewhere near the center of the sail, the plastic film began to rip. It was slowly driven outward by the radiation pressure, like smoke coiling upward from a fire. Within a quarter of an hour, nothing was left but the delicate tracery of the radial spars that had supported the great web. Once again there was a flare of rockets, as a launch moved in to retrieve the *Gossamer*'s capsule and her dejected crew.

"Getting rather lonely up here, isn't it?" said a conversational voice over the ship-to-ship radio.

"Not for you, Dimitri," retorted Merton. "You've still got company back there at the end of the field. I'm the one who's lonely, up here in front." It was not an idle boast; by this time *Diana* was three hundred miles ahead of the next competitor, and her lead should increase still more rapidly in the hours to come.

Aboard *Lebedev*, Dimitri Markoff gave a good-natured chuckle. He did not sound, Merton thought, at all like a man who had resigned himself to defeat.

"Remember the legend of the tortoise and the hare," answered the Russian. "A lot can happen in the next quarter-million miles."

It happened much sooner than that, when they had completed their first orbit of Earth and were passing the starting line again—though thousands of miles higher, thanks to the extra energy the Sun's rays had given them. Merton had taken careful sights on the other yachts and had fed the figures into the computer. The answer it gave for *Woomera* was so absurd that he immediately did a recheck.

There was no doubt of it—the Australasians were catching up at a completely fantastic rate. No solar yacht could possibly have such an acceleration, unless . . .

A swift look through the periscope gave the answer. *Woomera*'s rigging, pared back to the very minimum of mass, had given way. It was her sail alone, still maintaining its shape, that was racing up behind him like a handkerchief blown before the wind. Two hours later it fluttered past, less than twenty miles away; but long before that, the Australasians had joined the growing crowd aboard the Commodore's launch.

So now it was a straight fight between *Diana* and *Lebedev*—for though the Martians had not given up, they were a thousand miles astern and no longer counted as a serious threat. For that matter, it was hard to see what *Lebedev* could do to overtake *Diana*'s lead; but all the way around the second lap, through eclipse again and the long, slow drift against the Sun, Merton felt a growing unease.

He knew the Russian pilots and designers. They had been trying to win this race for twenty years—and, after all, it was only fair that they should, for had not Pyotr Nikolaevich Lebedev been the first man to detect the pressure of sunlight, back to the very beginning of the twentieth century? But they had never succeeded.

And they would never stop trying. Dimitri was up to something—and it would be spectacular.

Aboard the official launch, a thousand miles behind the racing yachts, Commodore van Stratten looked at the radiogram with angry dismay. It had traveled more than a hundred million miles, from the chain of solar observatories swinging high above the blazing surface of the Sun; and it brought the worst possible news.

The Commodore—his title was purely honorary, of course; back on Earth he was Professor of Astrophysics at Harvard—had been half expecting it. Never before had the race been arranged so late in the season. There had been many delays; they had gambled—and now, it seemed, they might all lose.

Deep beneath the surface of the Sun, enormous forces were gathering. At any moment the energies of a million hydrogen bombs might burst forth in the awesome explosion known as a solar flare. Climbing at millions of miles an hour, an invisible fireball many times the size of Earth would leap from the Sun and head out across space.

The cloud of electrified gas would probably miss the Earth completely. But if it did not, it would arrive in just over a day. Spaceships could protect themselves, with their shielding and their powerful magnetic screens; but the lightly built solar yachts, with their paper-thin walls, were defenseless against such a menace. The crews would have to be taken off, and the race abandoned.

John Merton knew nothing of this as he brought *Diana* around the Earth for the second time. If all went well, this would be the last circuit, both for him and for the Russians. They had spiraled upward by thousands of miles, gaining energy from the Sun's rays. On this lap, they should escape from the Earth completely, and head outward on the long run to the Moon. It was a straight race now; *Sunbeam*'s crew had finally withdrawn exhausted, after battling valiantly with their spinning sail for more than a hundred thousand miles.

Merton did not feel tired; he had eaten and slept well, and *Diana* was behaving herself admirably. The autopilot, tensioning the rigging like a busy little spider, kept the great sail trimmed to the Sun more accurately than any human skipper could have. Though by this time the two square miles of plastic sheet must have been riddled by hundreds of micrometeorites, the pinhead-sized punctures had produced no falling off of thrust.

He had only two worries. The first was shroud line number eight, which could no longer be adjusted properly. Without any warning, the reel had jammed; even after all these years of astronautical engineering, bearings sometimes seized up in vacuum. He could neither lengthen nor shorten the line, and would have to navigate as best he could with the others. Luckily, the most difficult maneuvers were over; from now on, *Diana* would have the Sun behind her as she sailed straight down the solar wind. And as the old-time sailors had often said, it was easy to handle a boat when the wind was blowing over your shoulder.

His other worry was *Lebedev,* still dogging his heels three hundred miles astern. The Russian yacht had shown remarkable maneuverability, thanks to the four great panels that could be tilted around the central sail. Her flipovers as she rounded the Earth had been carried out with superb precision. But to gain maneuverability she must have sacrificed speed. You could not have it both ways; in the long, straight haul ahead, Merton should be able to hold his own. Yet he could not be certain of victory until, three or four days from now, *Diana* went flashing past the far side of the Moon.

And then, in the fiftieth hour of the race, just after the end of the second orbit around Earth, Markoff sprang his little surprise.

"Hello, John," he said casually over the ship-to-ship circuit. "I'd like you to watch this. It should be interesting."

Merton drew himself across to the periscope and turned up the magnification to the limit. There in the field of view, a most improbable sight against the background of the stars, was the glittering Maltese cross of *Lebedev,* very small but very clear. As he watched, the four arms of the cross slowly detached themselves from the central square, and went drifting away, with all their spars and rigging, into space.

Markoff had jettisoned all unnecessary mass, now that

he was coming up to escape velocity and need no longer plod patiently around the Earth, gaining momentum on each circuit. From now on, *Lebedev* would be almost un-steerable—but that did not matter; all the tricky navigation lay behind her. It was as if an old-time yachtsman had de-liberately thrown away his rudder and heavy keel, know-ing that the rest of the race would be straight downwind over a calm sea.

"Congratulations, Dimitri," Merton radioed. "It's a neat trick. But it's not good enough. You can't catch up with me now."

"I've not finished yet," the Russian answered. "There's an old winter's tale in my country about a sleigh being chased by wolves. To save himself, the driver has to throw off the passengers one by one. Do you see the analogy?"

Merton did, all too well. On this final straight lap, Dim-itri no longer needed his copilot. *Lebedev* could really be stripped down for action.

"Alexis won't be very happy about this," Merton replied. "Besides, it's against the rules."

"Alexis isn't happy, but I'm the captain. He'll just have to wait around for ten minutes until the Commodore picks him up. And the regulations say nothing about the size of the crew—*you* should know that."

Merton did not answer; he was too busy doing some hurried calculations, based on what he knew of *Lebedev*'s design. By the time he had finished, he knew that the race was still in doubt. *Lebedev* would be catching up with him at just about the time he hoped to pass the Moon.

But the outcome of the race was already being decided, ninety-two million miles away.

On Solar Observatory Three, far inside the orbit of Mer-cury, the automatic instruments recorded the whole history of the flare. A hundred million square miles of the Sun's surface exploded in such blue-white fury that, by comparison, the rest of the disc paled to a dull glow. Out of that seething inferno, twisting and turning like a living creature in the magnetic fields of its own creation, soared the electrified plasma of the great flare. Ahead of it, moving at the speed of light, went the warning flash of ultraviolet and X rays. That would reach Earth in eight minutes and was relatively harmless. Not so the charged atoms that were following behind at their leisurely four million miles an hour—and which, in just over a day, would engulf Diana, Lebedev, and their accompanying little fleet in a cloud of lethal radiation.

The Commodore left his decision to the last possible minute. Even when the jet of plasma had been tracked past the orbit of Venus, there was a chance that it might miss the Earth. But when it was less than four hours away, and had already been picked up by the Moon-based radar network, he knew that there was no hope. All solar sailing was over, for the next five or six years—until the Sun was quiet again.

A great sigh of disappointment swept across the solar system. *Diana* and *Lebedev* were halfway between Earth and Moon, running neck and neck—and now no one would ever know which was the better boat. The enthusiasts would argue the result for years; history would merely record: "Race canceled owing to solar storm."

When John Merton received the order, he felt a bitterness he had not known since childhood. Across the years, sharp and clear, came the memory of his tenth birthday. He had been promised an exact scale model of the famous spaceship *Morning Star,* and for weeks had been planning how he would assemble it, where he would hang it in his bedroom. And then, at the last moment, his father had broken the news. "I'm sorry, John—it cost too much money. Maybe next year . . ."

Half a century and a successful lifetime later, he was a heartbroken boy again.

For a moment, he thought of disobeying the Commodore. Suppose he sailed on, ignoring the warning? Even if the race was abandoned, he could make crossing to the Moon that would stand in the record books for generations.

But that would be worse than stupidity; it would be suicide—and a very unpleasant form of suicide. He had seen men die of radiation poisoning, when the magnetic shielding of their ships had failed in deep space. No—nothing was worth that. . . .

He felt as sorry for Dimitri Markoff as for himself. They had both deserved to win, and now victory would go to neither. No man could argue with the Sun in one of its rages, even though he might ride upon its beams to the edge of space.

Only fifty miles astern now, the Commodore's launch was drawing alongside *Lebedev,* preparing to take off her skipper. There went the silver sail, as Dimitri—with feelings that he would share—cut the rigging. The tiny capsule would be taken back to Earth, perhaps to be used again; but a sail was spread for one voyage only.

He could press the jettison button now, and save his rescuers a few minutes of time. But he could not do it; he wanted to stay aboard to the very end, on the little boat that had been for so long a part of his dreams and his life. The great sail was spread now at right angles to the Sun, exerting its utmost thrust. Long ago, it had torn him clear of Earth, and *Diana* was still gaining speed.

Then, out of nowhere, beyond all doubt or hesitation, he knew what must be done. For the last time, he sat down before the computer that had navigated him halfway to the Moon.

When he had finished, he packed the log and his few personal belongings. Clumsily, for he was out of practice, and it was not an easy job to do by oneself, he climbed into the emergency survival suit. He was just sealing the helmet when the Commodore's voice called over the radio.

"We'll be alongside in five minutes, Captain. Please cut your sail, so we won't foul it."

John Merton, first and last skipper of the sun yacht *Diana,* hesitated a moment. He looked for the last time around the tiny cabin, with its shining instruments and its neatly arranged controls, now all locked in their final positions. Then he said into the microphone: "I'm abandoning ship. Take your time to pick me up. *Diana* can look after herself."

There was no reply from the Commodore, and for that he was grateful. Professor van Stratten would have guessed what was happening—and would know that, in these final moments, he wished to be left alone.

He did not bother to exhaust the air lock, and the rush of escaping gas blew him gently out into space. The thrust he gave her then was his last gift to *Diana.* She dwindled away from him, sail glittering splendidly in the sunlight that would be hers for centuries to come. Two days from now she would flash past the Moon; but the Moon, like the Earth, could never catch her. Without his mass to slow her down, she would gain two thousand miles an hour in every day of sailing. In a month, she would be traveling faster than any ship that man had ever built.

As the Sun's rays weakened with distance, so her acceleration would fall. But even at the orbit of Mars, she would be gaining a thousand miles an hour in every day. Long before then, she would be moving too swiftly for the Sun itself to hold her. Faster than a comet had ever streaked in from the stars, she would be heading out into the abyss.

The glare of rockets, only a few miles away, caught Merton's eye. The launch was approaching to pick him up—at thousands of times the acceleration that *Diana* could ever attain. But its engines could burn for a few minutes only, before they exhausted their fuel—while *Diana* would still be gaining speed, driven outward by the Sun's eternal fires, for ages yet to come.

"Good-bye, little ship," said John Merton. "I wonder what eyes will see you next, how many thousand years from now?"

At last he felt at peace, as the blunt torpedo of the launch nosed up beside him. He would never win the race to the Moon; but his would be the first of all man's ships to set sail on the long journey to the stars.

ARTHUR STERNBACH BRINGS THE CURVEBALL TO MARS

Kim Stanley Robinson

Kim Stanley Robinson sold his first story in 1976 and quickly established himself as one of the most respected and critically acclaimed writers of his generation. His story "Black Air" won the World Fantasy Award in 1984, and his novella The Blind Geometer *won the Nebula Award in 1987. His novel* The Wild Shore *was published in 1984 and was quickly followed up by other novels such as* Icehenge, The Memory of Whiteness, A Short, Sharp Shock, The Gold Coast, *and* The Pacific Shore, *and by collections such as* The Planet on the Table, Escape from Kathmandu, *and* Remaking History.

Robinson's already distinguished literary reputation would take a quantum jump in the decade of the '90s, though, with the publication of his acclaimed "Mars" trilogy, Red Mars, Green Mars, *and* Blue Mars; Red Mars *would win a Nebula Award, both* Green Mars *and* Blue Mars *would win Hugo Awards, and the trilogy would be widely recognized as the genre's most accomplished, detailed, sustained, and substantial look at the colonization and terraforming of another world, rivaled only by Arthur C. Clarke's* The Sands of Mars. *Robinson's latest books are the novel* Antarctica, *and a collection of stories and poems set on his fictional Mars,* The Martians. *He lives with his family in Davis, California.*

The Mars Trilogy will probably associate Robinson's

name forever with the Red Planet. Here he takes us to a future terraformed Mars for a charming little story that's about just what it says it's about, and that shows us that, where baseball is concerned, the more things change, the more they stay the same.

He was a tall, skinny Martian kid, shy and stooping. Gangly as a puppy. Why they had him playing third base I have no idea. Then again they had me playing shortstop and I'm left-handed. And can't field grounders. But I'm American, so there I was. That's what learning a sport by video will do. Some things are so obvious people never think to mention them. Like never put a lefty at shortstop. But on Mars they were making it all new. Some people there had fallen in love with baseball, and ordered the equipment and rolled some fields, and off they went.

So there we were, me and this kid Gregor, butchering the left side of the infield. He looked so young I asked him how old he was, and he said eight and I thought Jeez you're not *that* young, but realized he meant Martian years of course, so he was about sixteen or seventeen, but he seemed younger. He had recently moved to Argyre from somewhere else, and was staying at the local house of his co-op with relatives or friends, I never got that straight, but he seemed pretty lonely to me. He never missed practice even though he was the worst of a terrible team, and clearly he got frustrated at all his errors and strikeouts. I used to wonder why he came out at all. And so shy; and that stoop; and the acne; and the tripping over his own feet, the blushing, the mumbling—he was a classic.

English wasn't his first language, either. It was Armenian, or Moravian, something like that. Something no one else spoke, anyway, except for an elderly couple in his co-op. So he mumbled what passes for English on Mars, and sometimes even used a translation box, but basically tried never to be in a situation where he had to speak. And made error after error. We must have made quite a sight—me about waist-high to him, and both of us letting grounders pass through us like we were a magic show. Or else knocking them down and chasing them around, then winging them past the first baseman. We very seldom made an out. It would have been conspicuous except everyone else was the same way. Baseball on Mars was a high-scoring game.

But beautiful anyway. It was like a dream, really. First of all the horizon, when you're on a flat plain like Argyre, is only three miles away rather than six. It's very noticeable to a Terran eye. Then their diamonds have just over normal-sized infields, but the outfields have to be huge. At my team's ballpark it was nine hundred feet to dead center, seven hundred down the lines. Standing at the plate the outfield fence was like a little green line off in the distance, under a purple sky, pretty near the horizon itself—what I'm telling you is that the baseball diamond about covered *the entire visible world*. It was so great.

They played with four outfielders, like in softball, and still the alleys between fielders were wide. And the air was about as thin as at Everest base camp, and the gravity itself only bats .380, so to speak. So when you hit the ball solid it flies like a golf ball hit by a big driver. Even as big as the fields were, there were still a number of home runs every game. Not many shutouts on Mars. Not till I got there, anyway.

I went there after I climbed Olympus Mons, to help them establish a new soil sciences institute. They had the sense not to try that by video. At first I climbed in the Charitums in my time off, but after I got hooked into baseball the game took up most of my spare time. Fine, I'll play, I said when they asked me. But I won't coach. I don't like telling people what to do.

So I'd go out and start by doing soccer exercises with the rest of them, warming up all the muscles we would never use. Then Werner would start hitting infield practice, and Gregor and I would start flailing. We were like matadors. Occasionally we'd snag one and whale it over to first, and occasionally the first baseman, who was well over two meters tall and built like a tank, would catch our throws, and we'd slap our gloves together. Doing this day after day, Gregor got a little less shy with me, though not much. And I saw that he threw the ball pretty damned hard. His arm was as long as my whole body, and boneless it seemed, like something pulled off a squid, so loosewristed that he got some real pop on the ball. Of course sometimes it would still be rising when it passed ten meters over the first baseman's head, but it was moving, no doubt about it. I began to see that maybe the reason he came out to play, beyond just being around people he didn't have to talk to, was the chance to throw things really hard. I saw, too, that he wasn't so much shy as he was surly. Or both.

Anyway our fielding was a joke. Hitting went a bit better. Gregory learned to chop down on the ball and hit grounders up the middle; it was pretty effective. And I began to get my timing together. Coming to it from years of slow-pitch softball, I had started by swinging at everything a week late, and between that and my shortstopping I'm sure my teammates figured they had gotten a defective American. And since they had a rule limiting each team to only two Terrans, no doubt they were disappointed by that. But slowly I adjusted my timing, and after that I hit pretty well. The thing was their pitchers had no breaking stuff. These big guys would rear back and throw as hard as they could, like Gregor, but it took everything in their power just to throw strikes. It was a little scary because they often threw right at you by accident. But if they got it down the pipe then all you had to do was time it.

And if you hit one, how the ball flew! Every time I connected it was like a miracle. It felt like you could put one into orbit if you hit it right, in fact that was one of their nicknames for a home run. Oh, that's orbital, they would say, watching one leave the park headed for the horizon. They had a little bell, like a ship's bell, attached to the backstop, and every time someone hit one out they would ring that bell while you rounded the bases. A very nice local custom.

So I enjoyed it. It's a beautiful game even when you're butchering it. My sorest muscles after practice were in my stomach from laughing so hard. I even began to have some success at short. When I caught balls going to my right I twirled around backward to throw to first or second. People were impressed though of course it was ridiculous. It was a case of the one-eyed man in the country of the blind. Not that they weren't good athletes, you understand, but none of them had played as kids, and so they had no baseball instincts. They just liked to play. And I could see why—out there on a green field as big as the world, under a purple sky, with the yellow-green balls flying around—it was beautiful. We had a good time.

I started to give a few tips to Gregory, too, though I had sworn to myself not to get into coaching. I don't like trying to tell people what to do. The game's too hard for that. But I'd be hitting flies to the outfielders, and it was hard not to tell them to watch the ball and run under it and then put the glove up and catch it, rather than run all the way with their arms stuck up like the Statue of Liberty's. Or when they took turns hitting flies (it's harder than it looks) giving them batting tips. And Gregor and I played catch all the time during warm-ups, so just watching me—and trying to throw to such a short target—he got better. He definitely threw hard. And I saw there was a whole lot of movement in his throws. They'd come tailing in to me every which way, no surprise given how loose-wristed he was. I had to look sharp or I'd miss. He was out of control, but he had potential.

And the truth was, our pitchers were bad. I loved the guys, but they couldn't throw strikes if you paid them. They'd regularly walk ten or twenty batters every game, and these were five-inning games. Werner would watch Thomas walk ten, then he'd take over in relief and walk ten more himself. Sometimes they'd go through this twice. Gregor and I would stand there while the other team's runners walked by as in a parade, or a line at the grocery store. When Werner went to the mound I'd stand by Gregor and say, You know Gregor you could pitch better than these guys. You've got a good arm. And he would look at me horrified, muttering No no no no, not possible.

But then one time warming up he broke off a really mean curve and I caught it on my wrist. While I was rubbing it down I walked over to him. Did you see the way that ball curved? I said.

Yes, he said, looking away. I'm sorry.

Don't be sorry, That's called a curveball, Gregor. It can be a useful throw. You twisted your hand at the last moment and the ball came over the top of it, like this, see? Here, try it again.

So we slowly got into it. I was all-state in Connecticut my senior year in high school, and it was all from throwing junk—curve, slider, split-finger, change. I could see Gregor throwing most of those just by accident, but to keep from confusing him I just worked on a straight curve. I told him Just throw it to me like you did that first time.

I thought you weren't to coach us, he said.

I'm not coaching you! Just throw it like that. Then in the games throw it straight. As straight as possible.

He mumbled a bit at me in Moravian, and didn't look me in the eye. But he did it. And after a while he worked up a good curve. Of course the thinner air on Mars meant

there was little for the balls to bite on. But I noticed that
the blue dot balls they played with had higher stitching
than the red dot balls. They played with both of them as if
there was no difference, but there was. So I filed that away
and kept working with Gregor.

We practiced a lot. I showed him how to throw from the
stretch, figuring that a windup from Gregor was likely to
end up in knots. And by midseason he threw a mean curve
from the stretch. We had not mentioned this to anyone else.
He was wild with it, but it hooked hard; I had to be really
sharp to catch some of them. It made me better at shortstop, too. Although finally in one game, behind twenty to
nothing as usual, a batter hit a towering pop fly and I took
off running back on it, and the wind kept carrying it and I
kept following it, until when I got it I was out there
sprawled between our startled center fielders.

Maybe you should play outfield, Werner said.

I said Thank God.

So after that I played left center or right center, and I
spent the games chasing line drives to the fence and throwing them back in to the cutoff man. Or more likely, standing there and watching the other team take their walks. I
called in my usual chatter, and only then did I notice that
no one on Mars ever yelled anything at these games. It was
like playing in a league of deaf-mutes. I had to provide the
chatter for the whole team from two hundred yards away
in center field, including, of course, criticism of the plate
umpires' calls. My view of the plate was miniaturized but
I still did a better job than they did, and they knew it, too.
It was fun. People would walk by and say, Hey there must
be an American out there.

One day after one of our home losses, 28 to 12 I think
it was, everyone went to get something to eat, and Greg-
or was just standing there looking off into the distance.
You want to come along? I asked him, gesturing after the
others, but he shook his head. He had to get back home

and work. I was going back to work myself, so I walked with him into town, a place like you'd see in the Texas panhandle. I stopped outside his co-op, which was a big house or little apartment complex, I could never tell which was which on Mars. There he stood like a lamp-post, and I was about to leave when an old woman came out and invited me in. Gregor had told her about me, she said in stiff English. So I was introduced to the people in the kitchen there, most of them incredibly tall. Gregory seemed really embarrassed, he didn't want me being there, so I left as soon as I could get away. The old woman had a husband, and they seemed like Gregor's grandparents. There was a young girl there, too, about his age, looking at both of us like a hawk. Gregor never met her eye.

Next time at practice, I said, Gregor, were those your grandparents?

Like my grandparents.

And that girl, who was she?

No answer.

Like a cousin or something?

Yes.

Gregor, what about your parents? Where are they?

He just shrugged and started throwing me the ball.

I got the impression they lived in another branch of his co-op somewhere else, but I never found out for sure. A lot of what I saw on Mars I liked—the way they run their businesses together in co-ops takes a lot of pressure off them, and they live pretty relaxed lives compared to us on Earth. But some of their parenting systems—kids brought up by groups, or by one parent, or whatever—I wasn't so sure about those. It makes for problems if you ask me. Bunch of teenage boys ready to slug somebody. Maybe that happens no matter what you do.

Anyway we finally got to the end of the season, and I was going to go back to Earth after it. Our team's record was three and fifteen, and we came in last place in the regular season standings. But they held a final weekend tournament for all the teams in the Argyre Basin, a bunch of three-inning games, as there were a lot to get through. Immediately we lost the first game and were in the losers' bracket. Then we were losing the next one, too, and all because of walks, mostly. Werner relieved Thomas for a time, then when that didn't work out Thomas went back to the mound to rerelieve Werner. When that happened I ran all the way in from center to join them on the mound. I said Look you guys, let Gregor pitch.

Gregor! they both said. No way!

He'll be even worse than us, Werner said.

How could he be? I said. You guys just walked eleven batters in a row. Night will fall before Gregor could do that.

So they agreed to it. They were both discouraged at that point, as you might expect. So I went over to Gregor and said Okay, Gregor, you give it a try now.

Oh no, no no no no no no no. He was pretty set against it. He glanced up into the stands where we had a couple hundred spectators, mostly friends and family and some curious passersby, and I saw then that his like grandparents and his girl something-or-other were up there watching. Gregor was getting more hangdog and sullen every second.

Come on, Gregor, I said, putting the ball in his glove. Tell you what, I'll catch you. It'll be just like warming up. Just keep throwing your curveball. And I dragged him over to the mound.

So Werner warmed him up while I went over and got on the catcher's gear, moving a box of blue dot balls to the front of the ump's supply area while I was at it. I could see Gregor was nervous, and so was I. I had never caught before, and he had never pitched, and bases were loaded and no one was out. It was an unusual baseball moment.

Finally I was geared up and I clanked on out to him. Don't worry about throwing too hard, I said. Just put the curveball right in my glove. Ignore the batter. I'll give you the sign before every pitch; two fingers for curve, one for fastball.

Fastball? he says.

That's where you throw the ball fast. Don't worry about that. We're just going to throw curves anyway.

And you said you weren't to coach, he said bitterly.

I'm not coaching, I said, I'm catching.

So I went back and got set behind the plate. Be looking for curveballs, I said to the ump. Curve ball? he said.

So we started up. Gregor stood crouched on the mound like a big praying mantis, red-faced and grim. He threw the first pitch right over our heads to the backstop. Two guys scored while I retrieved it, but I threw out the runner going from first to third. I went out to Gregor. Okay, I said, the bases are cleared and we got an out. Let's just throw now. Right into the glove. Just like last time, but lower.

So he did. He threw the ball at the batter, and the batter bailed, and the ball cut right down into my glove. The umpire was speechless. I turned around and showed him the ball in my glove. That was a strike, I told him.

Strike! he hollered. He grinned at me. That was a curveball, wasn't it.

Damn right it was.

Hey, the batter said. What was that?

We'll show you again, I said.

And after that Gregor began to mow them down. I kept putting down two fingers, and he kept throwing curveballs. By no means were they all strikes, but enough were to keep him from walking too many batters. All the balls were blue dot. The ump began to get into it.

And between two batters I looked behind me and saw that the entire crowd of spectators, and all the teams not playing at that moment, had congregated behind the backstop to watch Gregor pitch. No one on Mars had ever seen a curveball before, and now they were crammed back there to get the best view of it, gasping and chattering at every hook. The batter would bail or take a weak swing and then look back at the crowd with a big grin, as if to say Did you see that? That was a curveball!

So we came back and won that game, and we kept Gregor pitching, and we won the next three games as well. The third game he threw exactly twenty-seven pitches, striking out all nine batters with three pitches each. Bob Feller once struck out all twenty-seven batters in a high school game; it was like that.

The crowd was loving it. Gregor's face was less red. He was standing straighter in the box. He still refused to look anywhere but at my glove, but his look of grim terror had shifted to one of ferocious concentration. He may have been skinny, but he was tall. Out there on the mound he began to look pretty damned formidable.

So we climbed back up into the winner's bracket, then into a semifinal. Crowds of people were coming up to Gregor between games to get him to sign their baseballs. Mostly he looked dazed, but at one point I saw him glance up at his co-op family in the stands and wave at them, with a brief smile.

How's your arm holding out? I asked him.

What do you mean? he said.

Okay, I said. Now look, I want to play outfield again this game. Can you pitch to Werner? Because there were a couple of Americans on the team we played next, Ernie and Caesar, who I suspected could hit a curve. I just had a hunch.

Gregor nodded, and I could see that as long as there was a glove to throw at, nothing else mattered. So I arranged it with Werner, and in the semi-finals I was back out in right-center field. We were playing under the lights by this time, the field like green velvet under a purple twilight sky. Looking in from center field it was all tiny, like something in a dream.

And it must have been a good hunch I had, because I made one catch charging in on a liner from Ernie, sliding to snag it, and then another running across the middle for what seemed like thirty seconds, before I got under a towering Texas leaguer from Caesar. Gregor even came up and congratulated me between innings.

And you know that old thing about how a good play in the field leads to a good at-bat. Already in the day's games I had hit well, but now in this semifinal I came up and hit a high fastball so solid it felt like I didn't hit it at all, and off it flew. Home run over the center field fence, out into the dusk. I lost sight of it before it came down.

Then in the finals I did it again in the first inning, back-to-back with Thomas—his to left, mine again to center. That was two in a row for me, and we were winning, and Gregor was mowing them down. So when I came up again the next inning I was feeling good, and people were calling out for another homer, and the other team's pitcher had a real determined look. He was a really big guy, as tall as Gregor but massive-chested as so many Martians are, and he reared back and threw the first one right at my head. Not on purpose, he was out of control. Then I barely fouled several pitches off, swinging very late, and dodging his inside heat, until it was a full count, and I was thinking to myself, Well heck, it doesn't really matter if you strike out here, at least you hit two in a row.

Then I heard Gregor shouting Come on, coach, you can do it! Hang in there! Keep your focus! All doing a passable imitation of me, I guess, as the rest of the team was laughing its head off. I suppose I had said all those things to them before, though of course it was just the stuff you al-

ways say automatically at a ball game, I never meant anything by it, I didn't even know people heard me. But I definitely heard Gregor, needling me, and I stepped back into
the box thinking, Look I don't even like to coach, I played
ten games at shortstop trying not to coach you guys, and I
was so irritated I was barely aware of the pitch, but ham-
mered it anyway out over the right field fence, higher and
deeper even than my first two. Knee-high fastball, inside.
As Ernie said to me afterward, You *drove* that baby. My
teammates rang the little ship's bell all the way around the
bases, and I slapped hands with every one of them on the
way from third to home, feeling the grin on my face. Afterward I sat on the bench and felt the hit in my hands. I
can still see it flying out.

So we were ahead 4–0 in the final inning, and the other
team came up determined to catch us. Gregor was tiring at
last, and he walked a couple, then hung a curve and their
big pitcher got into it and clocked it far over my head. Now
I do okay charging liners, but the minute a ball is hit over
me I'm totally lost. So I turned my back on this one and
ran for the fence, figuring either it goes out or I collect it
against the fence, but that I'd never see it again in the air.
But running on Mars is so weird. You get going too fast
and then you're pinwheeling along trying to keep from
doing a faceplant. That's what I was doing when I saw the
warning track, and looked back up and spotted the ball
coming down, so I jumped, trying to jump straight up, you
know, but I had a lot of momentum, and had completely
forgotten about the gravity, so I shot up and caught the
ball, amazing, but found myself *flying right over the fence.*

I came down and rolled in the dust and sand, and the
ball stayed stuck in my glove. I hopped back over the fence
holding the ball up to show everyone I had it. But they
gave the other pitcher a home run anyway, because you
have to stand inside the park when you catch one, it's a
local rule. I didn't care. The whole point of playing games

is to make you do things like that anyway. And it was good that the pitcher got one, too.

So we started up again and Gregor struck out the side, and we won the tournament. We were mobbed, Gregor especially. He was the hero of the hour. Everyone wanted him to sign something. He didn't say much, but he wasn't stooping either. He looked surprised. Afterward Werner took two balls and everyone signed them, to make some kind of trophies for Gregor and me. Later I saw half the names on my trophy were jokes, "Mickey Mantle" and other names like that. Gregor had written on it, "Hi, Coach Arnold, Regards, Greg." I have the ball still, on my desk at home.

MAN-MOUNTAIN
GENTIAN

Howard Waldrop

*Here's a wry, funny, and yet oddly poignant look at a pos-
sible future development in the sport of sumo wrestling,
one that only Howard Waldrop is likely to have even
thought of, let alone written. . . .*

*Howard Waldrop is widely considered to be one of the
best short-story writers in the business, and his famous
story "The Ugly Chickens" won both the Nebula and the
World Fantasy Awards in 1981. His work has been gathered in the collections:* Howard Who? All About Strange
Monsters of the Recent Past: Neat Stories by Howard Waldrop, *and* Night of the Cooters: More Neat Stories by
Howard Waldrop, *with more collections in the works. Waldrop is also the author of the novel* The Texas-Israeli War:
1999, *in collaboration with Jake Saunders, and of two solo
novels,* Them Bones *and* A Dozen Tough Jobs. *He is at
work on a new novel, tentatively titled* The Moon World.
His most recent book is a new collection, Going Home
Again. *A longtime Texas, Waldrop now lives in the tiny
town of Arlington, Washington, outside Seattle, as close to
a trout stream as he can possibly get without actually living in it.*

Just after the beginning of the present century it was
realized that some of the wrestlers were throwing
their opponents from the ring without touching them.

—Ichinaga Naya, *Zen-Suomo:*
Sport and Ritual (Kyoto: All-Japan
Zen-Sumo Association Books, 2014)

It *was the* fourteenth day of the January Tokyo tournament. Sitting with the other wrestlers, Man-Mountain Gentian watched as the next match began.

Ground Sloth Ikimoto was taking on Killer Kudzu.
They entered the tamped-earth ring and began their
shikiris. Ground Sloth, a *sumotori* of the old school, had
changed over from traditional to *zen-sumo* four years before. He weighed 180 kilos in his *mawashi*. He entered
at the white tassel salt corner. He clapped his huge
hands, rinsed his mouth, threw salt, rubbed his body with
tissue paper, then began his high leg lifts, stamping his
feet, his hands gripping far down his calves. The ring
shook with each stamp. All the muscles rippled on his
big frame. His stomach, a flesh-colored boulder, shook
and vibrated.

Killer Kudzu was small, and thin, weighing barely over
ninety kilos. On his forehead was the tattoo of his home-
land, the PRC, one large star and five smaller stars blazing
in a constellation. He also went into his ritual *shikiri,* but
as he clapped he held in one hand a small box, ten centimeters on a side, showing his intention to bring it into the
match. Sometimes these were objects for meditation,
sometimes favors from male or female lovers, sometimes
no one knew what. The only rule was that they could not
be used as weapons.

The wrestlers were separated from the onlookers by
four clear walls and a roof of plastic. Over this hung the
traditional canopy and tassels, symbolizing heaven and the

four winds. Through the plastic walls ran a mesh of fine wiring, connected to a six-volt battery next to the north-side judge.

A large number of 600X slow-motion video cameras were placed around the auditorium to be used by the judges if necessary.

Killer Kudzu placed the box on his side of the line. He returned to his corner and threw more salt.

Ground Sloth Ikimoto stamped once more, twice, went to his line, settled into position like a football lineman, legs apart, knuckles to the ground. His nearly bare buttocks looked like giant rocks. Killer Kudzu finished his *shikiri,* squatted at his line, where he settled his hand near his votive box, and glared at his opponent.

The referee, in his ceremonial robes, had been standing to one side during the preliminaries. Now he came to a position halfway between the wrestlers, his war fan down. He leaned away from the two men, left leg back to one side as if ready to run. He stared at the midpoint between the two and flipped his fan downward.

Instantly sweat sprang to their foreheads and shoulders, their bodies rippled as if pushing against great unmoving weights, their toes curled into the clay of the ring. They stayed immobile on their respective marks.

Killer Kudzu's neck muscles strained. With his left hand he reached and quickly opened the votive box.

Man-Mountain Gentian and the other wrestlers on the east side drew in their breaths.

Ground Sloth Ikimoto was a vegetarian and always had been. In training for traditional sumo, he had shunned the *chunko-nabe,* the communal stew of fish, chicken, meat, eggs, onions, cabbage, carrots, turnips, sugar, and soy sauce. Traditional *sumotori* ate as much as they could hold twice a day, and weight gain was tremendous.

Ikimoto had instead trained twice as hard, eating only

vegetables, starches, and sugars. Meat and eggs had never touched his lips.

What Killer Kudzu brought out of the box was a cheeseburger. With one swift movement he bit into it only half a meter from Ground Sloth's face.

Ikimoto blanched and started to scream. As he did, he lifted into the air as if chopped in the chest with an ax, arms and legs flailing, a Dopplering wail of revulsion coming from his emptied lungs. He passed the bales marking the edge of the ring, one foot dragging the ground, upending a boundary bale, and smashed to the ground between the ring and the square bales at the plastic walls.

The referee signaled Killer Kudzu the winner. As he squatted the *gyoji* offered him a small envelope signifying a cash prize from his sponsors. Kudzu, left hand on his knee, with his right hand made three chopping gestures from the left, right and above, thanking man, earth, and heaven. Kudzu took the envelope, then stepped through the doorway of the plastic enclosure and left the arena to rejoin the other west-side wrestlers.

The audience of 11,000 was on its feet, cheering. Across Japan and the world, 200 million viewers watched.

Ground Sloth Ikimoto had risen to his feet, bowed, and left by the other door. Attendants rushed in to repair the damaged ring.

Man-Mountain Gentian looked up at the scoring clock. The match had taken 4.1324 seconds. It was 3:30 in the afternoon on the fourteenth day of the Tokyo tournament.

The next match would pit Cast Iron Pekowski of Poland against Typhoon Takanaka.

After that would be Gentian's bout with the South African veldt wrestler Knockdown Krugerrand.

Man-Mountain Gentian stood at 13–0 in the tournament, having defeated an opponent each day so far. He wanted to retire as the first Grand Champion to win six tournaments in a row, undefeated. He was not very worried about his contest later this afternoon.

Tomorrow, though, the last day of the January tournament, he would face Killer Kudzu, who, after this match, also stood undefeated, at 14–0.

Man-Mountain Gentian was 1.976 meters tall and weighed exactly 200 kilos. He had been a sumotori for six years, had been yokozuna for the last two of those. He was twice holder of the Emperor's Cup. He was the highest-paid, the most famous zen-sumotori in the world.

He was twenty-three years old.

He and Knockdown Krugerrand finished their *shikiris*. They got on their marks. The *gyoji* flipped his fan.

The match was over in 3.1916 seconds. He helped Krugerrand to his feet, accepted the envelope and the thunderous applause of the crowd, and left the reverberating plastic enclosure.

"You are the wife of Man-Mountain Gentian?" asked a voice next to her.

Melissa put on her public smile and turned to the voice. Her nephew, on the other side, leaned around to look.

The man talking to her had five stars tattooed to his forehead. She knew he was a famous *sumotori*, though he was very slim and his *chon-mage* had been combed out and washed and his hair was now a fluffy explosion above his head.

"I am Killer Kudzu," he said. "I'm surprised you weren't at the tournament."

"I am here with my nephew, Hari. Hari, this is Mr. Killer Kudzu." The nephew, dressed in his winter Little League outfit, shook hands firmly. "His team, the Mitsubishi Zeroes play the Kawasaki Claudes next game."

They paused while a foul ball caused great excitement three rows down the bleachers. Hari leapt for it but some construction foreman of a father came up grinning with the ball.

"And what do you play?" asked Killer Kudzu.

"Utility outfield. When I play," said Hari, averting his eyes and sitting back down.

"Oh. How's your batting?"

"Pretty bad, .123 for the year," said Hari.

"Well, maybe this will be the night you shine," said Kudzu.

"I hope so," said Hari. "Half our team has the American flu."

"Just the reason I'm here," said Kudzu. "I was to meet a businessman whose son was to play this game. I find him not to be here, as his son has the influenza also."

It was hot in the domed stadium and Kudzu insisted they let him buy them Sno-Kones. Just as the vendor got to them, Hari's coach signaled and the nephew ran down the bleachers and followed the rest of his teammates into the warm-up area under the stadium.

Soon the other lackluster game was over and Hari's team took the field.

The first batter for the Claudes, a twelve-year-old built like an orangutan, got up and smashed a line drive off the Mitsubishi third baseman's chest. The third baseman had been waving to his mother. They carried him into the dugout. Melissa soon saw him up yelling again.

So it went through three innings. The Claudes had the Zeroes down by three runs, 6–3. In the fourth inning, Hari took right field, injuries having whittled the flu-ridden team down to the third-stringers.

One of the Claudes hit a high looping fly straight to right field. Hari started in after it, but something happened with his feet; he fell and the ball dropped a meter from his outstretched glove. The center fielder chased it

down and made the relay and by a miracle they got the
runner sliding into home plate. He took out the Zeroes
catcher doing it.

"It doesn't look good for the Zeroes," said Melissa.

"Oh, things might get better," said Killer Kudzu. "The
opera's not over till the fat lady sings."

"A *diva* couldn't do much worse out there," said
Melissa.

"They still don't like baseball in my country," he said.
"Decadent. Bourgeois, they say. As if anything could be
more decadent and middle-class than China."

"Yet you wear the flag?" She pointed toward his head.

"Call it a gesture to former greatness," he said.

Bottom of the sixth, last inning in Little League. The
Zeroes had the bases loaded but they had two outs in the
process. Hari came up to bat.

Things were tense. The outfielders were nearly falling
down from tension.

The pitcher threw a blistering curve that got the outside.
Hari was caught looking.

From the dugout the manager's voice saying unkind
things carried to the crowd.

Eight thousand people were on their feet.

The pitcher wound up and threw.

Hari started a swing that should have ended in a
grounder or a pop-up. Halfway through, it looked like
someone had speeded up a projector. The leisurely swing
blurred. Hari literally threw himself to the ground. The bat
cracked and broke in two at his feet.

The ball, a frozen white streak, cometed through the air
and hit the scoreboard 110 meters away with a terrific
crash, putting the inning indicator out of commission.

Everyone was stock-still. Hari was staring. Every
player was turned toward the scoreboard.

"It's a home run, kid," the umpire reminded Hari.
Slowly, unbelieving, Hari began to trot toward first base.

The place exploded, fans jumping to their feet. Hari's teammates on the bases headed for home. The dugout emptied, waiting for him to round third.

The Claudes stood fuming. The Zeroes climbed all over Hari.

"I didn't know you could do that more than once a day," said Melissa, her eyes narrowed.

"Who, me?" asked Kudzu.

"You're perverting your talent," she said.

"We're *not* supposed to be able to do that more than once every twenty-four hours," said Killer Kudzu, flashing a smile.

"I know that's not true, at least really," said Melissa.

"Oh, yes. You are *married* to a *sumotori,* aren't you?"

Melissa blushed.

"The kid seemed to feel bad enough about the dropped fly. Besides, it's just a game."

At home plate, Hari's teammates climbed over him, slapping him on the back.

The game was over, the scoreboard said 7–6, and the technicians were already climbing over the inning indicator.

Melissa rose. "I have to go pick up Hari. I suppose I will see you at the tournament tomorrow?"

"How are you getting home?" asked Killer Kudzu.

"We walk. Hari lives near."

"It's snowing."

"Oh."

"Let me give you a ride. My electric vehicle is outside."

"That would be nice. I live several kilometers away from—"

"I know where you live, of course."

"Fine, then."

Hari ran up. "Aunt Melissa! Did you see?! I don't know *what* happened! I just felt, I don't know. I just *hit* it!"

"That was wonderful." She smiled at him. Killer Kudzu

was looking up, very interested in the stadium support
structure.

The stable in which Man-Mountain Gentian trained was
being entertained that night. That meant that the wrestlers
would have to do all the entertaining.

Even at the top of this sport, Man-Mountain had never
gotten used to the fans. Their kingly prizes, their raucous
behavior at matches, their donations of gifts, clothing, vehicles, and in some cases houses and land to their favorite
wrestlers. It was all appalling.

It was a carryover from traditional sumo, he knew. But
zen-sumo had become a worldwide, not just a national
sport. Many saved for years to come to Japan to watch the
January or May tournaments. People here in Japan sometimes sacrificed at home to be able to contribute toward a
new *kesho-mawashi* apron for a wrestler entering the ring.
Money, in this business, flowed like water, appearing in
small envelopes in the mail, in the locker room, after feasts
such as the one tonight.

Once a month, Man-Mountain Gentian gathered them
all up and took them to his accountant, who had instructions to give it all, above a certain princely level, away to
charity. Other wrestlers had more, or less, or none of the
same arrangements. The tax men never seemed surprised
by whatever amount wrestlers reported.

He entered the club. Things were already rocking. One
of the hostesses took his shoes and coat. She had to put the
overcoat over her shoulders to carry it into the cloakroom.

The party was a haze of blue smoke, dishes, bottles, busi-
nessmen, wrestlers, and funny paper hats. Waitresses came
in and out with more food. Three musicians played unheard
on a raised dais at one side of the room. Someone was
telling a snappy story. The room exploded with laughter.

"Ah!" said someone. "Yokozuna Gentian has arrived."

Man-Mountain bowed deeply. They made two or three places for him at the low table. He saw that several of the host party were Americans. Probably one or more were from the CIA.

They and the Russians were still trying to perfect *zen-sumo* as an assassination weapon. They offered active and retired *sumotori* large amounts of money in an effort to get them to develop their powers in some nominally destructive form. So far, no one he knew of had. There were rumors about the Brazilians, however.

He could see it now, a future with premiers, millionaires, presidents, and paranoids in all walks of life wearing wire-mesh clothing and checking their Eveready batteries before going out each morning.

He had been approached twice, by each side. He was sometimes followed. They all were. People in governments simply did *not* understand.

He began to talk, while saki flowed, with Cast Iron Pekowski. Pekowski, now 12–2 for the tournament, had graciously lost his match with Typhoon Takanaka. (There was an old saying: In a tournament, no one who won more than nine matches ever beat an opponent who has lost seven. Which had been the case with Takanaka. Eight was the number of wins needed to retain current ranking.)

"I could feel him going," said Pekowski, in Polish. "I think we should talk to him about the May tournament."

"Have you mentioned this to his stablemaster?"

"I thought of doing so after the tournament. I was hoping you could come with me to see him."

"I'll be just another retired *sekitori* by then."

"Takanaka respects you above all the others. Besides, your *dampatsu-shiki* ceremony won't be for another two weeks. You'll still have your hair. And while we're at it, I still wish you would change your mind."

"Perhaps I could be Takanaka's dew-sweeper, if he decides."

"Good! You'll come with me then, Friday morning?"

"Yes."

The hosts were very much drunker than the wrestlers. Nayakano the stablemaster was feeling no pain but remained upright. Mounds of food were being consumed. A businessman tried to grab-ass a waitress. This was going to become every bit as nasty as all such parties.

"A song! A song!" yelled the head of the fan club, a businessman in his sixties. "Who will favor us with a song?"

Man-Mountain Gentian got to his feet, went over to the musicians. He talked with the samisen player. Then he stood facing his drunk, attentive audience.

How many of these parties had he been to in his career? Two, three hundred? Always the same, drunkenness, discord, braggadocio, on the part of the host clubs. Some fans really loved the sport, some lived vicariously through it. He would not miss the parties. But as the player began the tune he realized this might be the last party he would have to face.

He began to sing:

> *I met my lover by still Lake Biwa*
> *just before Taira war banners flew. . . .*

And so on through all six verses, in a clear pure voice belonging to a man half his size.

They stood and applauded him, some of the wrestlers in the stable looking away, as only they, not even the stablemaster, knew of his retirement plans and what this party probably meant.

He went to the stablemaster, who took him to the club host, made apologies concerning the tournament and a slight cold, shook hands, bowed and went out into the lobby, where the hostess valiantly brought him his shoes and overcoat. He wanted to help her, but she reshouldered the coat grimly and brought it to him. He handed her a tip and signed the autograph she asked for.

It had begun to snow outside. The neon made the sky a swirling multicolored smudge. Man-Mountain Gentian walked through the quickly emptying streets. Even the everpresent taxis scurried from the snow like roaches from a light. His home was only two kilometers away. He liked the stillness of the falling snow, the quietness of the city in times such as this.

"Shelter for a stormy night?" asked a ragged old man on a corner. Man-Mountain Gentian stopped.

"Change for shelter for an old man?" asked the beggar again, looking very far up at Gentian's face.

Man-Mountain Gentian reached in his pocket, took out three or four small ornate paper envelopes that had been thrust on him as he left the club.

The old man took them, opened one. Then another and another.

"There must be more than 800,000 yen here . . ." he said, very quietly and very slowly.

"I suggest the Imperial or the Hilton," said Man-Mountain Gentian. Then the wrestler turned and walked away.

The old man laughed, then straightened himself with dignity, stepped to the curb, and imperiously summoned an approaching pedicab.

Melissa was not home.

He turned on the entry light as he took off his shoes. He passed through the spartanly furnished low living room, turned off the light at the other switch.

He went to the bathroom, put depilatory gel on his face, wiped it off. He went to the kitchen, picked up half a ham and ate it, washing it down with three liters of milk. He returned to the bathroom, brushed his teeth, went to the bedroom, unrolled his futon, and placed his cinder block at the head of it.

He punched on the hidden tape deck and an old recording of Kimio Eto playing "Rukodan" on the koto quietly filled the house.

The only decoration in the sleeping room was Shuncho's print, "The Strongest and the Most Fair," showing a theater-district beauty and a *sumotori* three times her size, hanging on the far wall.

He turned off the light. Instantly the silhouettes of falling snowflakes showed through the paper walls of the house, cast by the strong streetlight outside. He watched the snowflakes fall, listening to the music, and was filled with *mono no aware* for the transience of beauty in the world.

Man-Mountain Gentian pulled up the puffed cotton covers, put his head on the building block, and drifted off to sleep.

They had let Hari off at his house. The interior of the runabout was warm. They were drinking coffee in the near-empty parking lot of Tokyo Sonic #113.

"I read somewhere you were an architect," said Killer Kudzu.

"Barely," said Melissa.

"Would you like to see Kudzu House?" he asked.

For an architect, it was like being asked to one of Frank Lloyd Wright's vacation homes, or one of the birdlike buildings designed by Eero Saarinen in the later twentieth century. Melissa considered.

"I should call home first," she said after a moment.

"I think your husband will still be at the Nue Vue Club, whooping it up with the moneymen."

"You're probably right. I'll call him later. I'd love to see your house."

The old man lay dying on his bed.

"I see you finally heard," he said. His voice was tired.

Man-Mountain Gentian had not seen him in seven years. He had always been old, but he had never looked this old, this weak.

Dr. Wu had been his mentor. He had started him on the path toward *zen-sumo* (though he did not know it at the time). Dr. Wu had not been one of those cryptic koan-spouting quiet men. He had been boisterous, laughing, playing with his pupils, yelling at them, whatever was needed to get them *to see*.

There had been the occasional letter from him. Now, for the first time, there was a call in the middle of the night.

"I'm sorry," said Man-Mountain Gentian. "It's snowing outside."

"At your house, too?" asked Dr. Wu.

Wu's attendant was dressed in Buddhist robes and seemingly paid no attention to either of them.

"Is there anything I can do for you?" asked Man-Mountain Gentian.

"Physically, no. This is nothing a pain shift can help. Emotionally, there is."

"What?"

"You can win tomorrow, though I won't be around to share it."

Man-Mountain Gentian was quiet a moment. "I'm not sure I can promise you that."

"I didn't think so. You are forgetting the kitten and the bowl of milk."

"No. Not at all. I think I've finally come up against something new and strong in the world. I will either win or lose. Either way, I will retire."

"If it did not mean anything to you, you could have lost by now," said Dr. Wu.

Man-Mountain Gentian was quiet again.

Wu shifted uneasily on his pillows. "Well, there is not much time. Lean close. Listen to what I have to say."

"The novice Itsu went to the Master and asked him: 'Master, what is the key to all enlightenment?'

"'You must teach yourself never to think of the white horse,' said the Master.

"Itsu applied himself with all his being. One day while raking gravel he achieved insight.

"'Master! Master!' yelled Itsu, running to his quarters. 'Master! I have made myself not think about the white horse!'

"'Quick!' said the Master. "When you were not thinking of the white horse, where was Itsu?'

"The novice could make no answer.

"The Master dealt Itsu a smart blow with his staff.

"At this, Itsu was enlightened."

Then Dr. Wu let his head back down on his bed.

"Good-bye," he said.

In his bed in the lamasery in Tibet, Dr. Wu let out a ragged breath and died.

Man-Mountain Gentian, standing on his futon in his bedroom in Tokyo, began to cry.

Kudzu House took up a city block in the middle of Tokyo. The taxes alone must have been enormous.

Through the decreasing snow, Melissa saw the lights. Their beams stabbed up into the night. All she could see from a block away was the tangled kudzu.

Kudzu was a vine, originally transplanted from China, raised in Japan for centuries. Its crushed root was used as a starch base, in cooking; its leaves were used for teas and medicines, its fibers to make cloth and paper. What kudzu was most famous for was its ability to grow over and cover anything which didn't move out of its way.

In the Depression thirties of the last century, it had been planted on road cuts in the southeastern United States to stop erosion. Kudzu had almost stopped progress there. In those ideal conditions it grew runners more than twenty meters long in a single summer, several to a root. Its vines climbed utility poles, hills, trees. It completely covered other vegetation, cutting off its sunlight.

Many places in the American South were covered three kilometers wide to each side of the highways with kudzu vines. The Great Kudzu Forest of central Georgia was a U.S. National Park.

In the bleaker conditions of Japan the weed could be kept under control. Except that this owner didn't want to. The lights playing into the snowy sky were part of the heating and watering system that kept vines growing year-round. All this Melissa had read before. Seeing it was something again. The entire block was a green tangle of vines and lights.

"Do you ever trim it?" she asked.

"The traffic keeps it back," said Killer Kudzu, and laughed. "I have gardeners who come in and fight it once a week. They're losing."

They went into the green tunnel of a driveway. Melissa saw the edge of the house, cast concrete, as they dropped into the sunken vehicle area.

There were three boats, four road vehicles, a hovercraft, and a small sport flyer parked there. Lights shone up into a dense green roof from which hundreds of vines grew downward toward the light sources.

"We have to move the spotlights every week," he said.

A butler met them at the door. "Just a tour, Mord," said Killer Kudzu. "We'll have drinks in the sitting room in thirty minutes."

"Very good, sir."

"This way."

Melissa went to a railing. The living area was the size of a bowling alley, or the lobby of a terrible old hotel. The balcony on the second level jutted out from the east wall. Killer Kudzu went to a console, punched buttons.

Moe and the Meanies boomed from dozens of speakers.

Killer Kudzu stood snapping his fingers for a moment. "O, send me! Honorable cats!" he said. "That's from Spike Jones, an irreverent American musician of the last century. He died of cancer," he added.

Melissa followed him, noticing the things everyone noticed—the Chrome Room, the Supercharger Inhalorium, the archery range ("the object is *not* to hit the targets," said Kudzu), the Mosasaur Pool with the fossils embedded in the sides and bottom.

She was more affected by the house and its tawdriness than she thought she would be.

"You've done very well for yourself."

"Some manage it, some give it away, some save it. I *spend* it."

They were drinking kudzu tea highballs in the sitting room, which was one of the most comfortable rooms Melissa had ever been in.

"Tasteless, isn't it?" asked Killer Kudzu.

"Not quite," said Melissa. "Well worth the trip."

"You could stay, you know?" said Kudzu.

"I thought I could." She sighed. "It would only give me one more excuse not to finish the dishes at home." She gave him a long look. "Besides, it wouldn't give you an advantage in the match."

"That really never crossed my mind."

"I'm quite sure."

"You are a beautiful woman."

"You have a nice house."

"Hmmm. Time to get you home."

"I'm sure."

They sat outside her house in the cold. The snow had stopped. Stars peeped through the low scud.

"I'm going to win tomorrow," said Killer Kudzu.

"You might," said Melissa.

"It is sometimes possible to do more than win," he said.

"I'll tell my husband."

"My offer is always open," he said. He reached over and opened her door on the runabout. "Life won't be the same after he's lost. Or after he retires."

She climbed out, shaking from more than the cold. He closed the door, whipped the vehicle in a circle, and was gone down the crunching street. He blinked his lights once before he drove out of sight.

She found her husband in the kitchen. His eyes were red; he was as pale as she had ever seen him.

"Dr. Wu is dead," he said, and wrapped his huge arms around her, covering her like an upright sofa.

He began to cry again. She talked to him quietly.

"Come, let's try to get some sleep," she said.

"No, I couldn't rest. I wanted to see you first. I'm going down to the stable." She helped him dress in his warmest clothing. He kissed her and left, walking the few blocks through the snowy sidewalks to the training building.

The junior wrestlers were awakened at 4 A.M. They were to begin the day's work of sweeping, cleaning, cooking, bathing, feeding and catering to the senior wrestlers. When they came in they found him, stripped to his *mawashi,* at the 300-kilo push bag, pushing, pushing, straining, crying all the while, not saying a word. The floor of the arena was torn and grooved. They cleaned up the area for the morning workouts, one following him around with the sand-trowel.

At 7 A.M. he slumped exhausted on a bench. Two of the *juryo* covered him with quilts and set an alarm clock beside him for 1 P.M.

"Your opponent was at the ball game last night," said Nayakano the stablemaster. Man-Mountain Gentian sat in the dressing rooms while the barber combed and greased his elaborate *chon-mage*. "Your wife asked me to give you this."

It was a note in a plain envelope, addressed in her beautiful calligraphy. He opened and read it. She warned him of what Kudzu said about "more than winning" the night before, and wished him luck.

He turned to the stablemaster.

"Has Killer Kudzu injured any opponent before he became *yokozuna* last tournament?"

Nayakano's answer was immediate. "No. That's unheard of. Let me see that note." He reached out.

Man-Mountain Gentian put it back in the envelope, tucked it in his *mawashi*.

"Should I alert the judges?"

"Sorry I mentioned it," said Man-Mountain Gentian.

"I don't like this," said the stablemaster.

Three hefty junior wrestlers ran in carrying Gentian's *kenzo-mawashi* between them.

The last day of the January tournament always packed them in. Even the maegashira and komusubi matches, in which young boys threw each other, or tried to, drew enough of an audience to make the novices feel good.

The call for the Ozeki class wrestlers came, and they

went through the grandiose ring-entering ceremony, wearing their great *kenzo-mawashi* aprons of brocade, silk, and gold while their dew-sweepers and swordbearers squatted to the sides. Then they retired to their benches, east or west, to await the call by the falsetto-voiced *yobidashi*.

Man-Mountain Gentian watched as the assistants helped Killer Kudzu out of his ceremonial apron, gold with silk kudzu leaves, purple flowers, yellow stars. His forehead blazed with the PRC flag. He looked directly at Gentian's place and smiled a broad smile.

There was a great match between Gorilla Tsunami and Typhoon Takanaka which went on for more than 30 seconds by the clock, both men straining, groaning, sweating until the *gyoji* made them stop, and rise, and then get on their marks again.

Those were the worst kinds of matches for the wrestlers, each opponent alternately straining, then bending with the other, neither getting advantage. There was a legendary match five years ago that took six 30-second tries before one wrestler bested the other.

The referee flipped his fan. Gorilla Tsunami fell flat on his face in a heap, then wriggled backward out of the ring.

The crowd screamed and applauded Takanaka.

Then the *yobidashi* said, "East—Man-Mountain Gentian. West—Killer Kudzu."

They hurried their shikiris. Each threw salt twice, rinsing once. Then Man-Mountain Gentian, moving with the grace of a dancer, lifted his right leg and stamped it, then his left, and the sound was like the double echo of a cannon throughout the stadium.

He went immediately to his mark.

Killer Kudzu jumped down to his mark, glaring across the meter that separated them.

The *gyoji*, off guard, took a few seconds to turn sideways to them and bring his fan into position.

In that time, Man-Mountain Gentian could hear the quiet hum of the electrical grid, hear muffled intake of breath from the other wrestlers, hear a whistle in the nostril of the north-side judge.

"Huuu!" said the referee and his fan jerked.

Man-Mountain Gentian felt like two freight trains had collided in his head. There was a snap as his muscles went tense all over and the momentum of the explosion in his brain began to push at him, lifting, threatening to make him give or tear through the back of his head. His feet were on a slippery sandy bottom, neck-high wave crests smashed into him, a rip tide was pushing at his shoulder, at one side, pulling his legs up, twisting his muscles. He could feel his eyes pushed back in their sockets as if by iron thumbs, ready to pop them like ripe plums. His ligaments were iron wires stretched tight on the turnbuckles of his bones. His arms ended in strands of noodles, his face was soft cheese.

The sand under him was soft, so soft, and he knew that all he had to do was to sink in it, let go, cease to resist.

And through all that haze and blindness he knew what he was not supposed to think about.

Everything *quit:* He reached out one mental hand, as big as the sun, as fast as light, as long as time, and he pushed against his opponent's chest.

The lights were back, he was in the stadium, in the arena, and the dull pounding was applause, screams.

Killer Kudzu lay blinking among the ring bales.

"Hooves?" Man-Mountain Gentian heard him ask in bewilderment before he picked himself up.

Man-Mountain Gentian took the envelope from the referee with the three quick chopping motions, then made a fourth to the audience, and they knew then and only then that they would never see him in the ring again.

The official clock said .9981 second.

"How did you do it, Man-Mountain?" asked the Tokyo *paparazzi* as he showered out his chon-mage and put on his clothes. He said nothing.

He met his wife outside the stadium. A lone newsman was with her, "Scoop" Hakimoto.

"For old times' sake," begged Hakimoto. "How did you do it?"

Man-Mountain Gentian turned to Melissa. "Tell him how I did it," he said.

"He didn't think about the white horse," she said. They left the newsman standing, staring.

Killer Kudzu, tired and pale, was getting in his vehicle. Hakimoto came running up. "What's all this I hear about Gentian and a white horse?" he asked.

Kudzu's eyes widened, then narrowed.

"No comment," he said.

That night, to celebrate, Man-Mountain Gentian took Melissa to the Beef Bowl.

He had seventeen orders and helped Melissa finish her second one.

They went back home, climbed onto their futons, and turned on the TV.

Gilligan was on his island. All was right with the world.

WINNING

Ian McDonald

British author Ian McDonald is an ambitious and daring writer with a wide range and an impressive amount of talent. His first story was published in 1982, and since then he has appeared with some frequency in Interzone, Asimov's Science Fiction, New Worlds, Zenith, Other Edens, Amazing, *and elsewhere. He was nominated for the John W. Campbell Award in 1985, and in 1989 he won the* Locus *"Best First Novel" Award for his novel* Desolation Road. *He won the Philip K. Dick Award in 1992 for his novel* King of Morning, Queen of Day. *His other books include the novels* Out on Blue Six, *and* Hearts, Hands, and Voices, Terminal Cafe, Sacrifice of Fools, *and the acclaimed* Evolution's Shore, *and two collections of his short fiction,* Empire Dreams *and* Speaking In Tongues. *His most recent book is a new novel,* Kirinya, *and a chapbook novella,* Tendeleo's Story, *both sequels to* Evolution's Shore. *Born in Manchester, England, in 1960, McDonald has spent most of his life in Northern Ireland, and now lives and works in Belfast. He has a Web site at http://www.lysator.liu.se/^unicorn/mcdonald/.*

In the vivid and inventive story that follows, he demonstrates that even in a high-tech future where a competitive edge is measured out in microseconds, there'll be many different kinds of winners and losers, all depending on your point of view. . . .

The beach is a white crescent of sand under the white crescent moon. Caught in the arms of the moon is a single bright star; a low-orbit manufactory. Below, the tourist ho-

tels and beachfront restaurants show a scatter of lights.
Tourists from Dahomey and Luzon and Costa Rica drink
and dance and snort designer synTHC and stalk in sexual
ambush among the pin lasers and multilayer video shriek.
It is many hours since they abandoned the casual nudity of
the beach to the moon and the stars and Hammadi.

He slips under the loose wire by the irrigation channel
outfall. The air is clean and cool, it has the crispness of au-
tumn and the end of the season: after these tourists have
checked out of their rooms and flown back to Dahomey
and Luzon and Costa Rica, there will be no more. In the
moonlight Hammadi limbers up using the isotonic flex
routine the Company taught him. In twenty seconds he is
ready. He slips out of the fleecy track suit. The repro shops
of Penang and Darwin produce good copies of professional bodysuits; skin smooth, patterned with patches of
bright primaries, sponsorship logos in all the right places.
They look good, but Hammadi has worn both and knows
the difference. A copy does not caress you, does not become one with you through eight thousand biomonitors
and sensory systems and interfacers. It does not feel like a
living skin. It feels like what it is: smooth stretch fabric
made up in the immigrant sweatshops of Vancouver and
Tananarive.

The wind is blowing off the mountains where snow has
lain for weeks: Hammadi shivers, breathes it in, lets it
blow through the hollow places of his body and soul. Tank-
taught disciplines take over, tyrosine and norepinephrine
levels in his bloodstream soar, pushing him into a state of
amplified awareness. His senses are so finely honed he can
count every grain of windblown sand against his cheek,
hear the roll and surge of the blood around his bones, see
the photons boiling from the lights of the tourist hotels and
beach clubs. He gathers the energy surging within him into
a tight cord, releases it. And he is running, past the hotels
and beachside clubs and closed-down restaurants, down

the long crescent of white sand. He is the Lion of God, the swift arrow of desire, he is the man Allah made fast so that he might delight to see him run.

It had always been his blessing and his curse, to have been specially gifted by God, for his father had used it as an excuse to exalt him above his brothers. At the dinner table, the only place where the lives of all the al-Bourhan family intersected, al-Bourhan Senior would bang the table and point at the inhumanly tall inhumanly beautiful bodies of the professional athletes that moved with liquid grace and power on the wall-mounted Sony flatscreen. Mouth full of couscous, he would berate his four other sons for their uselessness. "You think I don't hear, you think I am deaf, stupid, you think I am old and senile; that I don't hear you muttering how I am unfair, unjust, a bad father because I love Hammadi better than the rest of you? Well, I do not deny it. I love Hammadi the best, and you know why?" Crumbs of food would fly from his lips, he would stab his fingers at the figures drifting languidly around the track. "That is why. Because God has given him the chance of bettering himself, because he can hope for a life that is more than just getting a job and marrying a good woman and raising a family, a life that is more than serving drinks on a silver tray in a hotel or selling brass teapots to tourists until you die. That is why." When al-Bourhan spoke like this, Hammadi would leave the room. He could not look at his father or his brothers. He had not asked to be gifted by Allah. The inhumanly tall inhumanly beautiful figures of the athletes on the wallscreen kept drifting around the oval track beneath the tiered seats in the great stadium.

Jamila al-Bourhan was a woman who served God by serving men. She knew that men were stupid and vain creatures, capable of almost limitless stupidity in the name of their vanity, yet she married them, bore them, served them, even loved them, because she loved God more. Her work was her prayer, her kitchen her mosque. The law no longer required that women wear the veil, but some women can wear invisible veils all their lives. She watched al-Bourhan, the man God had made her to serve, wake Hammadi at five in the morning to train. She watched him take the boy out after his day at the garage to practice on the gritty, sweating streets. At night, when the cafés and bars were putting up the shutters, she watched him, on Haran's moped, pacing her son through the pools of hot green neon Arabic. She watched her family with the dispassionate detachment of Allah All Merciful, All Wise.

She was watching from the kitchen the day al-Bourhan presented the package at the dinner table. Everyone knew what it was, of course, but Hammadi pretended he did not as he opened the plastic wrap and held the brightly colored bodysuit up against himself.

"It's only a copy," al-Bourhan apologized, but she saw the look on his face that was at once shy and proud. She saw Hammadi bow his head to hide his embarrassment, she saw how her four sons bowed their heads to hide their disappointment and anger. That night Hammadi went running, brilliant as a bird beneath the glaring fluorescents, just like the professionals on the sports channels. His brothers sat around the table drinking mint tea and watching a Russian metal band on a music channel beamed by satellite from Singapore.

That night Jamila al-Bourhan spoke with the husband God had given her. "You will drive your sons away from you; they see how you look at Hammadi and how you look at them and they feel unworthy, they feel they are not sons to you."

"Wife," said the husband Allah had willed to her, "so many times I am explaining this and still you will not understand. Hammadi has been touched by the hand of God, and God's gifts are not to be wasted. It would be as wrong

for him not to run as it would be for me to kill a man. If I
push him to train, if I push him to his limits, and beyond,
if I make him hate me a little, I do it so that someday he
will be the one standing there on that track with the world
watching him. I do it only so that he may fulfill the will of
God for him."

"The will of Khedaffey al-Bourhan, you mean," said
the woman who loved Allah more than she loved men. "It
is an easy, and terrible, mistake to make, to think your will
is God's will."

But al-Bourhan was already shouting at his useless sons
to switch off that decadent rubbish and tune the set back to
IntRelay SattelSport. Hammadi's mother picked the discarded bodysuit off her son's bedroom floor. It felt like
something a snake had left behind.

That Sunday night al-Bourhan took Hammadi by black-
and-white moped cab to a street corner where the palm-
lined Boulevard of Heavenly Peace ran into the shanties
where the refugees from the war in the south had been hidden by the government. There were a number of other boys
already there, some in bodysuits like himself, some just in
shorts and vests. There was a large crowd of spectators,
people not just from Squattertown, but from all parts of the
city. Electric-thin men kept this side of starvation by government food handouts stood only a bodyguard away from
designer-muscled men and girls in paisley body paint. Al-
Bourhan paid the entrance fee to a man sitting on an up-
turned tangerine crate. Hammadi went to warm up with the
other runners. Excitement was a warm snake coiling in the
pit of his belly. All the hours driving himself along those
roads and pavements in those twilight hours, that chilly
predawn glow, in the weariness after hours of wrestling
with the innards of buses and trucks, had been for this electric thrill of *competition*. He saw his father haggling with a
small man in a crocheted hat who seemed to have a lot of
money in his hand.

The starter called them to order. There were no blocks, no lanes, no electronic timing, no hovering cameras, but crouching under the yellow floodlights the government had put up to reveal the lives of Squattertown, Hammadi felt he was in that great silver dome with the eyes of the world watching. "Fast as a cheetah," he whispered. "God's cheetah." Then the gun went off, and the spectators, rich and poor, rose as one with a roar, and Hammadi was burning along the boulevard under the tattered palm trees, blood bursting in his veins, to feel the tape brush across his chest. He returned to his father, who was receiving a large amount of cash from the man in the crocheted hat, high on victory.

"Nine-point-nine-seven," said al-Bourhan. "You can do better than that."

Every weekend there was a street race somewhere in the city, or in one of the neighboring cities. Al-Bourhan's winnings from the man in the crocheted hat, who went to all the races, grew smaller and smaller as the odds against his son grew shorter and shorter. He still made quite a lot of money out of Hammadi, but it was not riches he wanted, it was success.

The season traditionally concluded with the big meeting in the capital where the nation's youth met together in the Great Fellowship of Sport to have their endeavor rewarded with medals from the hand of the President. Medals from the hand of the President and the Great Fellowship of Sport were the farthest things from the minds of the athletes who traveled up to the capital: the talent scouts from the big corporations would be there with contracts in their thumb-lock impact-plastic cases.

The capital was an eight-hour bus journey distant. So that Hammadi might be fit and fresh, al-Bourhan booked them into a hotel close by the stadium. It was not a very expensive hotel, just grand enough to have prostitutes in the lobby bar. As Hammadi came down in the elevator for his evening run, they unfolded pneumatic thighs, smiled *diamante* smiles, and surrounded him in a nimbus of synthetic allure from their wrist-mounted pheromone enhancers. They ran cooing, purring fingers over the firm contours of his bodysuit. Hammadi was half hysterical with sexual confusion by the time his father shooed them away from his champion back to their stools by the bar. On his return they clicked their tongues and pursed their lips and hitched their rubber microskirts to flash dark vees of pubic hair at him. Hammadi's sleep that night was prowled by soft, writhing, fleshtone dreams.

Entering the stadium from the competitors' tunnel, Hammadi was overcome by a sudden disorientation. He was a street racer, a runner of the boulevards and the palm-lined avenues; surrounded by a curving wall of faces, tier upon tier upon tier of mothers fathers brothers sisters wives husbands lovers, he was reduced to a small and brilliantly colored insect creeping upon the smooth red running track. He searched the banked seats for his father. Impossible to find the one face in the ten thousand that meant anything to him. He was anonymous. He was nothing. The other runners came out onto the track and he saw their spirits shrivel as his had done, and they were all the same, equally handicapped, all street racers, night runners, poor boys on the round red track. Above the stadium blimp-borne laser projectors painted advertisements for the sponsoring companies across artificially generated clouds.

The starter called them to order. Hammadi prayed the prayer he always prayed before he ran, that God would make him fast today. All along the line the other runners completed their preparations physical and spiritual. The starter raised his gun. The flat crack filled the stadium one split second before the crowd rose in a wall of sound and Hammadi plunged from his blocks down the red tracks and across the line in one continuous thought.

He collected his medal from the President, who did not shake hands due to yet another public-health scare, and took it to show his father.

"You show me that? A bit of metal on a string and you think you have achieved something? Hammadi, meet Mr. Larsby. He is from Toussaint Mantene." A small white man in an expensive Penang suit took Hammadi's hand for a full minute and said a lot of things, none of which Hammadi could later remember. He was high on winning. On the way back to the hotel in the taxi Hammadi's father kept hugging him and saying how this was the proudest day in his life. The small white man in the Penang suit was waiting for them in their room. With him was a taller, thinner man in a Nehru suit. He was scanning the walls with a small hand-held unit.

"Purely routine," he said. "You never know, they get everywhere." He had the kind of voice Hammadi had only ever heard on the satellite channels. The small man opened his thumb-lock impact-plastic case and took out two thick sheaves of paper.

"Right here and here," he said. The small man placed his signature under Hammadi's graceful Arabic, and al-Bourhan and the man in the Nehru suit witnessed.

"Congratulations," said the small man, Larsby. "Welcome to Toussaint Mantene." Al-Bourhan was sitting on the bed in tears. The realization was only slowly penetrating Hammadi's victory high that he was not an amateur, a street racer, a boulevard runner anymore. He was on the other side of the television now. He was one of the inhumanly tall inhumanly beautiful figures that drifted around the silver dome. He was a professional.

His father was ecstatic. His brothers unsuccessfully tried to hide their jealousy. His mother concealed her pride behind fear for his spiritual well-being. But they all came with him to the big airport in the capital where Larsby and the man in the Nehru suit would take him onward on a sub-

orbital Sänger. The brothers watched the incredible shapes
of the aerospacers moving in the heathaze. Al-Bourhan
shouted at them for not being appreciative of their
brother's blessing. To Hammadi it was enough that they
had come. His mother nervously watched the streamlined
aircraft with the crescent moon and star of Islam on its tail
approach the airdock. She took her son's face in her hands,
and the intimacy of the gesture abolished every other person in the departure lounge.

"God has given you a gift," she said rapidly, for Larsby
and the man in the Nehru suit were approaching through
the aisles of seating. "Never forget that it is not yours, it is
only lent to you. Be true to the one who gave it to you.
Honor Allah and He will honor you."

Then Larsby and the man in the Nehru suit came and
took him through emigration control into another country.

He has settled into his stride now. All the motor and sensory faculties of his body are operating at optimum. He is
aware of the exact state and function of every muscle. He
can hear, like gunfire in the hills, the crack and fire of his
synapses, the seethe and surge of chemotransmitters along
the neural pathways. He feels he can run at this pace forever. He knows this is just a phase, in time he will pass
from it into the next when his body will begin to cry out in
protest at what his brain is forcing it to do. The muscles
will begin to burn, the lungs to strain for oxygen, the red
dots will explode softly, noiselessly in his vision. He will
want to give up; stop, give in to the pleading of the body.
But he will keep on, along that beach, and he will find that
suddenly the pain and the urge to give up will no longer
matter, his spirit will have risen above them, above all
things physical and psychological. He will perceive himself running on the crescent of white sand beneath the
lights of the orbital factories with the eye of God. He calls

this the "Sufi State," after those men who whirled themselves out of the flesh into the spirit. Running is not merely a conquering of space and time by the body, but also by the soul.

He has left the lights of the beachfront cafés and tourist hotels behind, his run now takes him past the condominiums of the rich: the government officials, the police chiefs, the drug squirarchs. Their low white houses huddle behind triple-strand electrified wire and thermal-imaging myotoxin dart throwers. A few lights burn on patios and by pool sides. He can hear the cries of the women as they are tumbled naked into the swimming pools and the bull laughter of the men who are tumbling them. The cool wind carries the smell of barbecuing meat and the sweet, glossy scent of synTHC. Close by the wire, dog eyes shine reflected long-red. The manufacturers of custom dogs supply implanted electronic surveillance systems as standard. Standard also the chips in their cerebral cortexes connected to a portable Behavior Control Unit. Implanted compressed gas lances that can blow an intruder's intestines out through his mouth and anus are extra. They watch the running figure in their artificial enhanced vision. They do not bark, they never bark, their vocal chords have been removed. Behind the biobeat and the *drastique* the cries of the women have taken on a new, insistent rhythm.

Hammadi runs on. His footprints in the damp sand by the sea edge slowly fill with black water.

They laughed when he asked where the windows were.

"It costs a billion apiece to build these things, you can't expect decoration," said Larsby. Hammadi was disappointed. If he was going to the edge of space, at least he wanted to see what it was like. Like a good Muslim he refused the hostess's offer of tranquilizers and was sick for the entire forty-minute suborbital flight.

The car from the airport had tinted windows, a bar, and
an office unit. It drove along an oceanfront boulevard lined
with ragged palms. There were tourists hotels and condominiums, there were street vendors and pedicab ranks,
there were people running and people walking little dogs,
there were beggars and security company prowl cars.
There were holographic advertisements for cameras and
computers and condoms and *cannabarillos*. The alphabet
was different. The other difference was the immense trun-
cated cone of a corporate arcology standing across the near
horizon like God. Hammadi could not have said what part
of the world he was in.

They gave him an apartment on the fifty-fifth floor with
a veranda overlooking the ocean. The only thing he did not
like about it was that he could not turn the television off.
He went out onto the balcony to look at the ocean and saw
that all the surrounding balconies were occupied by naked
fat women lying on their backs in the sun. Toward evening
a woman opened the door Larsby had told him only he
could open. She was dressed in a leather pouch and paisley bodytint.

"Excuse me, can I help you?" Hammadi asked. The
woman stood there a full minute, smiling at him in a way
that was both pitying and relieved. She closed the door and
he never saw her again. His training began the next day.

The first two weeks he did not run at all. He was measured, weighed, analyzed, sectioned, taken apart, and re-
assembled. He had electrodes connected to his skull and
sat for hours in a darkened room telling a synthetic voice
which of two lights flashed first, he arranged shapes and
matched up grids on holographic displays, he was lowered
into sensdep tanks and exposed to different-colored lights,
he was shot full of injections that made him feel angry or
sleepy or horny or induced bizarre hallucinations or made
him feel like crying continuously or that he had seen the
face of God and forgotten what it looked like. The man in

the Nehru suit made him sign a consent form, and when he woke up from surgery he was thirty centimeters taller and had plastic parallel interface ports under his ears and at the back of his neck and along his spine and inner thighs. He stroked the soft plastic with his fingers. It made him want to cry.

Every day he asked Larsby when he was going to run.

"You'll be in full training soon enough," Larsby said. "Don't worry, this is all just to find out what we need to design a training program specially for you that will bring you to your optimum performance peak. By the way, sign this." It was another consent form.

"What is it for?"

"It's just a general consent for us to introduce performance-enhancing agents into your food."

"Wait, please. Do you mean you want me to take drugs? Mr. Larsby, Islam prohibits the abuse of drugs."

Larsby pursed his lips. "Well, they're not exactly drugs; in fact, they're not drugs at all, they're naturally occurring chemicals, well, synthetic copies of them, found in the body, that stimulate muscle development, neural responses, and overall growth. Really, you shouldn't call them drugs at all."

Hammadi signed the form. He could not tell when they started to put the performance enhancers in his meals. At the end of the two weeks of testing Larsby sent Hammadi for five days of sun, sand, surf, sleep, and sex at a Company beach resort down the coast. When he returned, having enjoyed all of these bar one, Larsby summoned him to his office.

"Got something for you." A panel slid open in the wall. Hanging there, in this year's latest pastels and black, with all the logos in all the right places, was a Toussaint Mantene bodysuit. Hammadi tried it on in a small dressing room hidden behind another wooden panel in Larsby's office. As he sealed it shut he felt it move and settle around his contours, felt the temperature control mechanism adjust to his optimum heat-transfer pattern, felt the inbuilt film circuitry mesh with his parallel interfacers. Energy poured through him, burned up his spine, along his nerves and sinews. He had never experienced such a total, dynamic communion with his body before. He wanted to run and run and never stop. He looked at himself in the mirror, remembered the pride with which his father had presented him with the cheap Filipino copy.

The training began. Hammadi had thought he would be running every day with the other Company-sponsored athletes. Again he was wrong. Most of the competitive races were run in computer simulation. The few others he did meet in out-of-training hours were mostly boys like himself, lifted from lives of disadvantage and insignificance by the hand of Toussaint Mantene. Different skin, different hair, different eyes, same lives. They had too much in common to be able to communicate. Hammadi trained alone, under the silver dome with its tiers upon tiers of flipped-up seats and the lights that were supposed to stimulate sunlight but never quite did.

Larsby monitored the training sessions from a glass box that descended from the roof. It had not taken Hammadi long to realize that despite the whispered comments on the speaker they had implanted in his mastoid bone, Larsby was his coach only insofar as he was the man who had speculated in buying up the contract of a promising street runner and invested his time and effort in bringing him to the point where he might someday win him and the Company a lot of money. He had heard from the other Toussaint Mantene athletes of the fortunes in shares and influence points that changed hands at the intercorporate athletics meets.

His real coach was the computer. It regulated his calorific, mineral, nutrient, trace, and vitamin intake, it programmed his hours of sleep, it monitored his body

functions and vital signs from the moment he pulled his
bodysuit on in the morning to when he left it lying in a pile
outside the personal-hygiene cubicle at night, it produced
optimum performance parameters for every action he
made while running and programmed them into his muscles through the bodysuit interfacers, it compared his
movements and responses with a holographic ideal syn-
thesized from the performances of past champions, it
checked Hammadi's real-time performance against his optimized model a thousand times a second and tightened up
a neural firing curve here, flattened out a troublesome
brainwave pattern there, adjusted the levels of alpha
dopamines and K-endorphin groupings so that he was neither too happy nor too sad, too much in pain or not feeling
the burn enough.

He saw the other athletes flying off to competition
every other week and asked Larsby when he could run for
the Company.

"You've got a way to go yet, son," Larsby said in his always reasonable, always right voice. "Lot to learn, boy.
Lot of mistakes to put right. But you'll get there, don't you
worry about that."

"When?"

"When I say so."

Months passed, the passage of the anonymous seasons
apparent only in secondary, human responses: the changing fashions of the girls who roller-skated along the palm-
lined boulevards; the jet surfers and power skiers putting
on colorful wet suits, the fat peely women who sunbathed
naked on their balconies resetting their apartment lighting
to UVB and making appointments to have their
melanomas frozen off. Hammadi sent letters and flat-light
holograms of himself to his family. In the letters he received in reply his father would say how proud he was that
the son of such a humble man could hope to rise so high.
His mother would be constantly amazed at how tall he was

growing, how broad, how strong, why she hardly knew
him for the same Hammadi. She would always remind him
that God honored those who honored Him. Hammadi
looked at himself in the mirror in his personal-hygiene
cubicle, the long, deep look he had until now avoided. He
saw what the radical replacement surgery, the growth fac-
tors, the daily physiotherapy, the muscular development
hormones, the high-energy diet, the muscle-pattern opti-
mization treatment had done to him. He hardly recognized
himself for the same Hammadi.

Now when he trained, he was driven by a deep and dark
energy. It seemed like determination. It was anger, anger
that his father had always, only, loved him for what he
could become, not what he was. Larsby noticed the new,
driving energy. "So what's the secret then, boy?" he asked.
"The computer models never predicted you'd hit this kind
of form at this stage in training."

"I looked at myself in the mirror and saw that I was not
what I thought I was."

"You keep taking that look," said Larsby. "And keep
liking what you're seeing. I think maybe we might try you
at the next race meet."

Hammadi was flown in another windowless plane to
another arcology by another oceanside and another track
under its silver dome with tiers upon tiers of seats and
lighting that was meant to simulate daylight but never
quite did.

"You're entered in the two hundred," Larsby told him.
They were walking the track, letting the real-time analyz-
ers in Hammadi's shoes produce a model of the running
surface. "Given the range of entrants, the computer assigned the highest probability of an optimum performance
in that event. Friday. Twelve-thirty."

Hammadi stopped walking.

"Could you not have entered me in an event that is not
going to be run on a Friday?"

"You have some problem with Friday?"

Hammadi had known Larsby long enough to read a full spectrum of expressions into his practiced blandness.

"It's the Holy Day. I can't run on the Holy Day, it would be dishonoring to God."

Larsby looked at Hammadi as he might some dead thing washed up on the beach from deep in the ocean.

"Okay, so, I respect your religion, I respect every man who believes in something, but Hammadi: you say God's made you fast, that's the secret of your success, I can accept that, you have a remarkable talent, but answer this, which would honor God more, to use the gift he has given you to show a world which, frankly, does not believe, the strength of your belief, or let that light be hidden, so that no one will see what God can accomplish through you?"

"I don't know. I'll have to think about this. Give me time, will you?"

"Son, you take all the time you need."

Hammadi went to his apartment. He sat on the balcony overlooking the palms and the ocean. He thought about what his mother said about God honoring those who honored Him, and her accusations that her father had confused the will of Allah with his own will. He prayed. He waited on God, but no finger of fire wrote blazing letters across the yellow tropical storm clouds that clung to the horizon.

He went back to Larsby and said, "I'll run. If I am honoring God, He will bless me. If I am dishonoring God, I will not succeed."

Friday. Race day. Hammadi's bloodstream had been boosted with synthetic hemoglobin assistors and doped with adenosine triphosphates. By race time his nervous system was boiling with artificially induced fury. He ran onto the track, and as the trackside tech team ran final checks on his biological, physiological, and informational systems, the cameras looked on, hovering like blue flies on their silent ducted fans. Then the adenosine triphosphate

kicked in fully and all he cared about, all he lived for, was
to annihilate every other runner on that track. In the blocks
the pulser ticked in the corner of his field of vision, regis-
tering world, Pan-Olympic, Corporation, and personal
records. The starter was a ringing blip in his ears and a
flash of red across his vision. Cortical electrical activity
peaked momentarily to multivolt levels and sent him burning away from the blocks in a split second of controlled
epileptic spasm. The PCP pump in the base of his skull
trickled 3-4-morphatropine and tyrocine salicylate into his
brain stem; he felt he was growing in size until he filled the
entire stadium. He could compete the two hundred meters
in a single stride. Larsby's voice in his ear spoke through a
wash of mantras designed to erase everything unneedful
from his attention except winning. He was running like a
god, with the great easy strides Allah takes across Creation, galaxies in a single step. Yet, somehow, there were
others in front of him. Under his bodysuit his muscles
moved into new configurations as the interfacers fed new
response patterns to the changing tactical situation.

It was begun and ended in less than ten seconds.

He had come in third.

Larsby was ecstatic. "Third! Third! In your first competition! Boy, you beat runners been competing for three,
four, five years, runners who've won Pan-Olympic
medals. I don't know what it was you did, boy, but you ran
yourself right off our projections."

Hammadi was disconsolate. Third. He felt he had failed
father, God, Company. He had never felt the down after a
PCP high before. He picked his way through the other
crashed, shivering athletes for a place to hide and cry.

In his apartment there was a letter forwarded from his
father. There was a photograph of what looked like several
hundred people crammed into the front room of his old
home, all cheering and waving. His mother was nowhere
to be seen, presumably making mint tea for the men. He

might have honored everything else, but he had failed his mother.

He is beyond it now. Behind him lies the laughter of the condominiums and the dark, desperate pulse beat of the tourist hotels. The city is a cluster of lights, soft as powder, at the end of the beach, like the jeweled hilt of a sword. He runs on into the night, under the moon and the orbiting factories, past the dark olive groves and fig orchards and the houses of the humble, the olive farmers, the sardine fishermen, people whose lives have been largely passed over by the twenty-first century, except for the satellite dishes on their roofs and the squatter camps of refugees from the war in the south in the shade of their grandfather's olives. No lights here, these are a people who rise and set with the sun, but from the cardboard and plastic shanties Hammadi can hear the solar-charged televisions the government hands out. He wonders, do they recognize this running figure in its sleek primaries and corporate logos as the same man they cheered on to victory and national glory on those twenty-centimeter screens that are the only sources of light in the fetid, filthy shanties? The same sweet, glossy smell that haunts the condominiums carries to him from the shoreline squats. The condo people buy their highs with smartcards, the shanty people get them free, courtesy of the government as an exercise in social engineering, but they all end the same. Long-term synTHC users display symptoms similar to Alzheimer's. The government's generosity to its dispossessed gently shepherds the refugee problem to its own self-imposed final solution.

But Hammadi is the Sufi, the Dervish of Allah, translated into a purer, higher form of worship that gathers body mind emotion and spirit together in one living declaration of the power of God. This was the part of him the Company could never subcontract, the state of exaltation they could never simulate for all their chemicals and computers and conditioning, the part where divinity and humanity touched, the unknown fire that drove Hammadi al-Bourhan off their graphs and models and extrapolations.

Every other week he was flown to a competition against another company. Hammadi made steady progress up the ratings from also-ran and third to third and second to second and first. Larsby's wins on the credit-and-influence stakes grew smaller and smaller as the odds against Hammadi al-Bourhan grew shorter and shorter, but Larsby's eyes were set on a greater horizon. In ten months it would be the Pan-Olympiad and the chance of glory against the gathered corporations. Hammadi saw that horizon also, but his immediate concern was with a man called Bradley Nullabiri. He had met him first in a training simulation, the man who was to become his closest and deadliest rival. Bradley Nullabiri, Bayer-Mainoff GmBH, born December 21, 2002, Alice Springs, Australia, one of the final generation of pure-bred aboriginals: he studied that black man, ran and ran and ran that simulated two hundred meters against him until there was nothing about him as an athlete or a human that he felt he did not know. Then he flew on a suborbital Sänger with Larsby and his twenty-person tech team to run against him in the flesh.

He lost. They met again, in the return meet, when it was Bradley Nullabiri's turn to fly in with his coach and tech team. Hammadi lost. There was one more thing about Bradley Nullabiri that the files didn't cover: Bradley Nullabiri was also a man who had been touched by the hand of God, his gods, the stalking ones, the ancient ones, who had drawn his two-hundred-thousand-year heritage behind them out of the Dreamtime. In every respect they were the same. Except one, and that was the one that made Bradley Nullabiri unbeatable.

Bradley Nullabiri knew he was unbeatable.

"Question of attitude," Larsby said. "Nothing magical about it. You just got to believe you're more unbeatable than he is."

Hammadi spent the three weeks until their next meeting in the company of the psychologists who never got around to explaining what their tests were for or how he had scored in them. Team al-Bourhan was loaded into an aerospacer and disgorged after the forty-minute flight to do battle with Bradley Nullabiri. Media interest was by now so hyped they were charging two hundred thousand a minute for advertising. The race went to a freeze-frame finish. Hammadi lost by three-hundredths of a second.

"Forget Bradley Nullabiri," Larsby told a depressed Hammadi on the flight home. "You got to concentrate on the Pan-Olympics. Every waking and sleeping minute, you're thinking of nothing but Pan-Olympic gold, Pan-Olympic gold, Pan-Olympic gold."

"Bradley Nullabiri will be there."

"So will Hammadi al-Bourhan. Pan-Olympics are different."

His father, in his regular letters, gave the same advice: Allah would never permit the Godless to triumph over His Chosen, it was ordained that he would win gold at the Pan-Olympics and bring everlasting glory to Islam, his country, and the name of al-Bourhan. Incidentally, thanks to the money the Company put into a trust fund from his account, they had recently moved into a newer and bigger house, thank you, son.

Hammadi no longer replied to his father's letters.

Twenty minutes into the flight, just before the aerospacer went into free fall at the apex of its orbit, Hammadi realized that either he hadn't been told, or hadn't asked, where they were going. The new diamond-fiber doped ceramoplastic ankle joints that enabled him to withstand even more acceleration away from the blocks ached dully in free fall.

The antirejection drugs were abreacting with the free-g tranqs. He felt vast and vertiginous.

India. The room was the same, the television he could not turn off was the same, the balconies with the nude sun-bathing women were the same (except that here they were fat and brown rather than fat and pink), the palm-fringed ocean with its cargo of jet surfers and power skiers and body sailers was the same. But somewhere some geographical sense long abused by the mandatory uniformity of the world insisted this was *India*.

And this was the Pan-Olympiad. The youth of all nations gathered together in the Great Fellowship of Sport under the Eternal Flame and the Six Rings (one for each continent and one extra for the new orbital settlements). With the inevitable exceptions; some of the companies locked in takeover and merger battles were not sending teams, and T.S.A. Lagrange were boycotting the games as protest against the Pan-Olympic Council ruling that their technique of temporarily suspending their athletes' personalities through massive doses of PGCPE and ergominesterase and giving control of their bodies to the coaching computers was contrary to the Pan-Olympic tradition of sportsmanship.

Hammadi could not pronounce her name in her native language, but she told him it meant Swallow. He translated that into his native language and she said she liked the sound of it very much. She had been assigned to him by the organizing committee as his liaison and guide through the planetary party that was the Pan-Olympiad. He was mistrustful at first that she was a spy for a rival corporation; performance data was a highly negotiable commodity. He had no illusions that his training schedule had not been prepared with the help of black data. Larsby assured him of his hostess's impeccability.

"It's the Pan-Olympics, boy," he said twelve times a day every day. "Only comes 'round every four years, enjoy

it, make the most of it." It was unnecessary for him to add
that this might be Hammadi's only chance to enjoy it;
Hammadi understood how short an athlete's professional
life could be. In three years he expected to retire with at
least one world record to a condominium on the coast and
a life donating sperm to Toussaint Mantene's genetic engineering program at a million a year. So when he came out
from the closed training sessions, he was glad to let Swallow whirl him through the color and movement and gaudi-
ness and loudness of the Pan-Olympic city. She was the
perfect hostess; informative, spontaneous, with the intelligence to be a foil to Hammadi's curiosity, witty, pretty (he
could not deny that), fun to be with. She never made him
feel like a street-racing boy from the global boondocks.
The anticipation of her company after training put an extra
sparkle in his performance; with his probability models
improving every day, Larsby was happy to accede when
Hammadi asked if Swallow might be permitted into the
sessions. She sat with Larsby in his glass booth and
watched Hammadi pit himself against holographic enemies.

"You are so beautiful when you run," she told him. "So
alive, so you. You are like a big, graceful cat. Like a hunt-
ing cheetah."

Hammadi bowed his head and blushed as he had
learned to do when he was a boy and his father praised him
above his brothers. Within was a different heat altogether.

She slipped her tongue into his mouth for the first time
in Vidjaywada Shambalaya's, immersed in ethnobeat and
video shriek of interior bioscapes macroprojected from
nanocameras circling the bloodstreams of the club resident
drastique dancers. Further radical replacement surgery had
left Hammadi fifty centimeters taller and forty wider than
Swallow; pulling her to him to taste her again, he understood how easily he could have snapped her like the bird

from which she had taken her name. The smell of her enveloped him, erased the din of the club.

"You've never done anything like this before, have you?" she asked.

He shook his head shyly.

"This is your first time."

He nodded his head shyly.

"Mine, too."

Larsby had a singular honor to bestow upon Hammadi. He was to carry the Company Banner in the Grand Parade of All Athletes. Swallow thought he looked most impressive in his specially designed team uniform in the Toussaint Mantene colors. Parading into the stadium at the head of Team Toussaint Mantene under the gaze of two hundred thousand spectators and fifty global sat-tel networks, he looked long at the place where she had told him she would be sitting.

Later, she said she was so proud of him.

He said it had been nothing. Duty to the Company.

She said she thought he was beautiful.

He said no, she was beautiful, beautiful Swallow.

She said she had never felt about any other man the way she felt about him.

He said he had never known a woman who could make him feel the way he did right now.

She said did he want to make love to her?

And his will said no, but his body said yes, yes.

Of course, he came too early, before she even turned on. He was embarrassed, but she told him it was all right, everything was all right, it was just inexperience, this is new territory for them both, they would explore together, as a team. They made love again and this time it was a slow, attenuated coming together that had him roaring like a lion and whimpering like a dog and her growling guttural obscenities in the back of her throat. Afterward he told her he loved her, he loved her, he loved her, but she had fallen asleep like a small and graceful savannah cat. He woke her again with his penis to make love again. Outside in the submorning, blimps painted the clouds Day-Glo with holographic sponsorship messages and the never-ending world party coiled and uncoiled. The lights of the low orbitals, the new estate, rose to the ascendent and set.

He was too excited to sleep afterward, though the two-hundred-meter heats were only two days away. He sat in a soliform chair and thought about Swallow and thought about God. Sexual impurity had been the most heinous of his mother's library of sins. Yet what he had experienced had been so good and so holy that it could only have been a gift from God. Only when he had run himself into a state of sublime awareness had he ever experienced anything as divinely thrilling. He felt no guilt; two adult, responsible humans had been attracted to each other, as Allah had created them; had come together, as Allah had created them; had made love, as Allah had created them. He had enjoyed the creation of God. He had committed no sin. He had not dishonored God.

He crossed to the bed to look at her in the nakedness of sleep. He stroked her back, her thighs, her breasts, ran his fingers through her hair. His fingers stopped on the ridge of bone just behind her left ear.

Embossed in the flesh were three letters.

T.M.®

He knew those letters. He carried them himself, in the places where Toussaint Mantene had replaced his own bone and sinew with their diamond-fiber doped ceramoplastics.

He booked a ticket on a Sänger on the apartment unit. Team Toussaint Mantene Security came bursting in through the door they had told Hammadi only he could open to see just what the hell their prospective Pan-Olympic star thought he was doing, but he had already slipped away from them through the corridors and arcades and never-ending planetary party. In the acceleration seat he thought about the prostitutes in the almost grand hotel. The smile subtler, the costume less provocative, the enhanced pheromones less insistent, the approach less blatant. That was all.

He had told her that he loved her.

Despite the g-shock tranqs, he still threw up. The hostess swiftly vacuumed up the floating globules of vomit before gravity returned.

He sat on the balcony and looked at the sea and waited for Larsby. He was not long coming. It gave Hammadi a dry satisfaction to see the bland carelessness discarded like the mask it was. He let the small man scream himself hoarse, then asked, "Who was she?"

"Someone, anyone, no one, does it matter?"

"It matters."

Larsby had been defeated the moment he had walked through the door.

"Just a girl. From our Industrial Espionage Division. A Strength Through Joy girl. You would have recognized one of our own, so we had to do a little camouflaging surgery to, ah, fit her to the role."

"Don't blame her. It was you got careless."

Larsby grinned helplessly.

"Tell me why," Hammadi said.

"Because you still didn't believe in yourself. Because there was still an area in your life where you believed you were a failure."

"With women."

"It's all there in your file. PsychCorps saw it the first day you walked in here. You have a massive self-confidence problem with women, you don't believe you can be successful sexually. While that self-doubt remained, you could never have beaten Bradley Nullabiri. So we set you up with a woman who would be irresistibly attracted to you, go to bed with you, tell you she loved you so you would feel great enough about yourself—"

"I know!" Hammadi shouted. Then, more gently, "I know. . . ." He looked at Larsby. "Did she ever, do you know if, whether, she . . . felt anything?"

"Would it make a difference?"

"Not really."

"We needed you to beat Bradley Nullabiri."

"Winning is everything."

"Yes," said Larsby.

"You aren't even sorry," Hammadi said. "Well, it will just have to go down in history as one of the great unanswered questions in sport." He handed Larsby an envelope.

"You don't want to do this, boy."

"Oh, yes I do."

On the television you couldn't turn off, Bradley Nullabiri was running in the finals of the two hundred meters. He won. Hammadi did not feel a thing.

With regret the Company accepted Hammadi's resignation and took away his apartment with its view of the palms and the ocean and the naked sunbathing women. It suspended use of his *plastique* card and payment to his account and his parents' trust fund. It stripped him of the pastel-and-black bodysuit in which he was to have beaten Bradley Nullabiri. It put him into surgery and took back the PCP pump in his brain stem. It removed the sensory amplifiers and implanted neurochips and the biotech interfacers. It took out the diffusers and the synaptic controllers and the bioassay monitors and the mastoid speaker and the subvocal mike and the parallel ports and the serial muscular triggers and the subdermal blood scrubbers and left him with himself. It took all this away because it was and always had been and always would be Company property, on loan to him under the terms of the sponsorship contract.

That was what the man in the Nehru suit told him. The only thing the Company left him were the radical replacement ceramoplastic joints and shock absorbers. To have taken them away would have killed him. He stood two meters thirty in his skin, and the weight of his new mortality bore down in him. He felt like an angel cast out of heaven.

The deductions the Company made from his account for the reclamative surgery left him just enough for a Sänger flight home. The seatback flatscreen showed him the closing parade of All Athletes in the Great Fellowship of Sport in the silver stadium in Madras. Hammadi felt like he had died.

His father would not speak to him. Disowned him, disinherited him, ignored him, treated him as worse than dead. His brothers wanted to sympathize but were kept from doing so by fear of their father's wrath. His mother kept al-Bourhan from throwing Hammadi out of the house. She listened, long long hours in her mosque-kitchen as her son tried to explain why he had done what he had done. In the next room the television blared. His father's silence blared louder.

"I honored them, but they would not honor me," he said. "They pretended they cared about me, that they respected me as a man, as a Muslim, but all they respected was winning, all they wanted was a piece of meat that could run around a track faster than the other pieces of meat. And to please them I compromised myself, little by little. I became what they wanted me to be, not what God wanted me to be."

"You did not compromise," his mother said. "Not when it really mattered. In the end you honored God."

"And has God honored me?"

Jobs were easy for anyone who had done time with the Companies, even a failed star. Hammadi settled quickly into his post at the tourist-bus company arranging transfers between airport and hotels for the people from Dahomey

and Luzon and Costa Rica. His workmates soon learned
not to question this overtall, gangling freak about his racing days.

On his way home along the boulevards and palm-lined
avenues he would be passed by street-racing boys, out
practicing. He could not look at them. His eyes were like
lead. When he came home in these moods, his mother
would say, "God made you fast, God still makes you fast.
He still delights to see you run. He is not interested in
whether you win or not, just that you run for His pleasure."

It took many months for the truth of what she was saying to penetrate his sense of loss. But it was the truth, that
in winning he lost, that in losing he won. God had made
him not to win, or to lose, but to run. Now when he saw the
street runners, he would watch them, carefully noting, an-
alyzing, mentally commenting, correcting, coaching. One
night he found his old, old bodysuit draped on the bed.
Mother's intuition. He stroked the silky stretch fabric,
rubbed it against his cheek. He smiled at how ludicrously
outmoded it was. In the privacy of his room he stripped,
slipped it on.

It was nothing like a real bodysuit, of course, and it
clung oddly around his massively reengineered frame, but
it felt right. That night he found his way through the wire
mesh onto the private part of the beach and began to run,
slowly at first, but with gathering strength and speed,
along the white crescent of sand, for the glory and delight
of Allah.

It is nearly over now; the white crescent of sand is dwindling away between sea and stone to a horn, a sliver, to
nothing. He has left the people far behind, their cities, their
hotels and beach clubs and condominiums, their farms and
Squattertowns and satellite dishes and sardine boats. He is
among the eternal things; sea, sand, stone, sky, stars; un-

changing things, God-like things. At the end, where the beach peters out into jumbled rocks, he will stop, and then turn and jog slowly back beneath the moon and orbiting factories to the hole in the wire where he has left his tracksuit. But only at the end. Not before. He will run the race, he will go the distance. He glances at the fluorescent timer patch on the sleeve of his bodysuit. Not bad. Not what he would have hoped for, once. But not bad.

He is close now. The sand is running out beneath his feet, into the sea. He is tired, but it is a good tiredness. He is panting, but he still smiles. He is here. The end. The race is over. He stops, rests his hands on thighs, bends over, breath steaming in the cool air. He looks around him, at the white crescent of sand, at the white crescent moon, at the sea, at the lights of the tourist hotels and the condominiums, almost all gone out now, at the eternal glow of the city.

And he leaps into the air. Arms spread, fists raised to heaven. A leap of triumph, a leap of joy. The leap of a man who knows that God has taken pleasure in seeing him run, for Him, just for Him, under the stars and the moon, along the deserted beach. The leap of a man who has won.

THE DEAD

Michael Swanwick

Professional boxing has long been criticized for its corruption and soulless brutality, but as this mordant little look into the future of the sport demonstrates, hold on to your hats, because you ain't seen nothing *yet. . . .*

Michael Swanwick made his debut in 1980, and in the twenty-one years that have followed has established himself as one of SF's most prolific and consistently excellent writers at short lengths, as well as one of the premier novelists of his generation. He has several times been a finalist for the Nebula Award, as well as for the World Fantasy Award and for the John W. Campbell Award, and has won the Theodore Sturgeon Award and the Asimov's *Readers Award poll. In 1991 his novel* Stations of the Tide *won him a Nebula Award as well, and in 1995 he won the World Fantasy Award for his story "Radio Waves." In the past two years he's won back-to-back Hugo Awards—he won the Hugo in 1999 for his story "The Very Pulse of the Machine," and followed it up last year with another Hugo Award for his story "Scherzo with Tyrannosaur." His other books include his first novel,* In the Drift, *which was published in 1985, a novella-length book,* Griffin's Egg, *1987's popular novel* Vacuum Flowers, *and a critically acclaimed fantasy novel,* The Iron Dragon's Daughter, *which was a finalist for the World Fantasy Award* and *the Arthur C. Clarke Award (a rare distinction!). His most recent novel was* Jack Faust, *a sly reworking of the Faust legend that explores the unexpected impact of technology on society. Coming up is a new novel, featuring time travelers and hungry dinosaurs,* Bones of the Earth. *His short fiction has been assembled in* Gravity's Angels, A Geography of Un-*

known Lands, *and in a collection of his collaborative short work with other writers,* Slow Dancing through Time. *He's also published a collection of critical articles,* The Postmodern Archipelago. *His most recent books are three new collections,* Moon Dogs, Puck Aleshire's Abecedary, *and* Tales of Old Earth. *Swanwick lives in Philadelphia with his wife, Marianne Porter, and their son, Sean. He has a Web site at www.michaelswanwick.com/.*

Three boy zombies in matching red jackets bussed our table, bringing water, lighting candles, brushing away the crumbs between courses. Their eyes were dark, attentive, lifeless; their hands and faces so white as to be faintly luminous in the hushed light. I thought it in bad taste, but "This is Manhattan," Courtney said. "A certain studied offensiveness is fashionable here."

The blond brought menus and waited for our order.

We both ordered pheasant. "An excellent choice," the boy said in a clear, emotionless voice. He went away and came back a minute later with the freshly strangled birds, holding them up for our approval. He couldn't have been more than eleven when he died and his skin was of that sort connoisseurs call "milk glass," smooth, without blemish, and all but translucent. He must have cost a fortune.

As the boy was turning away, I impulsively touched his shoulder. He turned back. "What's your name, son?" I asked.

"Timothy." He might have been telling me the *specialité de maison*. The boy waited a breath to see if more was expected of him, then left.

Courtney gazed after him. "How lovely he would look," she murmured, "nude. Standing in the moonlight by a cliff. Definitely a cliff. Perhaps the very one where he met his death."

"He wouldn't look very lovely if he'd fallen off a cliff."

"Oh, don't be unpleasant."

The wine steward brought our bottle. "Château La Tour '17." I raised an eyebrow. The steward had the sort of old and complex face that Rembrandt would have enjoyed painting. He poured with pulseless ease and then dissolved into the gloom. "Good lord, Courtney, you *seduced* me on cheaper."

She flushed, not happily. Courtney had a better career going than I. She outpowered me. We both knew who was smarter, better connected, more likely to end up in a corner office with the historically significant antique desk. The only edge I had was that I was a male in a seller's market. It was enough.

"This is a business dinner, Donald," she said, "nothing more."

I favored her with an expression of polite disbelief I knew from experience she'd find infuriating. And, digging into my pheasant, murmured, "Of course." We didn't say much of consequence until dessert, when I finally asked, "So what's Loeb-Soffner up to these days?"

"Structuring a corporate expansion. Jim's putting together the financial side of the package, and I'm doing personnel. You're being headhunted, Donald." She favored me with that feral little flash of teeth she made when she saw something she wanted. Courtney wasn't a beautiful woman, far from it. But there was that fierceness to her, that sense of something primal being held under tight and precarious control that made her hot as hot to me. "You're talented, you're thuggish, and you're not too tightly nailed to your present position. Those are all qualities we're looking for."

She dumped her purse on the table, took out a single folded sheet of paper. "These are the terms I'm offering." She placed it by my plate, attacked her torte with gusto.

I unfolded the paper. "This is a lateral transfer."

"Unlimited opportunity for advancement," she said with her mouth full, "if you've got the stuff."

"Mmmm." I did a line-by-line of the benefits, all comparable to what I was getting now. My current salary to the dollar—Ms. Soffner was showing off. And the stock options. "This can't be right. Not for a lateral."

There was that grin again, like a glimpse of shark in murky waters. "I knew you'd like it. We're going over the top with the options because we need your answer right away—tonight preferably. Tomorrow at the latest. No negotiations. We have to put the package together fast. There's going to be a shitstorm of publicity when this comes out. We want to have everything nailed down, present the fundies and bleeding hearts with a *fait accompli*."

"My God, Courtney, what kind of monster do you have hold of now?"

"The biggest one in the world. Bigger than Apple. Bigger than Home Virtual. Bigger than HIVac-IV," she said with relish. "Have you ever heard of Koestler Biological?"

I put my fork down.

"Koestler? You're peddling corpses now?"

"Please. Postanthropic biological resources." She said it lightly, with just the right touch of irony. Still, I thought I detected a certain discomfort with the nature of her client's product.

"There's no money in it." I waved a hand toward our attentive waitstaff. "These guys must be—what?—maybe 2 percent of the annual turnover? Zombies are luxury goods: servants, reactor cleanups, Hollywood stunt deaths, exotic services"—we both knew what I meant—"a few hundred a year, maybe, tops. There's not the demand. The revulsion factor is too great."

"There's been a technological breakthrough." Courtney leaned forward. "They can install the infrasystem and controllers and offer the product for the factory-floor cost of a new subcompact. That's way below the economic threshold for blue-collar labor.

"Look at it from the viewpoint of a typical factory owner. He's already downsized to the bone and labor costs are bleeding him dry. How can he compete in a dwindling consumer market? Now let's imagine he buys into the program." She took out her Mont Blanc and began scribbling figures on the tablecloth. "No benefits. No liability suits. No sick pay. No pilferage. We're talking about cutting labor costs by at least two-thirds. Minimum! That's irresistible, I don't care how big your revulsion factor is. We project we can move five hundred thousand units in the first year."

"Five hundred thousand," I said. "That's crazy. Where the hell are you going to get the raw material for—"

"Africa."

"Oh, God, Courtney." I was struck wordless by the cynicism it took to even consider turning the sub-Saharan tragedy to a profit, by the sheer, raw evil of channeling hard currency to the pocket Hitlers who ran the camps. Courtney only smiled and gave that quick little flip of her head that meant she was accessing the time on an optic chip.

"I think you're ready," she said, "to talk with Koestler."

At her gesture, the zombie boys erected projector lamps about us, fussed with the settings, turned them on. Interference patterns moiréd, clashed, meshed. Walls of darkness erected themselves about us. Courtney took out her flat and set it up on the table. Three taps of her nailed fingers and the round and hairless face of Marvin Koestler appeared on the screen. "Ah, Courtney!" he said in a pleased voice. "You're in—New York, yes? The San Moritz. With Donald." The slightest pause with each accessed bit of information. "Did you have the antelope medallions?" When we shook our heads, he kissed his fingertips. "Magnificent! They're ever so lightly braised and then smothered in buffalo mozzarella. Nobody makes them better. I had the same dish in Florence the other day, and there was simply no comparison."

I cleared my throat. "Is that where you are? Italy?"

"Let's leave out where I am." He made a dismissive gesture, as if it were a trifle. But Courtney's face darkened. Corporate kidnapping being the growth industry it is, I'd gaffed badly. "The question is—what do you think of my offer?"

"It's . . . interesting. For a lateral."

"It's the start-up costs. We're leveraged up to our asses as it is. You'll make out better this way in the long run." He favored me with a sudden grin that went mean around the edges. Very much the financial buccaneer. Then he leaned forward, lowered his voice, maintained firm eye contact. Classic people-handling techniques. "You're not sold. You know you can trust Courtney to have checked out the finances. Still, you think: It won't work. To work, the product has to be irresistible, and it's not. It can't be."

"Yes, sir," I said. "Succinctly put."

He nodded to Courtney. "Let's sell this young man." And to me, "My stretch is downstairs."

He winked out.

Koestler was waiting for us in the limo, a ghostly pink presence. His holo, rather, a genial if somewhat coarse-grained ghost afloat in golden light. He waved an expansive and insubstantial arm to take in the interior of the car and said, "Make yourselves at home."

The chauffeur wore combat-grade photomultipliers. They gave him a buggish, inhuman look. I wasn't sure if he was dead or not. "Take us to Heaven," Koestler said.

The doorman stepped out into the street, looked both

ways, nodded to the chauffeur. Robot guns tracked our progress down the block.

"Courtney tells me you're getting the raw materials from Africa."

"Distasteful, but necessary. To begin with. We have to sell the idea first—no reason to make things rough on ourselves. Down the line, though, I don't see why we can't go domestic. Something along the lines of a reverse mortgage, perhaps, life insurance that pays off while you're still alive. It'd be a step toward getting the poor off our backs at last. Fuck 'em. They've been getting a goddamn free ride for too long; the least they can do is to die and provide us with servants."

I was pretty sure Koestler was joking. But I smiled and ducked my head, so I'd be covered in either case. "What's Heaven?" I asked, to move the conversation onto safer territory.

"A proving ground," Koestler said with great satisfaction, "for the future. Have you ever witnessed bare-knuckles fisticuffs?"

"No."

"Ah, now there's a sport for gentlemen! The sweet science at its sweetest. No rounds, no rules, no holds barred. It gives you the real measure of a man—not just of his strength but his character. How he handles himself, whether he keeps cool under pressure—how he stands up to pain. Security won't let me go to the clubs in person, but I've made arrangements."

Heaven was a converted movie theater in a run-down neighborhood in Queens. The chauffeur got out, disappeared briefly around the back, and returned with two zombie bodyguards. It was like a conjurer's trick. "You had these guys stashed in the trunk?" I asked as he opened the door for us.

"It's a new world," Courtney said. "Get used to it."

The place was mobbed. Two, maybe three hundred seats, standing room only. A mixed crowd, blacks and Irish and Koreans mostly, but with a smattering of uptown customers as well. You didn't have to be poor to need the occasional taste of vicarious potency. Nobody paid us any particular notice. We'd come in just as the fighters were being presented.

"Weighing two-five-oh, in black trunks with a red stripe," the ref was bawling, "the gang-bang *gang*sta, tha bare-knuckle *brawla,* the man with tha—"

Courtney and I went up a scummy set of back stairs. Bodyguard-us-bodyguard, as if we were a combat patrol out of some twentieth-century jungle war. A scrawny, pot-bellied old geezer with a damp cigar in his mouth unlocked the door to our box. Sticky floor, bad seats, a good view down on the ring. Gray plastic matting, billowing smoke.

Koestler was there, in a shiny new hologram shell. It reminded me of those plaster Madonnas in painted bathtubs that Catholics set out in their yards. "Your permanent box?" I asked.

"All of this is for your sake, Donald—you and a few others. We're pitting our product one-on-one against some of the local talent. By arrangement with the management. What you're going to see will settle your doubts once and for all."

"You'll like this," Courtney said. "I've been here five nights straight. Counting tonight." The bell rang, starting the fight. She leaned forward avidly, hooking her elbows on the railing.

The zombie was gray-skinned and modestly muscled, for a fighter. But it held up its hands alertly, was light on its feet, and had strangely calm and knowing eyes.

Its opponent was a real bruiser, a big black guy with classic African features twisted slightly out of true so that his mouth curled up in a kind of sneer on one side. He had gang scars on his chest and even uglier marks on his back that didn't look deliberate but like something he'd earned on the streets. His eyes burned with an intensity just this side of madness.

He came forward cautiously but not fearfully, and made a couple of quick jabs to get the measure of his opponent. They were blocked and countered.

They circled each other, looking for an opening.

For a minute or so, nothing much happened. Then the gangster feinted at the zombie's head, drawing up its guard. He drove through that opening with a slam to the zombie's nuts that made me wince.

No reaction.

The dead fighter responded with a flurry of punches, and got in a dancing blow to its opponent's cheek. They separated, engaged, circled around.

Then the big guy exploded in a combination of killer blows, connecting so solidly it seemed they would splinter every rib in the dead fighter's body. It brought the crowd to their feet, roaring their approval.

The zombie didn't even stagger.

A strange look came into the gangster's eyes, then, as the zombie counterattacked, driving him back into the ropes. I could only imagine what it must be like for a man who had always lived by his strength and stability to absorb punishment to realize that he was facing an opponent to whom pain meant nothing. Fights were lost and won by flinches and hesitations. You won by keeping your head. You lost by getting rattled.

Despite his best blows, the zombie stayed methodical, serene, calm, relentless. That was its nature.

It must have been devastating.

The fight went on and on. It was a strange and alienating experience for me. After a while I couldn't stay focused on it. My thoughts kept slipping into a zone where I found myself studying the line of Courtney's jaw, thinking about later tonight. She liked her sex just a little bit sick. There was always a feeling, fucking her, that there was something truly repulsive that she *really* wanted to do but lacked the courage to bring up on her own.

So there was always this urge to get her to do something she didn't like. She was resistant; I never dared try more than one new thing per date. But I could always talk her into that one thing. Because when she was aroused, she got pliant. She could be talked into anything. She could be made to beg for it.

Courtney would've been amazed to learn that I was not proud of what I did with her—quite the opposite, in fact. But I was as obsessed with her as she was with whatever it was that obsessed her.

Suddenly Courtney was on her feet, yelling. The hologram showed Koestler on his feet as well. The big guy was on the ropes, being pummeled. Blood and spittle flew from his face with each blow. Then he was down; he'd never even had a chance. He must've known early on that it was hopeless, that he wasn't going to win, but he'd refused to take a fall. He had to be pounded into the ground. He went down raging, proud and uncomplaining. I had to admire that.

But he lost anyway.

That, I realized, was the message I was meant to take away from this. Not just that the product was robust. But that only those who backed it were going to win. I could see, even if the audience couldn't, that it was the end of an era. A man's body wasn't worth a damn anymore. There wasn't anything it could do that technology couldn't handle better. The number of losers in the world had just doubled, tripled, reached maximum. What the fools below were cheering for was the death of their futures.

I got up and cheered, too.

•   •   •

In the stretch afterward, Koestler said, "You've seen the light. You're a believer now."

"I haven't necessarily decided yet."

"Don't bullshit me," Koestler said. "I've done my homework, Mr. Nichols. Your current position is not exactly secure. Morton-Western is going down the tubes. The entire service sector is going down the tubes. Face it, the old economic order is as good as fucking gone. Of course you're going to take my offer. You don't have any other choice."

The fax outed sets of contracts. "A Certain Product," it said here and there. Corpses were never mentioned.

But when I opened my jacket to get a pen, Koestler said, "Wait. I've got a factory. Three thousand positions under me. I've got a motivated workforce. They'd walk through fire to keep their jobs. Pilferage is at zero. Sick time practically the same. Give me one advantage your product has over my current workforce. Sell me on it. I'll give you thirty seconds."

I wasn't in sales and the job had been explicitly promised me already. But by reaching for the pen, I had admitted I wanted the position. And we all knew whose hand carried the whip.

"They can be catheterized," I said—"no toilet breaks."

For a long instant Koestler just stared at me blankly. Then he exploded with laughter. "By God, that's a new one! You have a great future ahead of you, Donald. Welcome aboard."

He winked out.

We drove on in silence for a while, aimless, directionless. At last Courtney leaned forward and touched the chauffeur's shoulder.

"Take me home," she said.

•   •   •

Riding through Manhattan I suffered from a waking hallu-
cination that we were driving through a city of corpses.
Gray faces, listless motions. Everyone looked dead in the
headlights and sodium vapor streetlamps. Passing by the
Children's Museum I saw a mother with a stroller through
the glass doors. Two small children by her side. They all
three stood motionless, gazing forward at nothing. We
passed by a stop-and-go where zombies stood out on the
sidewalk drinking forties in paper bags. Through upper-
story windows I could see the sad rainbow trace of virtu-
als playing to empty eyes. There were zombies in the park,
zombies smoking blunts, zombies driving taxies, zombies
sitting on stoops and hanging out on street corners, all of
them waiting for the years to pass and the flesh to fall from
their bones.

I felt like the last man alive.

Courtney was still wired and sweaty from the fight. The
pheromones came off her in great waves as I followed her
down the hall to her apartment. She stank of lust. I found
myself thinking of how she got just before orgasm, so desperate, so desirable. It was different after she came, she
would fall into a state of calm assurance; the same sort of
calm assurance she showed in her business life, the aplomb
she sought so wildly during the act itself.

And when that desperation left her, so would I. Because
even I could recognize that it was her desperation that
drew me to her, that made me do the things she needed me
to do. In all the years I'd known her, we'd never once had
breakfast together.

I wished there was some way I could deal her out of the
equation. I wished that her desperation were a liquid that I
could drink down to the dregs. I wished I could drop her in
a wine press and squeeze her dry.

At her apartment, Courtney unlocked her door and in

one complicated movement twisted through and stood facing me from the inside. "Well," she said. "All in all, a productive evening. Good night, Donald."

"Good night? Aren't you going to invite me inside?"

"No."

"What do you mean, no?" She was beginning to piss me off. A blind man could've told she was in heat from across the street. A chimpanzee could've talked his way into her pants. "What kind of idiot game are you playing now?"

"You know what no means, Donald. You're not stupid."

"No I'm not, and neither are you. We both know the score. Now let me in, goddamnit."

"Enjoy your present," she said, and closed the door.

I found Courtney's present back in my suite. I was still seething from her treatment of me and stalked into the room, letting the door slam behind me. So that I was standing in near-total darkness. The only light was what little seeped through the draped windows at the far end of the room. I was just reaching for the light switch when there was a motion in the darkness.

'Jackers! I thought, and all in a panic lurched for the light switch, hoping to achieve I don't know what. Creditjackers always work in trios, one to torture the security codes out of you, one to phone the numbers out of your accounts and into a fiscal trapdoor, a third to stand guard. Was turning the lights on supposed to make them scurry for darkness, like roaches? Nevertheless, I almost tripped over my own feet in my haste to reach the switch. But of course it was nothing like what I'd feared.

It was a woman.

She stood by the window in a white silk dress that could neither compete with nor distract from her ethereal beauty, her porcelain skin. When the lights came on, she turned toward me, eyes widening, lips parting slightly. Her breasts swayed ever so slightly as she gracefully raised a bare arm to offer me a lily. "Hello, Donald," she said huskily. "I'm yours for the night." She was absolutely beautiful.

And dead, of course.

Not twenty minutes later I was hammering on Courtney's door. She came to the door in a Pierre Cardin dressing gown and from the way she was still cinching the sash and the disarray of her hair I gathered she hadn't been expecting me.

"I'm not alone," she said.

"I didn't come here for the dubious pleasures of your fair white body." I pushed my way into the room. (But couldn't help remembering that beautiful body of hers, not so exquisite as the dead whore's, and now the thoughts were inextricably mingled in my head, death and Courtney, sex and corpses, a Gordian knot I might never be able to untangle.)

"You didn't like my surprise?" She was smiling openly now, amused.

"No, I fucking did not!"

I took a step toward her. I was shaking. I couldn't stop fisting and unfisting my hands.

She fell back a step. But that confident, oddly expectant look didn't leave her face. "Bruno," she said lightly. "Would you come in here?"

A motion at the periphery of vision. Bruno stepped out of the shadows of her bedroom. He was a muscular brute, pumped, ripped, and as black as the fighter I'd seen go down earlier that night. He stood behind Courtney, totally naked, with slim hips and wide shoulders and the finest skin I'd ever seen.

And dead.

I saw it all in a flush.

"Oh, for God's sake, Courtney!" I said, disgusted. "I can't believe you. That you'd actually . . . That thing's just an obedient body. There's nothing there—no passion, no connection, just . . . physical presence."

Courtney made a kind of chewing motion through her smile, weighing the implications of what she was about to say. Nastiness won.

"We have equity now," she said.

I lost it then. I stepped forward, raising a hand, and I swear to God I intended to bounce the bitch's head off the back wall. But she didn't flinch—she didn't even look afraid. She merely moved aside, saying, "In the body, Bruno. He has to look good in a business suit."

A dead fist smashed into my ribs so hard I thought for an instant my heart had stopped. Then Bruno punched me in my stomach. I doubled over, gasping. Two, three, four more blows. I was on the ground now, rolling over, helpless and weeping with rage.

"That's enough, baby. Now put out the trash."

Bruno dumped me in the hallway.

I glared up at Courtney through my tears She was not at all beautiful now. Not in the least. You're getting older, I wanted to tell her. But instead I heard my voice, angry and astonished, saying, "You . . . you goddamn, fucking necrophile!"

"Cultivate a taste for it," Courtney said. Oh, she was purring! I doubted she'd ever find life quite this good again. "Half a million Brunos are about to come on the market. You're going to find it a lot more difficult to pick up *living* women in not so very long."

I sent away the dead whore. Then I took a long shower that didn't really make me feel any better. Naked, I walked into my unlit suite and opened the curtains. For a long time I stared out over the glory and darkness that was Manhattan.

I was afraid, more afraid than I'd ever been in my life.

The slums below me stretched to infinity. They were a vast necropolis, a never-ending city of the dead. I thought of the millions out there who were never going to hold down a job again. I thought of how they must hate me—me and my kind—and how helpless they were before us. And yet. There were so many of them and so few of us. If they were to all rise up at once, they'd be like a tsunami, irresistible. And if there was so much as a spark of life left in them, then that was exactly what they would do.

That was one possibility. There was one other, and that was that nothing would happen. Nothing at all.

God help me, but I didn't know which one scared me more.

GAME OF THE CENTURY

Robert Reed

Here's a hard-hitting (literally!) look at the future of one of today's most popular sports, one that suggests that the past indeed is prologue . . . and that the future is going to be full of very unexpected surprises!

Robert Reed *sold his first story in 1986, and quickly established himself as a frequent contributor to* The Magazine of Fantasy and Science Fiction *and* Asimov's Science Fiction, *as well as selling many stories to* Science Fiction Age, Universe, New Destinies, Tomorrow, Synergy, Starlight, *and elsewhere. Reed may be one of the most prolific of today's young writers, particularly at short fiction lengths, seriously rivaled for that position only by authors such as Stephen Baxter and Brian Stableford. And—also like Baxter and Stableford—he manages to keep up a very high standard of quality* while *being prolific, something that is not at all easy to do. Reed stories such as "Sister Alice," "Brother Perfect," "Decency," "Savior," "The Remoras," "Chrysalis," "Whiptail," "The Utility Man," "Marrow," "Birth Day," "Blind," "The Toad of Heaven," "Stride," "The Shape of Everything," "Guest of Honor," "Waging Good," and "Killing the Morrow," among at least a half dozen others equally as strong, count as among some of the best short work produced by anyone in the '80s and '90s. Nor is he nonprolific as a novelist, having turned out eight novels since the end of the '80s, including* The Lee Shore, The Hormone Jungle, Black Milk, The Remarkables, Down the Bright Way, Beyond the Veil of Stars, An Exaltation of Larks, *and, most recently,* Beneath the Gated Sky. *His reputation can only grow as the years go by, and I suspect that he will become one of the big names of the first decade of the new century that lies ahead. Some of the best of his short work was collected in* The Dragons of Springplace. *His most recent book is* Marrow, *a novel-length version of his 1997 novella of the same name. Reed lives in Lincoln, Nebraska.*

The window was left open at midnight, January 1, 2041, and three minutes, twenty-one seconds later it was closed again by the decisive, barely legible signature of an elderly Supreme Court justice who reportedly quipped, "I don't know why I have to. Folks who like screwing sheep are just going to keep at it."

Probably so.

But the issues were larger than traditional bestiality. Loopholes in some badly drafted legislation had made it perfectly legal to manipulate the human genome in radical ways. What's more, said offspring were deemed human in all rights and privileges inside the U.S. of N.A. For two hundred and twelve seconds, couples and single women could legally conceive by any route available to modern science. And while few clinics and fewer top-grade hospitals had interest in the work, there were key exceptions. Some fourteen hundred human eggs were fertilized with tailored sperm, then instantly implanted inside willing mothers. News services that had paid minimal attention to the legislative breakdown took a sudden glaring interest in the nameless, still invisible offspring. The blastulas were dubbed the 1-1-2041s, and everything about their lives became the subject of intense public scrutiny and fascination and self-righteous horror.

Despite computer models and experiments on chimpanzees, there were surprises. Nearly a third of the fetuses were stillborn, or worse. Twenty-nine mothers were killed as a result of their pregnancies. Immunological problems, mostly. But in one case, a healthy woman in her midtwenties died when her boy, perhaps bothered by the drumming of her heart, reached through her uterine wall and intestines, grabbing and squeezing the offending organ with both of his powerful hands.

Of the nine hundred-plus fetuses who survived, almost 30 percent were mentally impaired or physically frail. Remarkably, others seemed entirely normal, their human genes running roughshod over their more exotic parts. But several hundred of the 1-1-2041s were blessed with perfect health as well as a remarkable stew of talents. Even as newborns, they astonished the researchers who tested their reflexes and their highly tuned senses. The proudest parents released the data to the media, then mixed themselves celebratory cocktails, stepping out onto their porches and balconies to wait for the lucrative offers to start flowing their way.

Marlboro Jones came with a colorful reputation. His father was a crack dealer shot dead in a dispute over footwear. With his teenage mother, Marlboro had lived at dozens of addresses before her mind failed and she leaped out of their bedroom window to stop the voices, and from there his life was a string of unbroken successes. He had coached, and won, at three different schools. He was currently the youngest head coach of a Top Alliance team. Thirty-six years old, he looked twenty-six, his chiseled features built around the bright, amoral eyes of a squirrel. Marlboro was the kind of handsome that made his charm appealing, and he was charming in a way that made his looks and mannerisms delightfully boyish. A laser mind lurked behind those eyes, yet in most circumstances he preferred playing the cultured hick, knowing how much it improved his odds.

"He's a fine-lookin' boy," the coach drawled. "Fine-lookin'."

The proud parents stood arm in arm, smiling with a frothy, nervous joy.

"May I?" asked Marlboro. Then without waiting for permission, he yanked the screen off the crib, reached in, and grabbed both bare feet. He tugged once, then again. Harder. "Damn, look at those legs! You'd think this boy'd be scampering around already. Strong as these seem . . . !"

"Well," said his mother, "he is awfully active."

"In a good way," the father cautioned.

"I believe it. I do!" Marlboro grinned, noticing that Mom looked awfully sweet in a tired-of-motherhood way, and it was too bad that he couldn't make a play for her, too. "Let me tell ya what I'm offering," he boomed. "A free ride. For the boy here—"

"Alan," Mom interjected.

"Alan," the coach repeated. Instantly, with an easy affection. Then he gave her a little wink, saying, "For Alan. A free education and every benefit that I'm allowed to give. Plus the same for your other two kids. Which I'm not supposed to offer. But it's my school and my scholarships, and I'll be damned if it's anybody's business but yours and mine!"

The parents squeezed one another, then with a nervous voice, the father made himself ask, "What about us?"

The coach didn't blink.

"What do you want, Mr. Wilde?" Marlboro smiled and said, "Name it."

"I'm not sure," the father confessed. "I know that we can't be too obvious—"

"But we were hoping," Mom blurted. "I mean, it's not like we're wealthy people. And we had to spend most of our savings—"

"On your little Alan. I bet you did." A huge wink was followed with, "It'll be taken care of. My school doesn't have that big college of genetics for nothing." He looked at the infant again, investing several seconds of hard thought into how they could bend the system just enough. Then he promised, "You'll be reimbursed for your expenses. Up front. And we'll put your son on the payroll. Gentlefolks in lab coats'll come take blood every half year or so. For a healthy, just-under-the-table fee. How's that sound?"

The father seemed doubtful. "Will the scientists agree to that?"

"If I want it done," the coach promised.

"Will they actually use his blood?" The father seemed uneasy. Even a little disgusted. "I don't like thinking of Alan being some kind of laboratory project."

Marlboro stared at him for a long moment.

Never blinking.

Then he said, "Sir." He said, "If you want, they can pass those samples to you, and you can flush them down your own toilet. Is that good enough?"

Nobody spoke.

Then he took a different course, using his most mature voice to tell them, "Alan is a fine, fine boy. But you've got to realize something. He's going to have more than his share of problems. Special kids always do." Then with a warm smile, Marlboro promised, "I'll protect him for you. With all my resources and my good country sense, I'll see that none of those predators out there get their claws in your little Alan."

Mom said, "That's good to hear. That's fine."

But Father shrugged, asking, "What about you? It'll be years before Alan can actually play, and you could have left for the pros by then."

"Never," Marlboro blurted.

Then he gave the woman his best wink and grin, saying, "You know what kind of talent I've been signing up. Do you really think I'd go anywhere else? Ever?"

She turned to her husband, saying, "We'll sign."

"But—?"

"No. We're going to commit."

Marlboro reconfigured the appropriate contracts, getting everyone's signature. Then he squeezed one of his recruit's meaty feet, saying, "See ya later, Alan."

Wearing an unreadable smile, he stepped out the front door. A hundred or so sports reporters were gathered on the small lawn, and through their cameras, as many as twenty million fans were watching the scene.

They watched Coach Jones smile and say nothing. Then he raised his arms suddenly, high overhead, and screamed those instantly famous words:

"The Wildman's coming to Tech!"

There was something about the girl. Perfect strangers thought nothing of coming up to her and asking where she was going to college.

"State," she would reply. Flat out.

"In what sport?" some inquired. While others, knowing that she played the game on occasion, would guess, "Are you joining the volleyball team?"

"No," Theresa would tell the latter group. Never patient, but usually polite. "I hate volleyball," she would explain, not wanting to be confused for one of those glandular, ritualistic girls. And she always told everyone, friends and strangers alike, "I'm going to play quarterback for the football team. For Coach Rickover."

Knowledgeable people were surprised and puzzled. Some would clear their throats and look up into Theresa's golden eyes, commenting in an offhand way, "But Rickover doesn't let women play."

That was a problem, sure.

Daddy was a proud alumnus of State and a letterman on the famous '33 squad. When Theresa was born, there was no question about where she was going. In '41, Rickover was only an assistant coach. Penises weren't required equipment. The venerable Coach Mannstein had shuffled into her nursery and made his best offer, then shuffled back out to meet with press and boosters, promising the world that he would still be coaching when that delightfully young lady was calling plays for the best team to ever take any field of play.

But six years later, while enjoying the company of a mostly willing cheerleader, Coach Mannstein felt a searing pain in his head, lost all feeling in his ample body, and died.

Rickover inherited the program.

A religious man driven by a quixotic understanding of the Bible, one of his first official acts was to send a letter to Theresa's parents, explaining at length why he couldn't allow their daughter to join his team. "Football," he wrote, "is nothing but ritualized warfare, and women don't belong in the trenches. I am sorry. On the other hand, Coach Terry is a personal friend, and I would be more than happy to have him introduce you to our nationally ranked women's volleyball program.

"Thank you sincerely."

"Coach."

The refusal was a crushing blow for Daddy.

For Theresa, it was a ghostly abstraction that she couldn't connect with those things that she truly knew and understood.

Not that she was a stupid child. Unlike many of her 1-1-2041 peers, her grades were respectably average, and in spatial subjects, like geometry and geography, she excelled. Also unlike her peers, Theresa didn't have problems with rage or with residual instincts. Dogs and cats didn't mysteriously vanish in her neighborhood. She was a good person with friends and her genuine admirers. Parents trusted her with their babies. Children she didn't know liked to beg for rides on her back. Once she was old enough to date, the boys practically lined up. Out of sexual curiosity, in part. But also out of fondness and an odd respect. Some of her boyfriends confided that they preferred her to regular girls. Something about her—and not just a physical something—set them at ease. Made them feel safe. A strange thing for adolescent males to admit, while for Theresa, it was just another circumstance in a life filled with nothing but circumstances.

In football, she always played quarterback. Whether on playground teams, or in the various midget leagues, or on the varsity squad in high school.

Her high school teams won the state championship three years in a row. And they would have won when she was a senior, except a mutant strain of parvovirus gave her a fever and chills, and eventually, hallucinations. Theresa started throwing hundred meter bullets toward her more compelling hallucinations, wounding several fans, and her coach grudgingly ordered her off the field and into a hospital bed.

Once State relinquished all claims on the girl, a steady stream of coaches and boosters and sports agents began the inevitable parade.

Marlboro Jones was the most persistent soul. He had already stockpiled a full dozen of the 1-1-2041s, including the premier player of all time: Alan, The Wildman, Wilde. But the coach assured Theresa that he still needed a quality quarterback. With a big wink and a bigger grin, he said, "You're going to be my field general, young lady. I know you know it, the same as I do . . . !"

Theresa didn't mention what she really knew.

She let Daddy talk. For years, that proud man had entertained fantasies of Rickover moving to the pros, leaving the door open for his only child. But it hadn't happened, and it wouldn't. And over the last few years, with Jones's help, he had convinced himself that Theresa should play instead for State's great rival. Call it justice. Or better, revenge. Either way, what mattered was that she would go somewhere that her talents could blossom. That's all that mattered, Daddy told the coach. And Marlboro replied with a knowing nod and a sparkling of the eyes, finally turning to his prospect, and with a victor's smile, asking, "What's best for you? Tour our campus first? Or get this signing crap out of the way?"

Theresa said, "Neither."

Then she remembered to add, "Sir," with a forced politeness.

Both men were stunned. But the coach was too slick to let it show. Staring at the tall, big-shouldered lady, he conjured up his finest drawl, telling her, "I can fix it. Whatever's broke, it can be fixed."

"Darling," her father mumbled. "What's wrong?"

She looked at her father's puffy, confused face. "This man doesn't want me for quarterback, Daddy. He just doesn't want me playing somewhere else."

After seventeen years of living with the girl, her father knew better than to doubt her instincts. Glaring at Marlboro, he asked flat out, "Is that true?"

"No," the man lied.

Instantly, convincingly.

Then he sputtered, adding, "That Mosgrove kid has too much chimp in his arm. And not enough touch."

There was a prolonged, uncomfortable silence.

Then Theresa informed both of them, "I've made up my mind, anyway. Starting next year, I'm going to play for State."

Daddy was startled and a bit frustrated. But as always, a little bit proud, too.

Coach Jones was, if anything, amused. The squirrel eyes smiled, and the handsome mouth tried not to follow suit. And after a few more seconds of painful silence, he said, "I've known Rickover for most of my adult life. And you know what, little girl? You've definitely got your work cut out for you."

•   •   •

Jones was mistaken.

Theresa believed.

A lifetime spent around coaches had taught her that the species was passionate and stubborn and usually wrong about everything that wasn't lashed to the game in front of them. But what made coaches ridiculous in the larger world helped them survive in theirs. Because they were stubborn and overblown, they could motivate the boys and girls around them; and the very best coaches had a gift for seducing their players, causing them to lash their souls to the game, and the next game, and every game to follow.

All Theresa needed to do, she believed, was outstubborn Coach Rickover.

State had a walk-on program. Overachievers from the Yukon to the Yucatán swarmed into campus in late summer, prepared to fight it out for a handful of scholarships. Theresa enrolled with the rest of them, then with her father in tow, showed up for the first morning's practice. An assistant coach approached. Polite and determined, he thanked her for coming, but she wasn't welcome. But they returned for the afternoon practice, this time accompanied by an AI advocate—part lawyer, part mediator—who spoke to a succession of assistant coaches with the quietly smoldering language of lawsuits and public relations nightmares.

Theresa's legal standing was questionable, at best. Courts had stopped showing interest in young ladies wanting to play an increasingly violent sport. But the threat to call the media seemed to work. Suddenly, without warning, the quarterback coach walked up to her and looked up, saying to her face, "All right. Let's see what you can do."

She was the best on the field, easily.

Pinpoint passes to eighty meters. A sprint speed that mauled every pure-human record. And best of all, the seemingly innate ability to glance at a fluid defense and pick it apart. Maybe Theresa lacked the elusive moves of some 1-1-2041s, which was the closest thing to a weakness. But she made up for it with those big shoulders that she wielded like dozer blades, leaving half a dozen strong young men lying flat on their backs, trying to recall why they ever took up this damned sport.

By the next morning, she was taking hikes with the varsity squad.

Coach Rickover went as far as strolling up to her and saying, "Welcome, miss," with that cool, almost friendly voice. Then he looked away, adding, "And the best of luck to you."

It was a trap.

During a no-contract drill, one of the second-string pure-human linebackers came through the line and leveled her when she wasn't ready. Then he squatted low and shouted into her face, "Bitch! Dog bitch! Pussy bitch! Bitch!"

Theresa nearly struck him.

In her mind, she left his smug face strewn across the wiry green grass. But then Rickover would have his excuse—she was a discipline problem—and her career would have encompassed barely one day.

She didn't hit the bastard, or even chew off one of his fingers.

Instead she went back to throwing lasers at her receivers and running between the tackles. Sometimes her blockers would go on vacation, allowing two or three rushers to drag her to the ground. Yet Theresa always got up again and limped back to the huddle, staring at the stubborn human eyes until those eyes, and the minds behind them, blinked.

It went on that way for a week.

Because she wouldn't allow herself even the possibility of escape, Theresa prepared herself for another four months of inglorious abuse. And if need be, another three years after that.

Her mother came to visit and to beg her daughter to give it up.

"For your sake, and mine. Just do the brave thing and walk away."

Theresa loved her mother, but she had no illusions: The woman was utterly, hopelessly weak.

Daddy was the one who scared her. He was standing over his daughter, watching as she carefully licked at a gash that came when she was thrown against a metal bench, her leg opened up from the knee to her badly swollen ankle. And with a weakling's little voice, he told her, "This isn't my dream anymore. You need to recon-sider. That, or you'll have to bury me. My nerves can't take any more twisting."

Picking thick golden strands of fur from her long, long tongue, Theresa stared at him. And hiding her sadness, she told him, "You're right, Daddy. This isn't your dream."

The war between player and coach escalated that next morning.

Nine other 1-1-2041s were on the team. Theresa was promoted to first team just so they could have a shot at her. She threw passes, and she was knocked flat. She ran side-ways, and minotaurs in white jerseys flung her backward, burying their knees into her kidneys and uterus. Then she moved to defense, playing AMBback for a few downs, and their woolly, low-built running back drove her against the juice cooler, knocking her helmet loose and chewing on one of her ears, then saying into that blood, "There's more coming, darling. There's always more coming."

Yet despite the carnage, the 1-1-2041s weren't deliver-ing real blows.

Not compared to what they could have done.

It dawned on Theresa that Rickover and his staff, for all their intimate knowledge about muscle and bone, had no idea what their players were capable of. She watched those grown men nodding, impressed with the bomblike impacts and spattered blood. Sprawled out on her back, waiting for her lungs to work again, she found herself studying Rickover: He was at least as handsome as Marlboro Jones, but much less attractive. There was something both analytical and dead about the man. And underneath it all, he was shy. Deeply and eternally shy. Wasn't that a trait that came straight out of your genetics? A trait and an affliction that she lacked, thankfully.

Theresa stood again, and she limped through the milling players and interns, then the assistant coaches, stepping into Rickover's line of sight, forcing him to look at her.

"I still want to play for you," she told him. "But you know, Coach . . . I don't think I'll ever like you . . ." And with that, she turned and hobbled back to the field.

Next morning, a decision had come down from On High.

Theresa was named the new first-string quarterback, and the former first-string—a tall, bayonet-shaped boy nicknamed Man o' War—was made rocketback.

For the last bits of summer and until the night before their first game, Theresa believed that her little speech had done its magic. She was so confident of her impression that she repeated her speech to her favorite rocketback. And Man o' War gave a little laugh, then climbed out of her narrow dormitory bed, stretching out on the hard floor, pulling one leg behind his head, then the other.

"That's not what happened," he said mildly. Smiling now.

She said, "What didn't?"

"It was the nine of us. The other 1-1-2041s." He kept smiling, bending forward until his chin was resting against his naked crotch, and he licked himself with a practiced deftness. Once finished, he sat up and explained, "We went to Coach's house that night. And we told him that if we were supposed to keep hurting you, we might as well kill you. And eat you. Right in the middle of practice."

She stared at her lover for a long moment, unsure what to believe.

Theresa could read human faces. And she could smell their moods boiling out of their hairless flesh. But no matter how hard she tried, she could never decipher that furry chimera of a face.

"Would you really have?" she finally asked.

"Killed you? Not me," Man o' War said instantly.

Then he was laughing, reminding her, "But those line-backers . . . you never can tell what's inside their smooth little minds . . . !"

Tech and State began the season on top of every sport reporter's rankings and the power polls and leading almost every astrologer's sure-picks. Since they had two more 1-1-2041s on their roster, including the Wildman, Tech was given the edge. Professional observers and fans, as well as AI analysts, couldn't imagine any team challenging either of them. On the season's second weekend, State met a strong Texas squad with its own handful of 1-1-2041s. They beat them by seventy points. The future seemed assured. Barring catastrophe, the two teams of the century would win every contest, then go to war on New Year's Day, inside the venerable Hope Dome, and the issue about who was best and who was merely second best would be settled for the ages.

In public, both coaching staffs and the coached players spouted all the hoary clichés. Take it one play at a time, and one game at a time, and never eat your chicken before it's cooked through.

But in private, and particularly during closed practices, there was one opponent and only one, and every mindless drill and every snake run on the stadium stairs and particularly every two-ton rep in the weight room was meant for Tech. For State. For glory and the championship and a trophy built from gold and sculpted light.

In the third week of the season, Coach Jones began using his 1-1-2041s on both sides of the line.

Coach Rickover told reporters that he didn't approve of those tactics. "Even superhumans need rest," he claimed. But that was before Tech devastated an excellent Alabama squad by more than a hundred and twenty points. Rickover prayed to God, talked to several physiologists, then made the same outrageous adjustment.

In their fourth game, Theresa played at quarterback and ABM.

Not only did she throw a school record ten touchdowns, she also ran for four more, plus she snagged five interceptions, galloping three of them back for scores.

"You're the Heisman front-runner," a female reporter assured her, winking and grinning as if they were girlfriends. "How does it feel?"

How do you answer such a silly question?

"It's an honor," Theresa offered. "Of course it is."

The reporter smiled slyly, then assaulted her with another silliness. "So what are your goals for the rest of the season?"

"To improve," Theresa muttered. "Every Saturday, from here on."

"Most of your talented teammates will turn professional at the end of the year." A pause. Then she said, "What about you, Theresa? Will you do the same?"

She hadn't considered it. The UFL was an abstraction, and a distraction, and she didn't have time or the energy to bother with either.

"All I think about," she admitted, "is this season."

A dubious frown.

Then the reporter asked, "What do you think of Tech's team?"

One play at a time, game at a time, and cook your chicken . . .

"Okay. But what about the Wildman?"

Nothing simple came into Theresa's head. She paused for a long moment, then told the truth, "I don't know Alan Wilde."

"But do you think it's right . . . ? Having a confessed killer as your linebacker and star running back . . . ?"

The reporter was talking about the Wildman. Vague recollections of a violent death and a famous, brief trial came to mind. But Theresa's parents had shielded her from any furor about the 1-1-2041s. Honestly, the best she could offer this woman was a shrug and her own smile, admitting, "It's not right to murder. Anyone. For any reason."

That simple declaration was the night's lead story on every sports network.

"Heisman hopeful calls her opponent a murderer! Even though the death was ruled justifiable homicide!"

Judging by the noise, it made for a compelling story.

Whatever the hell that means.

After the season's seventh week, a coalition of coaches and university presidents filed suit against the two front-runners. The games to date had resulted in nearly two hundred concussions, four hundred broken bones, and thirteen injuries so severe that young, pure-human boys were still lying in hospital beds, existing in protective comas.

"We won't play you anymore," the coalition declared.

They publicly accused both schools of recruiting abuses, and in private, they warned that if the remaining games weren't canceled, they would lead the pack in a quick and bloody inquisition.

Coach Rickover responded at his weekly press conference. With a Bible in hand, he gave a long, rambling speech about his innocence and how the playing fields were perfectly level.

Marlboro Jones took a different tack.

Accompanied by his school's lawyers, AI and human, he visited the ringleaders. "You goddamn pussies!" he shouted. "We've got contracts with you. We've got television deals with the networks. If you think we're letting your dicks wriggle free of this hook, you're not only cowards. You're stupid, too!"

Then he sat back, letting the lawyers dress up his opinion in their own impenetrable language.

But the opponents weren't fools. A new-generation AI began to list every known infraction: Payments to players and their families. Secretive changes of title for homes and businesses. Three boosters forming a charity whose only known function was to funnel funds to the topflight players. And worst by far, a series of hushed-up felonies connected to the 1-1-2041s under his care.

Marlboro didn't flinch.

Instead, he smiled—a bright, blistering smile that left every human in the room secretly trembling—and after a prolonged pause, he said, "Fine. Make it all public."

"The AI said, "Thank you. We will."

"But," said Marlboro, "here's what I'll take public. You pussies."

With precision and a perfect ear for detail, the coach listed every secret infraction and every camouflaged scandal that had ever swirled around his opponents' programs. Twenty-plus years in this industry, and he knew everything. Or at least that was the impression he gave. And then as he finished, he said, "Pussies," again. And laughed. And he glared at the Stanford president—the ringleader of this rabble—telling that piece of high-born shit, "I guess we're stuck. We're just going to have to kill each other."

Nobody spoke.

Moved, or even breathed.

Then the president managed to find enough air to whisper, "What do you propose?"

"Tech and State win our games by forfeit," the coach told them. "And you agree not to play us in court, either."

The president said, "Maybe."

Then with a soft, synthetic voice, his AI lawyer said, "Begging to differ, but I think we should pursue—"

Marlboro threw the talking box across the room.

It struck a wall, struck the floor. Then with an eerie calm, it said, "You cannot damage me, sir."

"Point taken." The coach turned to the humans. "Do we have a deal? Or don't we?"

Details were worked out; absolutely nothing was signed.

Near the end of negotiations, Marlboro announced, "Oh, and there's one last condition. I want to buy your lawyer." He pointed at the AI. "Bleed it of its secrets first. But I want it."

"Or what?" Stanford inquired.

"I start talking about your wives. Who likes it this way, who likes it that way. Just so everyone knows that what I'm saying is the truth."

The AI was sold. For a single dollar.

Complaining on and on with its thoughtful, useless voice, the box was thrown into the middle of Tech's next practice, and nothing was left afterward but gutted electronics pushed deep into the clipped green grass.

Tech's and State's regular season was finished. But that turned out to be a blessing as far as school coffers and the entertainment conglomerates were concerned. Hundred-point slaughters weren't winning the best ratings. In lieu of butchery, a series of ritualized scrimmages were held on Saturdays, each team dividing its top squads into two near-equal parts, then playing against themselves with enough skill and flair to bring packed stadiums and enormous remote audiences: all that helping to feed an accelerating, almost feverish interest in the coming showdown.

Sports addicts talked about little else.

While the larger public, caring nothing for the fabled gridiron, found plenty else to hang their interest on. The contrasting coaches, and the 1-1-2041s, and the debate about what is human, and particularly among girlfriends and wives, the salient fact that a female was the undisputed leader of one team.

Sports networks and digital wonderhouses began playing the games of the century early, boiling down its participants into algorithms and vectors and best guesses, then showing the best of their bloodless contests to surprisingly large audiences.

Eight times out of eleven, the digital Tech went away victors.

Not counting private and foreign betting, nearly ten billion reconstituted dollars had been wagered on the contest by Thanksgiving. By Christmas Eve, that figure had jumped another fivefold. Plus there were the traditional gubernatorial wagers of state-grown products: a ton of computer chips versus a ton of free-range buffalo.

Theresa spent Christmas at home with parents and grandparents, plus more than a dozen relatives who had managed to invite themselves. If anything, those cousins and uncles and assorted spouses were worse than a room full of reporters. They didn't know the rules. They expected disclosures. Confessions. The real and the dirty. And when Theresa offered any less-than-spectacular answer, it was met with disappointment and disbelief.

The faces said as much. And one little old aunt said it with her liquor-soddened mouth, telling her niece, "You're among family, darling. Why can't you trust us?"

Because she didn't know these people.

Over the past eighteen years, she had seen them spo-
radically, and all she remembered were their uncomfortable expressions and the careful words offered with quiet,
overly cautious voices.

Looking at her, some had said, "She's a lovely girl."

"Exotic," others volunteered.

"You're very lucky," to her parents.

Then out of pure-human earshot they would ask, "What
do you think is inside her? Dog? Dinosaur? What?"

Theresa didn't know which genes went into her creation. What was more, she hadn't felt a compelling need
to ask. But whatever chimerical stew made up her chro-
mosomes, she had inherited wonderful ears that could
pick up distant insults as well as the kindest, sweetest
words.

She was trying to be patient and charitable when one
idiot leaned forward, planted a drunken hand on her granite-
hard thigh, then told her with a resoundingly patronizing
tone, "I don't see what people complain about. Up close,
you're a beautiful creature. . . ."

Daddy heard those words, their tone.

And he detonated.

"What are you doing?" he screamed. "And get your
hand off your niece!"

Uncle John flinched, the hand vanishing. Then he stared
at his brother with a mixture of astonishment and building
rage, taking a deep breath, then another, before finding the
air to ask, "What did I say?"

"Why? Don't you remember?"

The poor fool sputtered something about being fair, for
God's sake.

The rest of the family stood mute, and stunned, and a
few began asking their personal clocks for the time.

"Leave," Daddy suggested.

To his brother, and everyone else, too.

He found the self-control to say, "Thank you for coming," but then added, "My daughter isn't a freak. She isn't, and remember that, and good night."

Christmas ended with a dash for the coats and some tenth-hearted, "Good lucks," lobbed in Theresa's direction.

Then it was just the three of them. And Daddy offered Theresa a sorrowful expression, then repeated his reasoning. "I've been listening to their contemptuous crap for nearly twenty years. You're not a monster, or a possession, and I get sick, sick, sick of it."

Theresa said nothing.

Mother said, "Darling," to one of them. Theresa wasn't sure who.

When nobody responded, Mother rose and staggered into the kitchen, telling the AI to finish its cooking, then store the meat and vegetables and mounds of stuffing for later this week, and into next year.

Theresa kept staring at her father, trying to understand why she was so disappointed, and angry, and sad.

He averted his eyes, then said, "I know."

What did he know?

"You're right," he confessed. "You caught me. You know!"

But Theresa couldn't make herself ask, "What am I right about?"

A citizen of unalloyed strength, yet she couldn't summon enough air to ask, "What is it, Father? What am I supposed to know?"

The Hope Dome was older than the players. Led by Miami, a consortium of cities had built that gaudy glass and carbon-fiber structure out on the continental shelf. Its playing field lay nearly fifty meters beneath the water's surface, and rising ocean levels combined with the new generation of hurricanes had caused problems. One of the bowl officials even repeated that tired joke that it was hope holding back the Atlantic. But then he winked slyly and said, "Don't worry." He unlocked a heavy door next to State's locker, revealing an enormous room filled with roaring bilge pumps whose only purpose, he boasted, was to send a river's worth of tiny leaks back into the sea.

In contrast to the palacelike Dome, the playing field was utterly ordinary.

Its dimensions and black earth and fluorescent-fed grass made it identical to a thousand other indoor facilities.

The day after Christmas, and both teams were given the traditional tour of the Dome and its field. To help extract the last greasy drama out of the blandness, Tech was still finishing its walk-through when State arrived. On the field together, with cameras and the world watching, the teams got their first naked-eye look at one another. And with a hundred million people waiting for anything, the two Heisman candidates met, and without any fuss, the two politely shook hands.

The Wildman offered Theresa several flavors of surprise.

The first surprise was his appearance. She had seen endless images of man-child, and she'd been near plenty of 1-1-2041s. But the running back was still impressive. There was bison in him, she had heard. And gorilla. And what might have been Siberian tiger genes. Plus something with an enormous capacity to grow bone. Elephant, perhaps. Something in the shape of his enormous head reminded her of the ancient mammoth skulls that she'd seen haunting the university museum.

The second surprise was the Wildman's mannerisms. A bowl official, nervous enough to shiver, introduced the two of them, then practically threw himself backward. But the boy was polite, and in a passing way, charming.

"We meet," he grunted. "Finally."

Theresa stared at the swollen incisors and the giant dog eyes, and telling herself not to stumble over her tongue, she offered her hand and said, "Hello," with the same pleasant voice she used on every new friend.

The Wildman took her hand gently. Almost too softly to be felt.

And with a thin humor, he said, "What do you think they would do? If we got down on our knees and grazed?"

Then the third surprise said, "Alan."

And the fourth surprise added, "You're just joking. Aren't you, son?"

Parents weren't normally allowed to travel with the players. But the Wildes appeared to be the exception. Theresa later learned that they accompanied him everywhere, always. Pulling her hand out of Alan's giant hand, she offered them a smile, and the mother said, "How are you, dear?"

The father offered, "I'm an admirer." His right hand was plastic. Lifelike, but not alive. Retrieving his hand, he added, "We're all admirers, of course."

How did he lose the limb? she wondered.

Because it was the polite thing to say, Theresa told them, "The best of luck to you. All of you."

Together, the Wildes wished her the same cliché. Then they said, "Alan," in a shared voice. Practiced, and firmly patient.

The boy stared at Theresa for a long moment, his face unreadable. Perhaps there was nothing there to read. Then with a deep bass voice, he said, "Later."

"Later," she echoed.

Two hundred kilos of muscle and armored bone pivoted, walking away with his tiny, seemingly fragile parents flanking him—each adult holding tightly to one of the hands and whispering. Encouragements, or sage advice. Or grave warnings about the world.

Even with her spectacular ears, Theresa couldn't hear enough to tell.

• • •

Days meant light practices, then the daily press conferences where every ludicrous question was asked and asked again with a linebacker's single-mindedness. Then the evenings were stuffed full of tightly orchestrated fun: Cookouts. A parade. Seats at a nuclear polka concert. Then a beach party held in both teams' honor.

It was on the beach that the Tech quarterback, Mosgrove, made a half-joking comment. "You know what we should do? Together, I mean." And he told the other 1-1-2041s, thinking they would laugh about it.

But instead of laughing, a plan was drawn up between the sea trout dinner and the banana split dessert.

On New Year's Eve, coaches put their teams to bed at ten o'clock. That was the tradition. And an hour later, exactly twenty-four of their players crept out of their beds and their hotel rooms, slipping down to the same beach to gather in two distinct groups.

At midnight and for the next three minutes and twenty-one seconds, no one said one word. With fireworks and laser arrays going off on all sides, their eyes were pointed at the foot-chewed sand, and every face grew solemn. Reflective. Then Theresa said, "Now," and looked up, suddenly aware of the electricity passing between them.

What was she feeling? She couldn't put a name to it. Whatever it was, it was warm, and real, and it felt closer even than the warm, salty air.

Still divided along team lines, the players quietly walked off the beach.

Theresa meant to return straight to bed, even though she wouldn't sleep. But she stopped first at the ladies' room, then happened past one of several hotel bars, a familiar face smiling out at her from the darkness, a thick hand waving her closer.

He was sitting alone in a booth, which surprised her.

With that slick, aw shucks voice, he asked, "Are my

boys finding their way home again? Or am I going to have to get myself a posse?"

"They'll end up in their rooms," she assured.

"Sit," said the coach. Followed by, "Please."

She squeezed her legs under the booth. Marlboro cuddled with his beer, but he hadn't been alone for long. The cultured leather beneath Theresa was still warm. But not the seat next to her, she noted. And she found herself wondering who was here first.

"Buy you a drink, young lady?"

She didn't answer.

He laughed with that easy charm, touched the order pad, and said, "Water, please. Just water."

"I really should leave," she told Marlboro.

But before she could make her legs move, he said, "You pegged me. That last time I came calling, you saw right through that brown shit I was flinging. About needing you for quarterback, and all that." A wink, then he added, "I was lying. Wasn't I?"

She didn't say one word.

Chilled water arrived, and Theresa found herself dipping into a strange paranoia. Mosgrove had suggested that meeting on the beach because Theresa had to come past this bar, and Coach Jones was waiting to ambush her, slipping some drug into her system so that tomorrow, in front of the entire world, she would fail.

A silly thought. But she found herself shuddering, if only because it was finally beginning to sink in . . . what was going to happen tomorrow. . . .

She didn't speak, but Marlboro couldn't let the silence continue. After finishing his beer and ordering another, he leaned over and spoke quietly, with intensity. He told her, "You saw through me. I'll give you that. But you know something, young lady? You're not the only shrewd soul at this table."

"No?" she replied.

Softly. With an unexpected tentativeness.

Then she forced herself to take a sip of her chilled water, licking her lips before asking, "What did you see in me!"

"Nothing," Marlboro said.

Then he leaned back and picked up the fresh beer glass, sucking down half of its contents before admitting, "I don't read you kids well. It's the muscles in your faces. They don't telephone emotions like they should."

She said, "Good."

He laughed again. Nothing was drunk about the man, but something about the eyes and mouth told her that he had been drinking for a long while. Nothing was drunk about the voice, but the words had even more sparkle and speed than usual. "Why do you think it is, young lady? All this noise and anguish about a game? A fucking little game that uses a hundred meters of grass and a ball that doesn't know enough to keep itself round?"

"I don't know—" she started.

"You're the favorite," he interrupted. "State is, I mean. According to polls, the general public hopes that I'm beat. You know why? Cause I've got twelve of you kids, and Rickover has only ten. And it takes eleven to play. Which means that on your team, at least one pure-human is always out there. He might be full of steroids and fake blood, and he's only going to last one set of downs, at most. But he's as close to being one of them butter-butts as anyone on either team. And those butter-butts, those fans of yours and mine, identify with Mr. Steroid. Which is why in their hearts they want Tech to stumble."

Theresa watched the dark eyes, the quick, wide mouth. For some reason, she couldn't force herself to offer any comment, no matter how small.

"And there's that matter of coaches," said Marlboro. "I'm the godless one, and Rickover is God's Chosen, and

I bet that's good enough for ten or twenty million church-goers. They're putting their prayers on the good man."

She thought of those days last summer—the pain and humiliation of practically begging for a spot on the roster, all while that good man watched from a distance—and she secretly bristled. Less secretly, she took a deep breath, looking away and asking him finally, "If it isn't me, who? Who do you see through?"

"Parents," he said. Point-blank.

"My folks?" she asked.

"And all the others, too," Marlboro promised. Then he took a pull of beer, grinned, and added, "They're pretty much the same. Sad fuck failures who want to bend the rules of biology and nature as much as they can, diluting their blood and their own talents, thinking that's what it takes for them to have genuinely successful children."

Theresa thought of her father's Christmas tantrum.

More beer, then Marlboro said, "Yeah, your parents. They're the same as the others. All of 'em brought you kids into existence, and only later, when it was too late, they realized what it meant. Like the poor Wildes. Their kid's designed for awesome strength and useful rage, and so much has gone so wrong that they can't get a moment's rest. They're scared. And with reason. They seem like nice people, but I guarantee you, young lady, that's what happens when you're torn up by guilt. You keep yourself sweet and nice, because if you falter, even for a second, who knows what you'll betray about your real self?"

Theresa sighed, then grudgingly finished her water. If there was a poison in this booth, it didn't come inside a thick blister of glass.

"Darling." A thick, slurring feminine voice broke the silence, saying, "Darling," a second time, with too much air. "Marl, honey."

A hand lay on the tabletop. Theresa found herself looking at it and at the fat diamond riding the ring finger. She asked herself what was wrong with that hand. It was too long, and its flesh wore a thin golden fur, and the fingernails were thick and curved and obviously sharp. Theresa blinked and looked up at the very young woman, and in that instant, the coach said, "My fiancée. Ivana Buckleman. Honey, this is the enemy, Theresa Varner—"

"How are you?" said the fiancée, a mouthful of cougar teeth giving the words that distinctive, airy sound. Then she offered the long hand, and the two women shook, nothing friendly about the gesture. With blue cat-eyes staring, Ivana asked, "Shouldn't you be asleep, miss? You've got a big day tomorrow."

Marlboro said nothing, drinking in the jealousy.

Theresa surrendered her place, then said, "Good luck, Coach."

He stared at her, and grinned, and finally said, "You know perfectly well, girl. There's no such bird."

Coach Rickover was famous for avoiding pregame pep talks. Football was war, and you did it. Or you didn't do it. But if you needed your emotions cranked up with colored lights, then you probably shouldn't be one of his players.

And yet.

Before the opening kickover, Rickover called everyone to the sideline. An acoustic umbrella was set up over the team, drowning out the roar of a hundred thousand fans and a dozen competing bands and the dull thunder of a passing storm. And with a voice that couldn't have been more calm, he told them, "Whatever happens tonight, I am extraordinarily proud of you. All of you. Ability is something given by God. But discipline and determination are yours alone. And after all my years in coaching, I can say without reservation, I've never been so proud and pleased with any team. Ever.

"Whatever happens tonight," he continued, "this is my

final game. Tomorrow morning, I retire as your coach. The Lord has told me it's time. And you're first to hear the news. Not even my wife knows. Not my assistant coaches. Look at their faces, if you don't believe me."

Then looking squarely at Theresa, he added, "Whatever happens, I want to thank you. Thank you for teaching an old man a thing or two about heart, and spirit, and passion for a game that he thought he already knew . . ."

The umbrella was dismantled, the various thunders descending on them.

Theresa still disliked the man. But despite that hard-won feeling, or maybe because of it, a lump got up into her throat and refused to go away.

The kickoff set the tone.

Man o' War received the ball deep in the end zone, dropped his head, and charged, skipping past defenders, then blockers—1-1-2041s, mostly—reaching his thirty-five-meter line with an avenue open to Tech's end zone. But the Wildman slammed into him from the side, flinging that long, graceful body across the sideline and into the first row of seats, his big-cat speed and the crack of pads on pads causing a hundred thousand fans to go silent.

State's top receiver couldn't play for the first set of downs. His broken left hand had to be set first, then secured in a cast.

Without Man o' War, Theresa worked her team down to the enemy's forty. But for the first time that season, the opening drive bogged down, and she punted the ball past the end zone, and Tech's first possession started at their twenty.

Three plays, and they scored.

Mosgrove threw one perfect pass. Then the Wildman charged up the middle twice, putting his shoulders into defenders and twisting around whatever he couldn't intimidate. Playing ABM, Theresa tackled him on his second run. But they were five meters inside the end zone, and a referee fixed his yellow laser on her, marking her for a personal foul—a bizarre call considering she was the one bruised and bleeding here.

Man o' War returned, and on the first play from scrimmage, he caught a sixty-meter bullet, broke two tackles, and scored.

But the extra point was blocked.

7–6, read every giant holo board. In flickering, flame-colored numbers.

The next Tech drive ate up nearly seven minutes, ending with a three-meter plunge up the middle. The Wildman was wearing the entire State team when he crossed the line—except for a pure-human boy whose collarbone and various ribs had been shattered, and who lay on the field until the medical cart could come and claim him.

14–6.

On the third play of State's next drive, Theresa saw linebackers crowding against the line, and she called an audible. The ball was snapped to her. And she instantly delivered it to Man o' War, watching him pull it in and turn upfield, a half step taken when a whippetlike ABM hit the broken hand with his helmet, splitting both helmet and cast, the ball bouncing just once before a second whippet scooped it up and galloped in for a touchdown.

Tech celebrated, and Theresa trotted to the sidelines. Rickover found her, and for the first time all year—for the first time in her life—her coach said, "That, young lady, was wrong. Was stupid. You weren't thinking out there."

21–6.

State's next possession ate up eight minutes, and it ended when the Wildman exploded through the line, driving Theresa into the ground and the ball into the air, then catching the ball as it fell into his chest, grinning behind the grillwork of his helmet.

Tech's following drive ended with three seconds left in the half.

28–6.

Both locker rooms were at the south end. The teams were leaving in two ragged lines, and Theresa was thinking about absolutely nothing. Her mind was as close to empty as she could make it. When a student jumped from the overhead seats, landing in the tunnel in front of her, she barely paused. She noticed a red smear of clothing, then a coarse, drunken voice. "Bitch," she heard. Then, "Do better! You goddamn owe me!" Then he began to make some comment about dog cocks, and that was when a massive hand grabbed him by an arm, yanking him off his feet, then throwing his limp body back into the anonymous crowd.

The Wildman stood in front of Theresa.

"She doesn't owe you fuck!" he was screaming. Looking up at hundreds of wide eyes and opened, horror-struck mouths, he shouted, "None of us owes you shit! You morons! Morons! Morons!"

Halftime needed to last long enough to sell a hundred happy products to the largest holo audience since the Mars landing, and to keep the energy level up in the dome, there was an elaborate show involving bands and cheerleaders from both schools, plus half a dozen puffy, middle-aged pop entertainers. It was an hour's reprieve, which was just enough time for Rickover to define his team's worst blunders and draw up elegant solutions to every weakness. How much of his speech sank home, Theresa couldn't say. She found herself listening more to the droning of the bilge pumps than to the intricacies of playing quarterback and ABM. A numbness was building inside her, spreading into her hands and cold toes. It wasn't exhaustion or fear. She knew how those enemies felt, and she recognized both festering inside her belly, safely contained. And it wasn't self-doubt, because when she saw Man o' War taking practice snaps in the back of the locker room, she leaped to her feet and charged Rickover, ready to say, "You can, but you shouldn't! Give me another chance!"

But her rocketback beat her to him. Flexing the stiff hand inside the newest cast, Man o' War admitted, "I can't hold it to pass. Not like I should."

Rickover looked and sounded like a man in absolute control.

He nodded, saying, "Fine." Then he turned to the girl and said, "We need to stop them on their opening drive, then hang close. You can, believe me, manage that."

Theresa looked at the narrowed corners of his eyes and his tight little mouth, the terror just showing. And she lied, telling him and herself, "Sure. Why not?"

Tech took the opening kickoff.

Coach Jones was grinning on the sidelines, looking fit and rested. Supremely confident. Smelling a blowout, he opened up with a passing attack. The long-armed Mosgrove threw a pair of twenty-meter darts, then dropped back and flung for the end zone. Theresa stumbled early, then picked herself up and guessed, running hard for the corner, the whippet receiver leaping high and her doing the same blind, long legs driving her toward the sky as she turned, the ball hitting her chest, then her hands, then bouncing free, tumbling down into Man o' War's long cupped arms.

State inherited the ball on the twenty.

After three plays and nine meters, they punted.

A palpable calm seemed to have infected the audience. People weren't exactly quiet, but their chatter wasn't directed at the game anymore. State supporters tucked into the south corner—where the piss-mouthed fellow had come from—found ways to entertain themselves. They chanted abuse at the enemy. "Moron, moron, moron!" they cried out as Tech moved down the field toward them. "Moron, moron, moron!"

If the Wildman noticed, it didn't show in the stony, inflexible face.

Or Theresa was too busy to notice subtleties, helping plug holes and flick away passes. And when the Wildman galloped up the middle, she planted and dropped a shoulder and hit him low on the shins.

A thousand drills on technique let her tumble the mountainous boy.

Alan fell, and Theresa's teammates would torpedo his exposed ribs and his hamstrings, using helmets as weapons, and sometimes more than helmets. One time, the giant man rose up out of the pile and staggered—just for a strange, what's-wrong-with-this-picture moment. A river of impossibly red blood was streaming from his neck. The field judge stopped the game to look at hands until he found long nails dipped in red, and a culprit. Tech was awarded fifteen meters with the personal foul, but for the next three plays, their running back sat on the sideline, his thick flesh being closed up by the team's medics.

Tech was on the eleven when he returned, breaking through the middle, into the open, then stumbling. Maybe for the first time in his life, his tired legs suddenly weighed what they really weighed. And when he went down hard, his ball arm was extended, and Theresa bent and scooped the treasure out of his hand and dashed twenty meters before one of the whippets leveled her.

For a long minute, she lay on her back on that mangled sod, listening to the relentless cheers, and trying to remember exactly how to breathe.

Tech's sideline was close. Pure-humans wearing unsoiled laser-blue uniforms watched her with a fanlike appreciation. This wasn't their game; they were just spectators here. Then she saw the Wildman trudge into

view, his helmet slightly askew, the gait and the slope of
his shoulders betraying a body that was genuinely, pro-
foundly tired. For the first time in his brief life, Alan Wilde
was exhausted. And Theresa halfway smiled, managing
her first sip of real air as Marlboro Jones strode into view,
cornering his star running back in order to tell him to goddamn please protect the fucking ball—

Alan interrupted him.

Growling. Theresa heard a hard, low sound.

Jones grabbed his player's face guard, and he managed
a chin-up, putting his face where it had to be seen. Then he
rode the Wildman for a full minute, telling him, "You don't
ever! Ever! Not with me, mister!" Telling him, "This is
your fucking life! It's being played out right here! Right
now!" Screaming at him, "Now sit and miss your life!
Until you learn your manners, mister! You sit!"

Four plays later, Theresa dumped a short pass into her
running back's hands, and he rumbled through a string of
sloppy tackles, all the way into the end zone.

State tried for a two-point conversion, but they were
stopped

The score looked sloppy on the holo boards, 28–12.

Tech's star returned for the next downs, but he was more
like Alan than like the mythical Wildman. In part, there
was a lack of focus. Theresa saw a confused rage in those
giant, suddenly vulnerable eyes. But it was just as much
exhaustion. Frayed muscles were having trouble lifting the
dense, overengineered bones, and the pounding successes
of the first half were reduced to three-meter gains and
gouts of sod and black earth thrown toward the remote
carbon-fiber roof.

State got the ball back late in the third quarter. Rickover
called for a draw play, which might have worked. But in

the huddle, Theresa saw how the defense was lining up, and she gave Man o' War a few crisp instructions.

As the play began, her receiver took a few steps back.

Theresa flung the ball at a flat green spot midway between them, and it struck and bounced high, defenders pulling to a stop when they assumed the play was dead. Then Man o' War grabbed the ball, and despite his cast, heaved the ball an ugly fifty meters, delivering its fluttering fat body into waiting hands.

Rickover wanted to try for two points.

Theresa called time-out, marched over to Rickover and said, "I can get us three." It meant setting up on the ten-meter line. "I can smell it," she said. "They're starting to get really tired."

"Like we aren't?" Man o' War piped in, laughing amiably as medics patched his cast.

The coach grudgingly agreed, then called a fumbleroosky. Theresa took the snap, bent low, and set the live ball inside one of the sod's deep gouges. And her center, a likable and sweet pure-human named Mitch Long, grabbed up the ball and ran unnoticed and untroubled into the end zone.

28–21, and nobody could think for all the wild, proud cheering of pure-humans.

State managed to hold on defense.

Mosgrove punted, pinning them deep at their end with ten minutes left.

Theresa stretched the field with a towering, uncatchable pass, then started to run and dump little passes over the middle. The Wildman was playing linebacker, and he tackled her twice, the second blow leaving her chin cut open and her helmet in pieces. Man o' War took over for a down. He bobbled the snap, then found his grip just in time for the Wildman to come over the center and throw an elbow into his face, shattering the reinforced mask as well as his nose.

Playing with two pure-humans at once, Theresa pitched to her running back, and he charged toward the sideline, wheeled, and flung a blind pass back across the field. She snagged it and ran forty meters in three seconds. Then a whippet got an angle, and at the last moment pushed her out of bounds. But she managed to hold the ball out, breaking the orange laser beam rising from the pylon.

Finally, finally, the game was tied.

Marlboro called time-out, then huddled with his 1-1-2041s. There wasn't even the pretense of involving the rest of the team. Theresa watched the gestures, the coach's contorting face. Then Tech seemed to shake off its collective fatigue, putting together a prolonged drive, the Wildman scoring on a tough run up the middle and Mosgrove kicking the extra point with just a minute and fifty seconds left.

35–28.

Rickover gathered his entire team around him, stared at their faces with a calming, messianic intensity. Then without uttering a word, he sent eleven of them out to finish the game.

The resulting drive consumed the entire one hundred and ten seconds.

From the first snap, Theresa sensed what was happening here and what was inevitable. When Man o' War dropped a perfect soft pass, she could assure him, "Next time." And as promised, he one-handed a dart over his shoulder on the next play, gaining fifteen. Later, following a pair of hard sacks, it was fourth and thirty, and Theresa scrambled and pumped faked twice, then broke downfield, one of the whippets catching her, throwing his hard little body at her belly. But she threw an elbow, then a shoulder, making their first down by nothing and leaving the defender unconscious for several minutes, giving the medics something to do while her team breathed and made ready.

Thirty meters came on a long sideline pattern.

Fifteen were lost when the Wildman drove through the line and chased Theresa back and forth for a week, then downed her with a swing of an arm.

But she was up and functioning first. Alan lay on the ground gasping, that wide elephantine face covered with perspiration and its huge tongue panting and an astonished glaze numbing the eyes.

Tech called time-out.

Mitch brought in the next three plays.

He lasted for one. Another pure-human was inserted the next down, and the next, and that was just to give them eleven bodies. The thin-skinned, frail-boned little boys were bruised and exhausted enough to stagger. Mitch vomited twice before he got back to the sidelines, bile and blue pills scattered on the grass. The next boy wept the entire time he was with them. Then his leg shattered when the Wildman ran over him. But every play was a gain, and they won their next first down, and there was an entire sixteen seconds left and forty meters to cross and Theresa calmly used their last time-out and joined Rickover, knowing the play that he'd call before he could say it.

She didn't hear one word from her coach, nodding the whole time while gazing off into the stands.

Fans were on their feet, hoarsely cheering and banging their hands together. The drunks in the corner had fashioned a crude banner, and they were holding it high, with pride, shouting the words with the same dreary rage.

"MORON, MORON, MORON," she read.

She heard.

The time-out ended, and Theresa trotted back out and looked at the faces in the huddle, then with an almost quiet voice asked, "Why are turds tapered?"

Then she said, "To keep our assholes from slamming shut."

Then she gave the play, and she threw twenty meters to

Man o' War, and the clock stopped while the markers
moved themselves, and she threw the ball into the sod,
halfway burying it to stop the universe once again.

Two seconds.

She called a simple crossing pattern.

But Coach Jones guessed it and held his people back in
coverage. Nobody was open enough to try forcing it,
which was why she took off running. And because everyone was sloppy tired, she had that advantage, twisting out
of four tackles and head-faking a whippet, then finding
herself in the corner with Alan Wilde standing in front of
her, barring the way to the goal line.

She dropped her shoulder, charging as he took a long
step forward and braced himself, pads and her collarbone
driving into the giant man's groin, the exhausted body
pitched back and tumbling and her falling on top of him,
lying on him as she would lie on a bed, then rolling, off the
ground until she was a full meter inside the end zone.

She found her legs and her balance, and almost too late,
she stood up.

Alan was already on his feet. She saw him marching
past one of the officials, his helmet on the ground behind
him, forgotten, his gaze fixed on that MORON banner and
the people brandishing it in front of him.

Some were throwing small brown objects at him.

Or maybe at all the players, it occurred to her.

Theresa picked up the bone-shaped dog treat, a part of
her astonished by the cruel, calculated planning that went
into this new game.

Carried by a blistering rage, Alan began running toward
the stands, screaming, "You want to see something funny,
fucks? Do you?"

Do nothing, and State would likely win.

But Theresa ran anyway, hitting Alan at the knees,
bringing him down for the last time.

A yellow laser struck her—a personal foul called by the panicked referee.

Theresa barely noticed, yanking off her helmet and putting her face against that vast, fury-twisted face, and like that, without warning, she gave him a long, hard kiss.

"Hey, Alan," she said. "Let's just have some fun here. Okay?"

A couple thousand Tech fans, wrongly thinking that the penalty ended the game and the game was won, stampeded into the far end of the field.

In those next minutes, while penalties and the crowd were sorted out, the 1-1-2041s stood together in the end zone, surrounding the still fuming Wildman. And watching the mayhem around them, Theresa said, "I wish." Then she said it again—"I wish!"—with a loud, pleading voice.

"What are you wishing for?" asked Man o' War.

She didn't know what she wanted. When her mouth opened, her conscious mind didn't have the simplest clue what she would say. Theresa was just as surprised as the others when she told them, "I wish they were gone. All these people. This is our game, not theirs. I want to finish it. By ourselves, and for ourselves. Know what I mean?"

The 1-1-2041s nodded.

Smiled.

The rebellion began that way, and it culminated moments later when a whippet asked, "But seriously, how can we empty this place out?"

Theresa knew one way, and she said it. Not expecting anything to come of her suggestion.

But Alan took it to heart, saying, "Let me do it."

He took a step, arguing, "I'm strongest. And besides, if I'm caught, it doesn't mean anything. It's just the Wildman's usual shit."

Police in riot gear were busy fighting drunks and bitter

millionaires. The running back slipped off in the direction of the locker room, as unnoticed as any blood-caked giant could be. Then after a few moments, as the crowds were finally herded back into the stands, Marlboro Jones came over and looked straight at Thēresa, asking everyone, "Where is he?"

No one spoke.

Rickover was waving at his team, asking them to join him.

Theresa felt a gnawy guilt as well as an effervescent thrill.

Marlboro shook his head, his mouth starting to open, another question ready to be ignored—

Then came the roaring of alarms and a fusillade of spinning red lights. Over the public-address system, a booming voice said, "There is nothing to worry about. Please, please, everyone needs to leave the dome *now! Now!* In an orderly fashion, please follow the ushers *now!*"

Within fifteen minutes, the dome was evacuated.

Coaching staffs and most of the players were taken to the helipad and lifted back to the mainland, following the media's hasty retreat.

Twenty minutes after the emergency began, the 1-1-2041s came out of their hiding places. The sidelines were under seawater, but the field itself was high enough to remain mostly dry. Security people and maintenance crews could be heard in the distance. Only emergency lights burned, but they were enough. Looking at the others, Theresa realized they were waiting for her to say something.

"This is for us," she told them. "And however it turns out, we don't tell. Nobody ever hears the final score. Agreed?"

Alan said, "Good," and glared at the others, his fists bleeding from beating all those bilge pumps to death.

Man o' War cried out, "Let's do it then!"

In the gloom, the teams lined up for a two-point play. State had ten bodies, and including the whippet still groggy from being unconscious, Tech had its full twelve.

Fair enough.

Theresa leaned low, and in a whisper, called the only appropriate play.

"Go out for a pass," she told her receivers and her running back. "I'll think of something."

She settled behind the minotaur playing center, and she nestled her hands into that warm, damp groin, and after a long gaze at the empty stands, she said, "Hey."

She said, "When you're ready. Give it here."

STREAK

Andrew Weiner

*Baseball has been widely popular here on Earth, crossing
lines of culture, language, and politics, so perhaps in the
future it will become just as popular* off *Earth as well.
Here we've taken Out to the Ball Game with some enig-
matic baseball fans from* very *far away in tow, to investi-
gate a red-hot streak that may be a little* too *good to be
true. . . .*

*Canadian author Andrew Weiner has made numerous
sales to* Asimov's Science Fiction, The Magazine of Fantasy & Science Fiction, Chrysalis, Full Spectrum, Northern
Frights, Prairie Fire, *and elsewhere. His short work has
been assembled in two collections,* Distant Signals and
Other Stories, *and, most recently,* This is the Year Zero. *He
is also the author of the critically acclaimed novel* Station
Gehenna. *He lives in Toronto, Canada.*

Victor Garmez was playing centerfield the day the aliens
came.

Last season, back in Double-A ball, he had mostly
played left field. The Chiefs had started him there, too. But
just a few weeks into the season there had been a rash of
injuries on the major league team, and the regular center-
fielder, Mel Hewlett, had been dispatched to Toronto to
join The Show.

Hewlett had been batting only .251 at the time, Garmez
.305. But Hewlett was management's blue-eyed boy, a
first-round pick in the college draft. Garmez was just another Dominican. Or so he imagined they thought of him,
when they thought of him at all.

Garmez did not miss Hewlett. But he did envy him, all the more so as the iron-gray sky over Syracuse opened up at the top of the third inning and the rain began to fall in torrents. Playing deep, he was soaked through by the time he made it back to the dugout.

They didn't get wet, up in Toronto. They just closed the roof on the dome.

In the dressing room, some of the players had resumed their endless card games. Others were watching daytime TV on the small monitor perched on top of one of the lockers. Garmez sat down to watch with them. He needed to improve his English.

The actors in the TV show were glossy and well-dressed and lived in palacelike homes. You never saw such people or such homes back in the Dominican Republic. Garmez's mother, along with his three sisters, lived in a two-room shack.

One day, though, he would make it to the big leagues, and build them a new house. If he didn't catch pneumonia and die first, this ghastly wet and chilly April.

"There's something you should know, Jill," a glossy, well-dressed man with fair wavy hair, who looked just a little like Mel Hewlett, was telling a glossy, well-dressed woman. And then, abruptly, the picture blanked.

"We interrupt this broadcast," said an authoritative-sounding voice, "to bring you this special bulletin."

War, Garmez thought. These Yankees have got themselves in another war. Or someone shot their president. . . .

The face of a newscaster filled the screen. At first glance, he looked like any other newscaster: dignified, sober, serious. But there was something wild about his eyes.

"Aliens," said the newscaster, "extraterrestrial visitors to our planet from another part of the galaxy, are currently meeting with world leaders in closed session at the United

Nations in New York. We take you now to Diane Kendrick at the UN Plaza. Are you there, Diane?"

Ken Brady stared in horror at his managing editor.

"You're assigning me *where?*"

"You heard me," Hugh Vernon said. "Sports desk."

"But I'm a science writer. I don't know anything about sports."

"And they don't know shit about science. I want you on the Garmez story."

"Garmez?"

Vernon looked at Brady with a mixture of scorn and awe.

"You don't know? You really don't know?"

"I've been doing stories on the aliens," Brady said. "Who's Garmez?"

"Victor Garmez," Vernon said. "Plays left field for the Blue Jays. Got called up from Triple-A in April as a backup. Got into a game and went 3-for-4. They kept him on the team and he kept on hitting. He's now hit safely in fifty-one consecutive games. . . ."

"And?"

"Fifty-one games," Vernon repeated. "Six more to get past Joe DiMaggio. That name ring any bells for you?"

"Sure. Wasn't there a song about him?"

"DiMaggio set the record for a hitting streak in 1941. No one else has even come close. Until this kid from the Dominican Republic."

"And this is a big deal?"

"A big deal?" Vernon echoed. "The greatest accomplishment in the history of baseball is on the line. I think you could say that was a big deal."

"Okay," Brady said. "But what does it have to do with me?"

"I want a think piece on probability theory. What are the

odds against a streak like this? Baseball fans eat up this statistical crap. I need two thousand words for Saturday. Front page of the sports section."

"What's so special about Saturday?"

"Jays finish up their home stand. And Garmez goes for number fifty-seven. Assuming he gets that far."

"And if he doesn't?"

Vernon shrugged. "We'll run it on the science page."

"I was supposed to finish this piece on the aliens."

"Screw the aliens," Vernon said. "The aliens are boring. *This* is the big story."

Boring. While Brady did not personally agree with his assessment, he could see how interest in the aliens might have begun to wear a little thin.

Following their meeting with world leaders, and a single, carefully orchestrated press conference, the aliens had been keeping a studiously low profile. They were here, they claimed, strictly in a touristic capacity. They wished only to obtain the requisite visas to come and go as they liked, along with a supply of native currencies. In exchange for this they had offered certain philosophical constructs and technological devices. Details of their offerings had not yet been revealed, but apparently the deal had been satisfactory to all concerned.

Afterward the aliens had flitted here, there, everywhere. They had been sighted buying jewelry at Tiffany's in New York, shopping for native art in Manila, dining on caviar in Moscow, observing the work of the Zurich sanitation department. There had even been reports, still unconfirmed, of aliens seen in Montreal, eating smoked meat, although so far none had been spotted in Toronto.

At their one press conference, the aliens had not been terribly forthcoming. They had declined to identify their planet of origin. Neither would they discuss the technology that had powered their ship. As to the nature of their own society, they offered only the barest clues. And they declined to be drawn into comment on Earthly ideological and religious squabbles.

It was not surprising that the aliens were evasive on these issues. But it made for rather thin gruel when you had to write background pieces on them. Brady was in some ways relieved to lay down the burden of speculating endlessly on the basis of little or no data. Even to have to write about *baseball,* of all things, a game about which he knew almost nothing and cared less.

"Garmez, yeah," said the hitting coach. "I expected good things of him, you know. But not this good."

"He didn't make the team in spring training," Brady said.

"Only just came up from Double-A. We thought he needed more seasoning. Still does, to tell you the truth. But when he's hitting like that . . . I mean, when you're hot, you're hot, right?"

"Right," Brady said.

"Garmez, he's a good little hitter. Reminds me of Wade Boggs."

"Wade Boggs never hit in fifty-one consecutive games."

The coach shrugged. "Streaks," he said. "I never understood them. I mean, not to take anything away from Garmez, but he's had some real luck along the way. Back around game twelve, he hits this little looper and it just drops in because the right fielder plays it too deep. Could have been scored an error, but they give him the hit. Another time he hits a chopper back to the mound and legs it out to first base. The umpire says safe, but it looks awfully close. Take away those hits and there's no streak, just a guy having a real good season."

"DiMaggio had some luck, too," Brady said. "From what I've read, there were a couple of very close judgment calls."

"Were there? Maybe that's true. But you know, I remember seeing DiMaggio when I was a kid. He was a giant, a real giant. . . . It's some strange kind of world where some green kid can come this close to topping DiMaggio. But don't print that, okay? The line around here is, we're right behind him."

Victor Garmez was tall and thin, with mournful eyes and a wispy mustache. According to team records, he had just turned twenty-two.

"I don't know what to tell you," he said. "Nothing like this ever happened to me before. Once I went eleven, maybe twelve games in winter ball. But fifty-one? It's crazy."

He spoke quietly, shyly. His vocabulary was quite good, but his accent was thick, and Brady had to strain to understand him.

"I guess you never expected anything like this to happen."

"Expected? I never expected to *be* here. It was a fluky thing, you know. One guy breaks an ankle, another guy gets the flu, another one runs into the wall trying to catch a ball and throws out his shoulder—" Garmez allowed himself a brief smile at the fate of Mel Hewlett "—no chance of catching it, he's just hotdogging. So they got to call me."

"You must have been pleased when you got the call."

"Stunned, more like. One minute I'm watching TV and they're talking about these aliens. And then the manager comes in and tells me to pack because I'm going to The Show. Between the aliens and The Show, my head was spinning so fast I thought it was going to fall off."

Garmez was cradling a bat in his arms, waiting to take batting practice. As they watched, the man in the batting cage smashed a home run ball into the upper deck. He turned, grinning broadly, and caught sight of Garmez and the journalist. The grin turned to a scowl.

"That guy," Garmez said. "Two million dollars a year. Cleanup hitter, he's supposed to be. And you know how many RBIs he hit in April? Three."

A week ago, Brady would not have known what an RBI was. Now, after studying the sacred texts of sabermetrics, he knew all too well. At night, when he closed his eyes, all he saw were tables of names and numbers.

"They hate me," Garmez said. "All these guys. Because I'm showing them up. Me and a couple of others, we're carrying this team."

He ran his hand along his bat.

"That bat," Brady said. "Is that the one you've been using? Kind of a lucky bat?"

Garmez shook his head. "I've used five, six different bats since I came up. A lot of guys, they got lucky bats and lucky socks and lucky Ninja Turtles, all kinds of lucky crap. But I don't believe in that stuff. What happens to me out there, it's down to me. And God."

"You think God is helping you?"

"I don't know. Maybe so." Garmez's voice trailed down to a whisper. "It's kind of hard to explain it any other way."

"How does it feel, taking on a legend like Joe DiMaggio?"

"I never heard too much about DiMaggio. Married Marilyn Monroe, right? They say he was a hell of a ballplayer."

"You think you're going all the way?" Brady asked

"I know it. You see, it's like they say: when you're hot, you're hot."

"Yes," Brady said. "Like they say."

They shook hands, and Garmez headed off to the bat-

ting cage. Then he turned back. "Hey," he said. "Maybe I
get to marry a movie star, too."

"Yeah," Brady said. "Maybe you do."

When you're hot, you're hot.

Victor Garmez believed that. So did his batting coach.
So did a lot of other people. And certainly it sounded plau-
sible: the more you succeeded, the more confident you felt,
and the better you did next time up.

The only problem, Brady thought, was that it wasn't
true. Not in baseball or any other sport. He had pored
over the studies, and they all pointed to the same conclusion.

There was a Stanford psychologist who had studied the
Philadelphia 76ers basketball team, tracking every basket
for more than a season. He found that the probability of
making a second basket did *not* rise after a successful shot.
The number of baskets made in succession was no greater
than you would predict on the basis of the laws of chance.
If your chance of making each basket was one in two, for
example, you would get five baskets in a row, on average,
once in thirty-two sequences.

Longer runs occurred, but there was no mystery to
them. A more talented basketball player might shoot at,
say, a 0.6 probability of success each time out. He would
get five in a row about once every thirteen sequences.

The same applied to baseball. There was almost no
statistic in the game, no sequence of wins or losses or hits
or strikeouts, that went beyond the frequency predicted
by the laws of chance. There was no "hot" or "cold"
about it: only skill intermeshing with the dance of probabilities.

Brady could have told Garmez this. But Garmez would
not have believed it. No athlete would. No sports fan, either. People didn't seem able to think in probabilistic

terms. They saw patterns emerging from the random flux of existence, and they rushed to impose meaning on them, to spin tales of heroism and villainy, or to look for the hand of God.

No, Garmez would not have believed it. No more than Brady's readers were going to believe it.

Besides, there *was* one exception to the rule. One gigantic, spooky exception: DiMaggio's fifty-six-game hitting streak. A sequence of events, as the biologist and baseball fan Stephen Jay Gould had once observed, *"so many standard deviations above the expected distribution that it should not have occurred at all . . . the most extraordinary thing that ever happened in American sports."*

Like DiMaggio, Victor Garmez was heading off the probabilistic map. And no one could predict where he might end up.

Brady had Saturday off. He rose early and picked up the newspaper from his front step. His own article was on the front page of the sports section. Obviously Garmez had come through with hit number fifty-six the night before.

Brady glanced briefly at his work, then tossed it aside. It was solid stuff, but he wasn't really satisfied with it. For all his research, he had finally been unable to penetrate the mystery of Garmez's streak.

Garmez would be going for number fifty-seven that afternoon. Fame and fortune—and perhaps the lifelong endorsement contract with the ketchup manufacturer that had finally eluded DiMaggio—beckoned.

Brady had liked the shy young Dominican, and wished him well. But he had no interest in seeing the game. Besides, he was supposed to meet Janice, his fiancée, at the Eaton Centre shopping mall to select a china pattern for

her forthcoming bridal shower. Janice believed in doing
things properly.

Brady was in the Eaton's china department with Janice
when he spotted the alien over in housewares, examining a
Eurostyle toaster.

The alien in housewares looked exactly like all the
other aliens Brady had seen on TV. He looked remarkably
humanoid, with only his exceptional tallness and thin-
ness—all the aliens were more or less seven feet tall—calling attention to his alien nature.

This was, to Brady's knowledge, the first alien to be
seen in Toronto. He found a store phone and called Hugh
Vernon to explain the situation.

"You want me to follow him?"

"Can't hurt," Vernon said. "First-person report on an
alien shopping spree. What's he bought so far?"

Brady craned his head to see the alien at the cash desk.

"Looks like a nonstick frying pan."

"Jeez," Vernon said. "This is already sounding like a
real thriller. But stay with it, you never know."

Abandoning Janice to select the china pattern, Brady
tailed the alien out of the department store and into the
mall proper. The alien led him into W. H. Smith's, a book-
seller. Like all the stores in the mall, it was nearly empty
this beautiful mid-June day. Half the population of the city
had headed out for their cottages. The rest were probably
glued to their TV sets, watching Victor Garmez go for hit
number fifty-seven.

The alien browsed for some time at the magazine racks,
at first flipping through the car magazines, then becoming
engrossed in *Playboy*. Brady wondered whether the alien
might be homesick for his own large-breasted alien wife,
back home on Arcturus 3 or wherever it was that they had
come from.

As far as anyone knew, there were no alien women on Earth. Or at least, all the aliens looked the same, and the general assumption was that they were male, although that assumption could have been quite unfounded. So far, none had been publicly forthcoming about their sexual natures, despite several multimillion-dollar offers for syndicated rights to such disclosures. Really, very little was known about the aliens.

Finally the alien left the store and headed for the escalator, making his way down to the lowest level. Brady realized that the alien was heading for the subway station. He followed the alien to the southbound platform. A train pulled up, and the alien got on. Brady got into the next car.

The alien disembarked at Union Station. After exiting the subway, he stood for a moment, apparently confused.

Brady seized the opportunity. "Need some help?" he said.

"Thank you, yes. Which way is SkyDome?" The alien spoke a fluent, accentless English.

"It's this way," Brady said, pointing. "I'm going there myself, I'll show you."

"That would be appreciated," the alien said. He was still holding the Eaton's shopping bag containing his nonstick frying pan.

"You're interested in baseball?"

"Very much so," said the alien. "In fact, you might describe this as the high point of our visit."

Aliens. Just when everything was going so well, some *aliens* had to come along and screw everything up.

Garmez got the story from Mel Hewlett soon after arriving at the ballpark. Earlier that week, the Canadian government had booked a block of tickets for the aliens, along with assorted federal, provincial, and city politicians. It was supposed to be kept secret until game time, for security reasons. But Hewlett had got the word from a secretary in the front office, and he seemed delighted to pass it on to Garmez.

"Why would aliens want to see a baseball game?"

"I don't know, Vic," Hewlett said, grinning. Garmez hated being called "Vic," as Hewlett well knew. "Maybe they're here to see *you*. Maybe your fame has spread throughout the galaxy."

Garmez had been feeling excited when he arrived at the stadium. It had been a pleasant excitement, full of anticipation. Now it turned into a dull agitation.

Aliens. Garmez had not had time to give much thought to the alien visitors. His own life had been moving ahead much too fast. But when he thought about them at all, it was with a kind of derision. If they were going to come all this way, you would think they would have something to tell us. Something important about God and life and the secrets of the universe. But from what he saw on the TV, they had nothing to say at all, except "that's nice" and "how much is that?"

Really, the aliens reminded Garmez of nothing so much as the North American tourists who streamed into the Dominican Republic every winter, buying all kinds of awful crap and burning themselves up on the beach and drinking themselves into oblivion.

It must be awfully boring, he thought, back where these aliens came from. To come all this way to see *us*.

And now, of all the things in the world to see or buy, they had to come *here*. Shaken, he went to see the team manager.

"How come you never told me about these aliens?" he demanded.

"Only found out myself a few hours ago," the manager said, mildly. "What you got to do now is forget about it. Forget about the aliens. Forget about your streak. Just go out there and play your normal game."

"My normal game, sure," Garmez said. He gazed out through the window at the stadium. It was beginning to fill up. "These aliens. What the hell they want here, anyway?"

"Someone invited them, I guess."

"You think they know about my streak?"

"I'm sure someone told them. Although it probably doesn't mean a hell of a lot to them. I mean, how could it?"

"Yeah," Garmez echoed. "How could it?"

Brady used his press credentials to gain entry into the ballpark. But instead of heading for the press box, he followed the alien to a special roped-off section. Within this section were dozens of aliens, along with various local dignitaries.

A security officer rose to bar his progress.

"It's all right," the alien said. "He's with me."

Gratefully, Brady sank down into an unoccupied seat next to his unexpected sponsor. He realized that he was staring at the thick, reddish neck of the prime minister of Canada in the seat ahead of him.

"Very kind of you," he told the alien.

"Think nothing of it, Mr. Brady."

"How do you know my name?"

"I saw it on your press pass."

Brady distinctly remembered that the alien had been ahead of him at the time. But perhaps he was wrong. Or perhaps the aliens were somehow possessed of 360-degree vision.

He could not help but wonder why the alien would knowingly invite a journalist to sit beside him. Since their initial press conference, the aliens had granted no further interviews to the media.

"I most enjoyed your article in this morning's *Tribune,*" the alien said, as if in answer to this unspoken question. "Highly insightful."

"You're interested in probability theory?"

"Fascinated by it."

The alien leaned forward in his seat to watch the proceedings on the field. The Red Sox were batting in the top of the second inning. There was no score as yet, but the Sox, with only one out in the inning, had runners at first and second.

"If there's anything you don't understand," Brady told the alien, "go ahead and ask."

This was rather a bold offer from a man who, for all his recent research, still had at best a dim understanding of the intricacies of the game.

"Thank you," said the alien, "but I am quite well acquainted with the game, having made a certain study of it. In some ways, it is much like our own . . ." Here he said something untranslatable into Earthly phonetics.

Mumblypobble, Brady scribbled into his notebook, this being the best approximation he could manage.

"Ah," said the alien. "I believe the Sox will certainly sacrifice in this situation, in all likelihood a bunt down the third-base line."

Brady scribbled down this alien prognosis.

"Games," said the alien, "are in a way the essence of a culture. The externalization of its most deeply held values about life, time, and existential meaning."

Polite applause rippled through the ground as the Red Sox hitter fulfilled the alien's prediction and gave himself up, laying down a bunt that moved the runners to second and third.

A new hitter took his place. He walked stiffly, and his hair was peppered with gray. "Batting .425 lifetime with runners in scoring position," murmured the alien. "But this will certainly be his last season. It's all so wildly nostalgic, is it not?"

"Nostalgic?"

The alien waved his hand in a disconcertingly human gesture. "The knowledge that each moment is precious precisely because it is ephemeral, and will never recur in quite the same way. The awareness of the fleetingness of life, the immediateness of death. The infinite poignancy of history in the making. Consider Victor Garmez." He gestured toward the Blue Jays' left fielder. "Will he ever have a finer moment than today?"

The alien smiled. It was a perfectly pleasant smile, yet it was also oddly chilling. Because somehow Brady knew that Victor Garmez would never have a finer moment. Ever, ever again.

A roar went up around the stadium as Victor Garmez stepped into the batter's box in the bottom of the second.

Sure, he thought. Today I'm their hero. But if I don't get a hit, it's back to being a bum. I'll be the guy who couldn't quite get past DiMaggio.

He stared sightlessly into the crowd to where the aliens were supposed to be sitting. He couldn't pick them out. Maybe they hadn't come. But of course, the aliens looked pretty much like humans.

The roar of applause continued. Some idiot was trying to get a wave going. Garmez called time-out and stepped back for a moment to review the situation. One out, a man on second, Red Sox leading five to nothing. A sacrifice fly would bring home the run, but one run would not make enough difference.

What he needed to do was get on base. He would look for the hit, but accept the walk.

"They're not going to give you anything to hit," the manager had told him. "They'd rather walk you than let you get number fifty-seven against them. If they offer the walk, take it."

"What if they walk me every time?"

"The way they count it now, the streak stays alive. You get another shot tomorrow."

"But what about then? How did they count it *then?*"

"For DiMaggio, you mean? Back then, it had to be consecutive games."

"Then that's how I got to do it, too."

Bold words. A lot bolder than he felt, right now, facing the ace of the Red Sox staff, a big, tough right-hander with a fastball averaging ninety-five miles per hour.

He watched, mesmerized, as the Boston pitcher went into his windup. And stood, transfixed, as the ball hurtled into his face.

"A close one," remarked the alien, as the hitter seemed to wait until the very last moment to weave out of the way of a high, tight fastball. "Very close. This is a game of surprising violence. And all so very much more vivid in its actuality."

"Actuality?" echoed Brady. "You mean, you used to watch it on TV?"

"Hush," said the alien. "Let us savor the opening round of this most fascinating duel."

Brady watched as, to applause and scattered boos, Garmez walked on four deliveries, without once having attempted contact with the ball.

The afternoon wore on. The Blue Jays picked up a couple of runs, cashing in Garmez's walk. Boston replied with another in the third. Garmez came out to bat again in the fourth with the bases empty, but grounded out to the shortstop. The next player up hit a solo home run.

The heat of the fierce afternoon sun was making Brady sleepy. He had difficulty keeping his eyes open during the scoreless fifth inning.

"Ah, baseball," the alien said. "Its hypnotic tedium, its mystic transformation of the immediate."

Brady stared at him blankly.

"Philip Roth," the alien said, apparently surprised. "*My Baseball Years.* Surely you've read it?"

"Actually, no."

"It breaks your heart," the alien said. "It is designed to break your heart. Bart Giamatti."

"Who?"

The alien shook his head in apparent disappointment, and returned his attention to the game.

In the sixth, Garmez walked again but was left stranded. The Red Sox continued to lead, six to three.

The Blue Jays scored another run in the seventh and threatened to score more, as the starting pitcher began to tire, but a relief pitcher came on and shut them down.

"You think Garmez is going to do it?" Brady asked during the seventh-inning stretch.

"Surely," the alien said, "you wouldn't want me to spoil it for you?"

Neither side scored in the eighth.

There was an almost palpable air of expectation in the alien section now, as the Red Sox went quietly in the top of the ninth.

The first Blue Jay hitter of the ninth grounded out to first base. Waiting in the on-deck circle was Victor Garmez.

"Why are there so many of you here?" Brady asked.

The alien seemed surprised at this question.

"To see Victor Garmez, of course. As your article points out, this man defies probability. Against astounding odds, he achieves continuity in a universe of flux. In a sense, he defies death. For all of us."

The alien leaned forward in his seat as Garmez took his

stance in the batter's box. "Besides," the alien said, "you
wouldn't expect us to miss this? To miss the wonderful
aching poignancy of it all?"

The crowd gasped as Garmez swung at and missed a
breaking ball in the dirt. But Brady was not watching. He
was consumed, suddenly, by a terrible situation.

"Wait a minute," he said. "You're not aliens at all!
You're *time travelers,* isn't that right? On some kind of
baseball junket."

"We are indeed aliens," the alien said, "by any possible
yardstick you could imagine. There is a certain quality of
brilliance to your deduction, but I am really not at liberty
to discuss it with you. At any rate, I now wish to turn my
fullest attention to this most diverting spectacle."

Behind 0 and 2. One more strike and it would be over, the
whole crazy circus.

Maybe it was better that way, Garmez thought. Better to
be a footnote in baseball history than the man who beat
DiMaggio. There would be less to live up to afterward.

He wiped the sweat from his brow, took his stance,
waggled the bat. Easy, he told himself. Nice and easy.

Curveball, floating way outside. 1 and 2.

Breaking ball, in the dirt.

Fastball, high and inside, jackknifing him off the plate.

A full count. Another walk? If it came, it came. He
watched the pitcher go into his windup.

He's got to throw me a strike, Garmez thought. Streak
or not, he doesn't want to bring up the tying run. Got to be
a fastball straight down the middle.

He watched it coming all the way, as though it were
traveling in slow motion. He felt as if he had all the time
in the world. The cheers of the crowd damped down to a
dull roar as he brought his bat around. There was a satisfying crack, and he watched the ball streaking into the

right-field corner. Then he was rounding second base and being waved on to third.

As the crowd sank back into their seats to watch the next batter, the aliens remained standing. Then they began to file out of the grounds.

"Don't you want to see who wins?" Brady asked his alien seatmate.

The alien shrugged. "It doesn't really matter who wins. Either way, the outcome is well within the normal distribution. We've seen quite enough, thank you."

Brady realized that the prime minister had turned around in his seat and was watching this exchange.

"Surely you're staying for the reception?" the prime minister asked, a little petulantly.

"Oh, no," the alien said. "This has been extremely entertaining, but it really is time to be moving on."

The departure of the aliens caused considerable discussion among the crowd. The umpires called time-out as they waited for the noise to subside. Garmez stood patiently at third base.

"Aliens," the third-base coach said. "Go figure them."

With the help of Garmez's triple, the Blue Jays tied up the game in the ninth, sending it into extra innings. The Red Sox, however, finally prevailed in the twelfth. Brady, slumped low in his seat, stayed until the end. It was the first and last major-league baseball game he would ever attend.

Garmez's streak was broken off the following night, at County Stadium in Milwaukee. But he continued to hit well, and was named Rookie of the Year. Endorsement contracts, including offers from rival ketchup manufacturers, poured in. He was able to build a house for his family in the Dominican Republic, and another for himself in Florida. He did not, however, marry a movie star.

Brady married Janice, but they separated a year later. She took the china, which he had never liked.

The aliens, after their visit to SkyDome, were not seen again.

Life, within the normal distribution, continued.

Author's note: I am indebted to Stephen Jay Gould's lucid and poetic article "The Streak of Streaks" (New York Review of Books, August 16, 1988) *for the information on sports probabilities used in this story.*

THE HOLY STOMPER VS. THE ALIEN BARREL OF DEATH

R. Neube

New writer R. Neube (and no, it's not a pseudonym!) has made frequent sales to Asimov's Science Fiction *in the past few years, as well as to* Tales of the Unanticipated, *and elsewhere. He lives in Covington, Kentucky.*

Here, he gives us ringside seats for the fast-paced, funny, and action-packed story of a professional wrestler who must face his greatest challenge in an arena far from this Earth, in a match with the fate of millions at stake, and on a mission that will redefine our definitions of diplomacy forever.

No sooner had I limped off the Greyhound shuttle than a pair of suits snagged me. They escorted my weary bones through the corridors of the good ship *Mead* to a crowded foyer next to an airlock. One of the suits pushed me into a reception line. Had I known, I would have worn shoes.

A petite woman popped into line beside me. Her fingers fussed with the rumpled lay of my jacket. "I'm glad you've finally arrived. What timing! This will be the first time the aliens have left their ship."

"First contact?" I asked, still groggy from a week of flying to this nowhere.

"*Second* contact. They ate the two anthropologists we sent into *their* ship."

"I prefer sociologists myself, but I have a good recipe for anthros. It all depends on the sauce."

It irritated me how she casually dumbed down her jargon for my benefit. Anthropologists studied people, xenopologists studied aliens. Sadder still, she did not even notice that she had insulted my intelligence.

"Don't say *any*thing," she repeated twice. "Just follow my lead and your common sense." She scurried to the front of the line, where she began conferring with a mob of suits and uniforms.

I grinned and did a few knee bends to loosen up after the cramped flight up to the *Mead.* They hadn't told me why I was here, but their check was generous. Having wrestled the circuit through the Dyb' worlds, I understood how to entertain aliens. Perhaps they wanted me to arrange an exhibition for this new species.

The airlock hissed open. The alien resembled a barrel with far too many limbs. A tailor would be driven to commit suicide trying to fit its four uneven arms. A tank on its back pumped a vile concoction through clear tubes stuck here and there into skin the consistency of bark. Its stench brought tears to my eyes. It shuffled by the uniforms, suits, and the petite woman without deigning to stop. It shambled directly to me, then paused, looking me over. It rocked back on four legs, its legion of kneecaps crackling like frying bacon.

I realized that the critter planned to slam that lump of a head into my chin. My instincts took over. I butted *my* forehead into that featureless lump *first.* We both staggered.

Whereupon, it turned and shambled back to the airlock.

I grinned. Having gotten through the ritual uneaten, I assumed the good guys had won.

•   •   •

"What breed of moron are you?" shouted the General.

"I may not be Aristotle, but I know who he was," I replied as an MP shoved me into a chair at the conference table.

"What's the moron prattling about?"

"It's Greek to me."

I straightened in my chair, craning to see who had made that last crack. It was the petite woman from the reception line, now wearing a badge declaring herself the Chief Xenopologist aboard the *Mead*. The simple fact that someone had a sense of humor in this tomb cheered me.

"Moron!" growled the General. His chestful of medals tinkled whenever he moved. General Windchime. He probably wore them to bed.

"Moron," agreed the Senator in the same tone he deployed for the hostile media.

"Couldn't you find anyone more *appropriate?*"

Clyde Keller, my sponsor, cringed from the General. A toupee slipped off his sweating brow to reveal an array of sensory implants. Maybe he saw something in the infrared that I missed. Poor Clyde took a trembling breath, his face aglow, verging on a blown fuse or a major clot.

"There was no time, sir. He was the only one I could locate who passed the immunological screening." Clyde's voice didn't crack, it shattered.

"*Why* did you strike the Ambassador?" General Windchime waved a fist in my direction as he sputtered.

"It was not the Ambassador. It was the Messiah's personal aide." The Xeno waved a disk at the General.

"Lookit," I said. "I may talk slow, but I'm not stupid. Everybody told me to follow my instincts—so I did."

"Idiot!" Coffee mugs hopped when the General's fist slammed against the table.

"I'm impressed with your mastery of synonyms. Look, it was the *alien* who initiated the head butt. I reacted. If A, then B. His exoskeleton spooked me at first, but now I know my head is just as hard." I touched the bandage a medico had sprayed on my gashed forehead. "What a *great* noise it made! Did anyone record it? I want a copy for my sounds-effects library."

"Their brains aren't located in the skull feature. He didn't hurt the Pek." The Xeno tossed her disk on the table. "Baxter and Sloane were experts, and *they* got butchered during the contact phase. We must try a different approach, or abandon this expedition."

Shaking his head, a lanky bloke cleared his throat. Given his rail-thin, crushed posture, I pegged him as a Spacer. "If we abandon them, they die. Their vessel is falling apart. It was designed for a useful life of three, maybe four centuries. If Intelligence is correct, it has been flying for more than eight hundred years."

"What exactly are you doing for them?" I asked the Spacer to annoy General Windchime. I promised myself I would annoy these yerps at every opportunity.

The Spacer flashed a dazzling smile. "We've attached work blisters to their hull. I modify our hardware to re-place equipment they've allowed to deteriorate. I scrounge parts off every ship that stops here. We're becoming a reg-ular tourist attraction, you know. Their life support is a monster—they require eleven arsenic compounds in their atmosphere."

The General's thousand-watt glower shut him up. The Spacer stared at his feet, which drew my attention to them. Despite their high shine, his boots were disintegrating. Hairy feet protruded from holes. His jumpsuit was thread-bare and patched.

"Why have we brought Citizen Muscle here on board?" asked a burly man wearing a GE corporate uni-form. "I could have used the money to buy a new com-pressor assembly. You *must* increase my department's budget! I—"

"Another Tech heard from," observed the Senator. Acolytes laughed in unison.

"Why *is* he here?" bellowed Windchime, bayoneting in my direction with a gnarled forefinger.

I responded with a more eloquent digit.

The Xeno stood. She spoke slowly, as if weighing each word. "We believe Citizen Scorpio can provide us with insights from his vocation, which has evolved into a religious aspect of Pek life. I wanted—"

"Moron," chorused a cast of dozens. The General launched into sound bites worthy of a championship grudge match.

I pulled out my chip plate and caught Clyde's eye. He produced his.

I CAN DO A FUND-RAISER FOR THE PEK, I typed, my pinkie on the broadcast button. LAST YEAR, I PUT TOGETHER A CARD FOR MARS FOREST, INC., AND FILLED STANTON ARENA. WE RAISED $700K FOR THEM. TALK TO ME LATER.

Clyde nodded as my message appeared on his chipper. He smiled like he was going to cry before he slipped into the corridor.

"This is a waste of *my* time. Carver, see that—" the General waved in my direction, shooing me "—our new moron gets the standard briefing in his cabin. Ito, have you finished your analysis of the radiation emission? Is it a leak or an exhaust by-product? Matrice, I expect a full report within the hour."

"*Matarice,*" screamed the Xeno with a whisper. "My name is Matarice."

Clyde had promised me "comparable" quarters. Comparable to what? A jail cell? Most jails I had experienced were far larger, far more homey. I felt blessed to have a toilet, doubly blessed to have a ventilation slot. Between thumps, an occasional whiff of putative fresh air graced my cabin.

I plugged into the comm port and dumped messages for my various enterprises into the ship's computer for later broadcast. My paper factory on Nok was of particular concern, since the union was suing me for "unfair labor practices" after I gave 80 percent of my stock to the workers.

"You can't win, boyo. Next time, bribe the union prez and be done with it!"

It was fortunate that the *Mead* expedition had approached me in October. Over-the-hill for steady wrestling, I made a point of vacationing and healing during my birth month. However, I *was* responsible for assembling a Thanksgiving card for the Liu Arena on Nok. The Barbarian continued to hang tough, insisting on points of the gate before he would sign a contract to wrestle.

"Yeah, like I make money giving away points," I grumbled while typing my fingers raw. "You get a few shots on prime time and you think you're a superstar!"

Stretching atop my spartan cot, I opened an MRE carton. I couldn't tell whether dinner was chocolate cake or steak. The *Mead*'s galley had incinerated after a tech stripped its sensors for the alien ship. The crew now dined on surplus military field rations.

Did General Windchime dine on this muck? Sure, sell me a Martian ice cap, too!

The screen on my wall beeped, announcing the start of my briefing. They spared no expense, showing me the *Monitor* episode about the Pek and their odyssey. Nothing like being educated by a children's news program—fortunately, it was my favorite show.

The Peks' generation ship swept into Sol System at .6 light speed, a pitted, gray cylinder twenty klicks in length. Probes were dispatched from the Pek ship. The atmosphere of Mars was too tenuous, Earth was too wet, and Venus fitted even an alien's definition of hell. Before using the sun as a slingshot, however, their sensory matrix captured three hours of 1957 television—a soap opera, the local news from Cincinnati, the CBS evening news, and a wrestling fest from Texas.

Their third Messiah spent the rest of his/her (Don't you hate omnisexual aliens? Would impregnating yourself be incest?) life studying those programs. The Peks had fled their sin-choked world for a paradise promised by their *original* Messiah. They'd scoured twenty-one stellar systems without discovering Eden—then they tuned into championship wrestling.

Poor critters.

A few years shy of two centuries later, the *Mead* stumbled onto the Pek gen ship while flying to study primitives on Quince III. The ailing generation ship was snailing along at a third of light speed, gradually slowing and falling apart in the largest void in this end of the galaxy. The *Mead* followed it cautiously until they confirmed that the Pek vessel no longer possessed external sensors. They attached surveillance modules to its hull and began collecting data.

This process was aided by the fact that the Peks were broadcasting TV programming of their *own* creation. Around the clock, a cornucopia of Pek history, religion, and culture filled the airwaves, formatted as news, soaps, and wrestling. Performance offerings to their supreme deity.

I nodded out during the cultural stuff. My eyes cracked open during a static-filled Pek soap opera. The aliens added snow to their pristine pictures in order to imitate those holy signals of yore—from back in 1957. Barrel-shaped, quad-limbed actors lumbered across the screen. Eight joints per limb made their arms more expressive than their whistling voices. Tall gray ones waved and whistled about infidelity. Short blue ones pushed thin orange ones who whined about their drinking problems. What the plot lacked in sense, the actors compensated for with boundless energy.

I resumed my slumber.

My day began with the usual aches, not unusual for someone who had broken 106 bones in his career. My contract specified room service. The personnel on the other end of the phone line pretended not to understand. Clyde Keller refused to accept my call; his secretary claimed he had flown back to Mars.

Checking my e-mail, I found that the Barbarian had caved, but wanted a five-grand signing bonus. The check from the Sol Trade Commission to pay for my transportation to the middle of nowhere had cleared. However, my paycheck from Mead University Research, Inc., had bounced.

Typical! Folks always tried to take advantage of me.

The Xeno arrived with a bucket of Cajun kelp sticks. "I am Citizen Tiffany Matarice. Citizen Scorpio, may I call you Romney?"

"Sure thing, Tiff," I replied, scarfing the kelp. "Your check bounced."

"That is not important. You passed muster. Romney, the Peks have requested that you wrestle for them!"

"Unless every one of the eighteen clauses in my contract is fulfilled, I'm not moving from this cabin. This isn't professional."

"There, uh"—she paused to stare at the scars around my neck where Bubba Brochoski cut my throat with a broken bottle during a Texas brawl match—"there must be a mix-up at the bank."

I looked at her for a long moment. "Folks assume I'm stupid because I'm big. Folks enjoy taking advantage of stupid people. It makes them feel better about their own miserable lives. I want my money, Tiff. But, before you snacker off, tell me how to score a decent breakfast on this scow."

Matarice was a gray gamine—skin and hair dyed to match her gunfighter's eyes. She moved with too much spring under the ship's half-standard grav, reinforcing the gamine illusion. Silence was her game. She stood and stared holes through me.

Gray lady, stormy glare. I forgot the rest of the poem.

Sitting on my cot, I prepared for a long game. I blanked my mind, no mean task considering the dearth of breakfast aboard the *Mead*. Eventually, I nodded off.

Shortly after I woke, an orderly delivered a small box. It was filled with Martian bucks and Taylor dollars, Nok hundred-dollar coins and finger-sized Dyb' cash ingots, a sealed plasticard of antique rubles, and credit-card vouchers. Took me half an hour with a currency exchange chart to tally my pelf.

I decided not to charge my usual bad-check fee. My generous nature has ever been my bane.

Despite my nose filters, the alien's smell reminded me of the Avondale riots of my youth. Burning tires, summer sweat, and charred flesh—the stench followed the Pek like a smog bank. I sidled, then dropped for a knee-walk, spooking my barrel-shaped opponent to the other side of the ring. I winked at the camera, strutting mime I'd mastered from Charlie Chaplin films.

During my study of Pek wrestling technique, I'd noticed that they didn't play to the camera and the future revenue the home audience represented. Daresay they never suffered nightmares about ratings.

The yerp threw one of its triangular feet at me. I had been waiting for that move. Ducking beneath the blow, I

balanced its second thigh atop my shoulder and commenced circle dancing. The sucker had three other feet and
would kick my teeth in the instant it regained its balance.

A nifty thing about an opponent with eight joints per
limb was the opportunity to grab the captive foot and beat
the Pek with it. Gorgeous George and Goshawk Geoffrey
could only have dreamt of such sterling schtick. After the
audience grew bored of me flailing that lump with its own
foot, I backstepped and drop-kicked the sucker over the
top rope.

Time for a bow and a kiss toward the camera.

I prayed that my VCR aboard the *Mead* was recording
true. There wasn't a vid promoter in Sol System who
wouldn't fork over $100K for a copy of this match. The
word "auction" echoed through my brain's greed center.

I grinned at the ref until it turned away from me.
Whereupon, I drop-kicked the ref over the ropes, too. The
crowd's uproar made the racket in Deimos Square Gardens sound like a kitten's fart. My victory prance kept
them whistling. As my opponent came to its feet, I threw
myself through the ropes and splattered the yerp to the
metal deck.

Mass times velocity equaled ratings cubed.

Rolling off my foe, I "accidentally" swept the ref's legs
from beneath it. The aliens shared their joy by throwing
green, squishy fruit at me. Stealing the Masked
Manchurian's trademark, I backflipped from the apron into
the center of the ring.

I loved low grav!

In lieu of the tobacco smoke the aliens had seen filling
the wrestling arena in their intercepted vid, the Pek burnt
compost for their sacred ambiance. It was perfume compared to the aliens' reek. Using the reduced grav, I sprang
into the overhead lights, hung, then made a double flip
down to the ring. My staggering impact was less than perfect, but the Peks went wild.

Performance offerings. I danced for the camera. Yeah, I could double my appearance fee after this vid hit the networks. Triple!

I made the mistake of allowing the Pek back into the ring. It came at me like a missile, bayoneting its nonhead into my belly. My spleen leapt into my sinus cavity. Its mitts raked my face, trying to rip the filters from my nose.

Trying to *kill* me!

Breaking free, I collapsed into a corner. Rocketing in again, the Pek bounced off my size-sixteen boot. Scooping the yerp up, I staggered to lift it as my vertebrae compressed. The throw was sheer luck. I couldn't have *aimed* the squirming lump for a direct hit on the referee. The deck rang like a bell.

"Give me some real competition!" I screamed at camera three in my stilted Pek. Xeno Tiff had rehearsed me a hundred times, getting the phrase whistle-perfect. My throat filter felt funny. Had it dislodged? I began hacking worse than an escapee from a TB colony.

The taste of arsenic reminded me of the eighth grade when the Freemont Razors tried to drown me in a rusty toilet before home room.

The ref rolled under the ropes. My foe followed. It rolled, I rocked. I hopped up and down on the alien until its shell cracked, the yerp screaming like a puppy in a garbage crusher. (Another trick the Razors taught me. Poor Rover. I could never bear to own another pet.)

The bell rang. Pulling me off my opponent, the ref wrapped a belt around my waist. It was silver, the same color as Pek blood.

The ex-champ's tag-team partner raced down the aisle and hopped into the ring. Pure stereotype. I swept its legs out from under it and kicked it until my toes ached. Backing off, I waited for the Pek to rise before scoop-slamming the fool over the top and onto the unforgiving metal deck.

The studio audience went ape, showering me with something ooshy that resembled fish guts.

My next cough sprayed blood.

They ambushed me as soon as I boarded the Mead. The General and his staff got in my face. Dizzy and puny, I slumped against the bulkhead, hacking and cursing. They stayed in my face. I blew out my nasal filters. Green snot earned me some breathing space.

"Moron!" bellowed General Windchime.

"It's like breathing broken glass. You people are paying for my replacement lungs."

Windchime tried to slap me. He screamed when I snapped his forearm. His aide went for her side arm. She screamed, too, once I broke her wrist. Some might have considered my response childish, but sucking arseno-hydrocarbon poisons gave me an attitude.

A dozen MPs swarmed me with their electroprods. At least the voltage twitched my spleen back into place.

Matarice waited in my cabin. She expressed no surprise when the uniformed gangsters dumped me at her feet. She patiently bided her time until my spasms subsided. I sat upright and grinned. She kicked my brain loose.

"You were *not* supposed to kill it!" she screamed, and kicked and kicked.

I recovered enough to parry the final blows. Despite artificial grav, long-term spacing sapped folks' endurance.

"Is someone dumping steroids in your water supply?" I asked politely.

"I'll have you up on charges of murder!"

"It was self-defense. They only saw the vid. They haven't a clue about the reality. If I hadn't—" I burst out in laughter, a miracle considering the way my lungs crawled into my throat. Arsenic wasn't a bad buzz, a cross between good pot and a baseball bat upside the head.

"Moron!"

"What? Is that word a *Mead* tradition?"

"You murdered a nonhuman! We can't cover up something like that. We're trying to *save* them, not stomp them to death!"

"Yeah, life is a rerun of *Star Whatsit,* and I'm trashing the prime bloody directive. Beam down to reality, Tiff! Did Baxter and Sloane go meekly to their slaughter? Lookit, we have more important matters to discuss."

"Murderer!" Her eyes flickered, swirling darker shades of gray.

"These barrel bum are a species known only from these seven thousand religious fanatics. They're so weirded out that they've stopped fixing their ship. They're trying to *blackmail* their deity into action! Their wrestlers are killing each other like Aztecs sacrificing to their gods. If they pray hard enough . . . *if* their performance offerings are sincere enough . . . if, if, if! Those bizarre yerps are—"

"You cannot judge another species. That is racist. Moron! You cannot—"

"Lookit, Tiff, they weren't too tightly wrapped *before* they spent the last five generations in space. Why do they broadcast their offerings? They're telling their deity that they have received the communication and understand— but they *don't.* They're faking it out of desperation. I think—"

"That is one of a myriad exclusive theories, Citizen Scorpio. You are not qualified—"

"To exercise my common sense? They refuse to discuss their religion with you people because they're waiting for one of *us,* a pro wrestler, one of their deity's messengers, to explain the mysteries to them. We're there Hermes."

The Gray Woman sputtered. "My peers and I have invested *years* deconstructing, dissecting every frame of their broadcasts. We have identified their symbology. We have learned their language, and have a good idea about the motifs behind their crypto-TV culture. Yet *you* dare saunter in, commit murder, and announce *your* solution!"

"That's the size of it, meka." I remoted the TV. The Pek news appeared, the *Mead*'s masterputer providing awkward English subtitles.

"It was *my* idea to bring you here," she said glumly. "The Trade Commission will probably have me fired. The Pek will never listen to us again. Do you have any *idea* what you've destroyed?" The Gray Woman slumped onto a toadstool and stared at the screen.

"If I'm wrong, you can blame Clyde Keller. Just as well, since the coward hightailed out of here on the last shuttle. Just watch the screen. I'll let the Pek do my arguing for me."

The anchor-alien wore a blond wig. The Pek spoke of a fire in the warehouse district, a shooting in front of a house of ill repute, and a six-car pileup blocking rush hour. It proceeded as most rituals did—smooth and confident, mimicking the recording of yore without a clue of what repute (sick or well) or a rush hour might be.

"Wrong about what? What are you saying?" she whispered, staring at the screen.

I coughed into my fist, spraying a fine mist of arsenic-laced blood. The coughing came with such intensity that my toes shortened. I'd count myself fortunate if my lungs were the only things requiring replacement.

Clips from my match appeared, intercut with mouthings from the current Messiah. Matarice froze, gray eyes growing wide, glowing in the light of the screen.

"The Messiah *never* appears on broadcasts. *Never!* What have you *done?*"

The alien spoke so rapidly that the subtitles failed to keep pace. But the Messiah called me holy. I could envision my new moniker on the marquee—The Holy Stomper.

I hadn't expected the xenopologist to throw up on my

carpet. Actually, it was an improvement on the fiber's color. I patted her back.

"What have you done to my Peks?" she moaned. "What kind of maniac *are* you?"

"I grew up on the wrong side of the trailer park," I explained to annoy my guest. Anyone who kicked me in the head deserved to be tortured by my life's story. "My mom was crazy over her God like the Pek are over theirs. That's why I understand them."

"I don't wish to listen to your personal history," she hissed through clenched teeth, each word intoned as a curse.

"Ah, but from history blooms knowledge! I grew up on the streets. When I was seventeen, Howard 'The Blade' Smith took it in his head to kill me. Never did figure why."

"I know why," she growled.

"I broke into the Razor's clubhouse and hid under his bed. When he went to sleep, I crawled out and used the ax I'd been hugging for hours. He had $50K in his pillowcase.

"While I was waiting for the next bus out of town, I took measure of myself. The money was a onetime shot, so I had to strike gold my first time out. I was too lazy for business, not smart enough for college, not vicious enough for crime. I went down the checklist. And, in the end, I went straight from the Chi-town bus station to a cosmetic surgeon and bought a muscle job.

"I own mines on Mars, a paper factory on Nok, and export companies on three different poleis. I could have retired years ago, but I love being silly. It's my talent, my greatest strength. And people underestimate me because I look stupid—that's my greatest asset. You people have studied the Pek to death, but you treat them like microbes under a microscope. They might be aliens, but they enjoy being silly, too!

"Believe me, I know what I'm doing."

She threw up again.

I hadn't thought about Mom in years. She would have understood ceasing maintenance on a spacecraft to show her faith in God. Her God's "Plan" called for her husband to abandon her and robbers to rape and butcher her. "His Plan," she babbled over dinner every night, explaining the latest disaster to overtake her. Her eyes sparkled when she spoke about her deity, the way a junkie's eyes sparkled after dosing.

Once Matarice left, I gingerly avoided the puddles she left behind on my way to my chip plate. I tapped into the comm system, then tapped a message for my accountants to score everything they could on the *Mead*'s finances. It felt important to discover why their check had bounced.

When an opponent was too fast, you attacked his legs. When they were too strong, you had to be faster. When they were generals and fuzzy scientists, you had to hire *smarter* people.

I love my Gold Card!

There was precious little difference between locker rooms, be they aboard the Pek gen ship or Lunar Square Gardens. Although here, the grotty sock stench was replaced by a grotty arsenic stench.

I squeezed my nose, feeling the tips of my nasal filters; I squeezed my throat, feeling the lump of that filter. A secondary sheet filter I wrapped around my mouth and nose. Three layers was as much as I could do and still breathe. With luck, the wrap would divert my opponent's attention and keep the alien from yanking out my internal filters.

With luck . . .

"Four scope and seben yeaps," I said through my mask. You couldn't wrestle unless you could curse. That was a Law of Nature.

Aliens moved as quietly as Martian muggers. I glanced up to find myself surrounded by half a dozen of the tall

Grays—the dangerous ones. Their reek clogged my nostrils, defying the filters. The Pek swayed as they whistled. Wasn't that the old *Lassie* theme? I unwrapped my mouth, then replied with the same, earning a round of applause.

"Will you tell us?" asked a small blue Pek, elbowing through the crowd.

I sidled, getting my back against the wall. The Grays kowtowed to the Blue. It smelled different—fill an old tire with roses and ignite it with kerosene. The Grays squatted and slapped their mitts on the deck. It echoed like thunder.

"Will you reveal the Secrets?" the Blue asked in perfect English as it tugged at my sweats.

I winked at the critter. They liked winking. Lacking eyelids, or anything that might pass as eyes, they suffered eyelash envy. "You speak the lingo well."

"My English is good to the last drop, like the Marlboro House Man," replied the alien proudly. "Will you share the Secrets?"

"Do you understand the word 'rigged'?"

Apparently the Blue did, whistling a quick translation to its comrades. I would have sworn it was the theme from *The Andy Griffith Show*. I snapped my fingers at the appropriate moment. All those video history telecourses I took while on the circuit were paying dividends.

"Predetermined?"

"Close enough. I am told. My opponent is told. The Boss decides who will win the big matches."

"Told by *your* Prophet?" The Blue advanced, tilting its body in a querulous fashion. Its limbs made clicking noises. The other Pek grew agitated, stomping their feet as they milled.

"*Everything* is predetermined. If A, then B. Soap operas are written to a formula. If A, then B. The news is about folks. Folks react in the same way, given the same circumstances. If A, then B. The Boss studies the market demographics and decides who will earn the most money by drawing the largest crowd. If Audience, then Bucks. One way or the other, *every*thing is rigged!"

More Blues appeared. A mob of Grays filled the doorway. Whistling grew in volume until my teeth ached. Limbs waved and whacked. I picked up a container of talc and surreptitiously unscrewed its cap. However feeble, any diversion would be better than none, should the natives decide to make me into a Slim Jim.

"Who is The Boss?" asked the smallest of the Blues. It lacked a leg and two arms, not to mention sporting a massive dent in its barrel body. The veteran must have lost more than a few bouts.

"It depends. Different arenas have different Bosses."

The maimed Blue eased forward, the others parting to give him/her plenty of room. This Pek wore a massive belt of silver. I intuited it was their current Messiah, despite it not resembling the one I saw on TV. I bowed. My fingers pulled the belt I'd won off the bench. Bowing again, I offered the belt to the Messiah, smiling like a village idiot.

"Every Boss has a Boss. The trick is to find someone who can rig the Boss. Allow me to explain. . . ."

The Messiah snapped its arm joints while I spoke. First the Blues, then the Grays, slapped their bodies in unison, in reply. It might have been a happy sound to them. It reminded me of a tray of silver spoons being tossed across a tile floor.

"What the hell have you *done?* They haven't left the Prayer Arena in two days! Intell says—" Matarice excelled at storming into a room.

"Is N. Tell any relation to Willie Tell? I 'rastled him on New Berne once."

"*Intelligence,* you lump! They've tapped into every system on the ship. They can tell how often the Pek flush their toilets."

"So much for your putative sense of humor. Huh, come to think of it, there weren't any toilets in the locker room. Do Peks have bowel mo—"

"I don't care! What did you *tell* them? They *never* cancel a night of wrestling! Now they've stopped broadcasting altogether." She spoke loud and slow, as if I were stupid and deaf.

"I told them the truth, of course."

I kept one eye on the monitor. Figures marched down the screen in tidy columns. Legions of numbers had been the focus of my attention for hours. My accountants had ordered the *Mead*'s four previous budgets directly from the Trade Commission's Depository, then sent me the germane files. My bouncing check had been the source of the original afflatus, but I was light-years beyond that.

"*Which* truth?" Matarice's gray face contorted, bringing to mind Reaper McGuire after he'd ruptured himself during a mistimed Boston Squash.

"Which truth, Romney?" This time honey dripped from the question. You would not find her smile in the dictionary under "sincere" unless a shark wrote it.

"Did you know someone is peculating from the *Mead*'s grant money?" I said. "The hard copy is next to the lamp. Take notice how 17.3 percent of the budget for wages is transferred into a 'General Accounts' fund. From there, it is deposited into the account of Citizen Frederick Brooks, FN2914-336-8106 as a consultancy fee. Valid code, but no such person exists—this is one slick crime."

"What? What qualifies *you* to—No, money isn't important. What did you tell the *Pek?* Stop avoiding the question."

"You think I'm just another pretty face? I earned a degree in accounting to keep track of my businesses. When you're always on the road, you have all this time on your hands. Aren't telecourses great? You people have lost over thirty million, Tiff. Pretty soon, that could add up to some serious money."

"The Pek! What did you tell them?"

"A basic truth. When the game is fixed, you must hire yourself a Fixer."

Her face twitched. People with gray-dyed skin should never blush. "Game? Aliens cannot distinguish the nuisances of English. I—"

"You mean *nuances*. What's the prob? You have failed for years to find common ground with the Pek. I *have*. All their praying is begging overtime that their new Champion will win the big match."

"Champion?"

I scooted away from the gray gamine, mindful of her penchant for painting the carpet with lunch, as well as kicking like a rabid mule.

I grinned. My petition had percolated through the Trade Commission's Audit Committee by now. The Martian media moguls had digested my revelations and would shortly open the bidding war on the rest of the story. Phil Crockett, aka The Stomper, president of Crockett Construction Ltd., would still be debating whether the profit inherent in the gimmick of the century would offset the cost of building a home for my new clients. Best of all, General Windchime would soon discover that I had bribed one of his officers for an hour's unsupervised access to the communication center.

All the burners were on high. My pots were boiling. Chief Scorpio was preparing a feast, though I had yet to figure out who I was having for supper.

"If you're smart, you can use this disaster to your benefit, Tiff. The embezzlements can be blamed for your failure with the Pek. If you and the other scientists come down on the Trade Commission's side, they will be grateful. As PR-minded as the Commission is, the *Mead* might even get their research expanded. I, for one, will be requesting your aid. I'll need your people for another year or two to get everything working properly."

"What are you saying?"

"You people play the villain, and I play the righteous Champion. We fight—you people lose."

"*What?*"

"What do you think 10 percent of a civilization is worth? By the way, we'll be suing the Trade Commission and your university for malfeasance and social sodomy. Okay, I don't know the legal terms. That's why I've retained Peterson, Danson, and Grier."

"But, but—"

"There will be an army of politicians eager to join our cause. Everybody hates the Commission."

"Suing? But, the *Mead*—"

"Don't worry, that's just for the consumption of the press. We're going after the deep pockets, not you people."

"Wa-what?" moaned Matarice.

I smiled at her. "Isn't that an agent's job?" I said brightly.

It was going to be a *hell* of a good fight. And the ratings would be out of this world!

Literally!

STROBOSCOPIC

Alastair Reynolds

*Here's a taut, inventive, and fast-paced story that specu-
lates that the newish realm of computer game design will
eventually merge with the field of daredevil exhibitions of
the jump-over-a-canyon-on-a-rocketsled sort, to produce a
sport where everything can change in the blink of an eye—
sometimes with fatal results.*

*New writer Alastair Reynolds is a frequent contributor
to* Interzone, *and also has sold to* Asimov's Science Fiction, Spectrum SF, *and elsewhere. His first novel,* Revelation Space, *was widely hailed as one of the major SF books
of the year. His most recent novel is a sequel to* Revelation
Space, *also attracting much notice,* Chasm City. *A professional scientist with a Ph.D. in astronomy, he comes from
Wales but lives in the Netherlands, where he works for the
European Space Agency.*

"Open the box."

I wasn't making a suggestion. Just in case the tone of
my voice didn't make that clear, I backed up my words
with an antique but functional blunderbuss; something
won in a gaming tournament half a lifetime earlier. We
stood in the airlock of my yacht, currently orbiting Venus:
me, my wife, and two employees of Icehammer Games.

Between us was a gray box the size of a child's coffin.

"After all this time," said the closest man, his face hidden behind a mirrored gold visor on a rococo white helmet.
"Still don't trust us?"

"First rule of complex systems," I said. "You can't tell
friends from enemies."

"Thanks for the vote of confidence, Nozomi."

But even as he spoke, White knelt down and fiddled with the latches on the lid of the box. It opened with a gasp of air, revealing a mass of translucent protective sheeting wadded around something very cold. After pausing the blunderbuss to Risa, I reached in and lifted out the package, feeling its bulk.

"What is it?

"An element of a new game," said the other man, Black. "Something called *Stroboscopic*."

I carried the package to a workbench. "Never heard of it."

"It's hush-hush," Black said. "Company hopes to have it up and running in a few months. Rumor is it's unlike anything else in Tycho."

I pulled back the last layer of wadding.

It was an animal packed in ice; some kind of hard-shelled arthropod; like a cross between a scorpion and a crab—all segmented exoskeletal plates and multijointed limbs terminating in various specialized and nasty-looking appendages. The dark carapace was mottled with patches of dirty white, sparkling with tiny reflections. Elsewhere it shone like polished turtleshell. There were ferocious mouth parts but nothing I recognized as an eye, or any kind of sensory organ at all.

"Looks delicious," I said. "What do I cook it with?"

"You don't eat it, Nozomi. You play it." Black shifted nervously as if wary of how much he could safely disclose. "The game will feature a whole ecology of these things—dozens of other species; all kinds of predator-prey relationships."

"Someone manufactures them?"

"Nah." It was White speaking now. "Icehammer found 'em somewhere outside the system, using the snatcher."

"Might help if I knew where."

"Tough titty. They never told us; we're just one of dozens of teams working on the game."

I couldn't help but laugh. "So you're saying, all I have to go on is one dead animal, which might have come from anywhere in the galaxy?"

"Yeah," White said, his helmet nodding. "Except it isn't dead."

The mere fact that I'd seen the creature, of course, meant that I'd have an unfair advantage when it came to playing the game. It meant that I, Nozomi, one of the dozen or so best-known gamers in the system, would be cheating. But I could live with that. Though my initial rise to fame had been driven mainly by skill, it was years since I'd played a game without having already gained an unfair edge over the other competitors.

There were reasons.

I could remember a time in my childhood when the playing of games was not the highest pinnacle of our culture; simply one means by which rich immortals fought boredom. But that was before the IWP commenced the first in a long series of wars against the Halo Ideologues, those scattered communities waging dissent from the system's edge. The Inner Worlds Prefecture had turned steadily more totalitarian, as governments generally do in times of crisis. Stealthily, the games had been pushed toward greater prominence, and shady alliances had been forged between the IWP and the principal gaming houses. The games enthralled the public and diverted their attentions from the Halo wars. And—unlike the arts—they could not be used as vehicles for subversion. For gamers like myself it was a near-utopian state of affairs. We were pampered and courted by the houses and made immensely rich.

But—maybe because we'd been elevated to such loftiness—we also saw what was going on. And turning a blind eye was one of the few things I'd never been good at.

One day, five years ago, I was approached by the same individuals who'd brought the box to my yacht. Although they were officially working for Icehammer, they were also members of an underground movement with cells in all the gaming houses. Its lines of communication stretched out to the Ideologues themselves.

The movement was using the games against the IWP. They'd approach players like myself and offer to disclose material relating to games under development by Icehammer or other houses; material that would give the player an edge over their rivals. The player in turn would siphon a percentage of their profit into the movement.

The creature in the box was merely the latest tip-off.

But I didn't know what to make of it, except that it had been snatched from somewhere in the galaxy. Wormhole manipulation offered instantaneous travel to the stars, but nothing larger than a beachball could make the trip. The snatcher was an automated probe that had retrieved biological specimens from thousands of planets. Icehammer operated its own snatcher, for obtaining material that could be incorporated into products.

This time, it seemed to have brought back a dud.

"It just sits there and does nothing," Risa said when the Icehammer employees had left, the thing resting on a chilled pallet in the sick bay.

"What kind of game can they possibly build around it?"

"Last player to die of boredom wins?"

"Possible. Or maybe you throw it? It's heavy enough, as though the damn thing is half-fossilized. Those white patches look like quartz, don't they?"

Maybe the beast wouldn't do *anything* until it was

placed into the proper environment—perhaps because it needed olfactory or tactile cues to switch from dormancy.

"Black said the game was based on an ecology?" I said.

"Yeah, but how do you think such a game would work?" Risa said. "An ecology's much too chaotic to build into a game." Before she married me she'd been a prominent games designer for one of the other houses, so she knew what she was talking about. "Do you know how disequilibriate your average ecology is?"

"Not even sure I can pronounce it."

"Ecologies aren't kids's stuff. They're immensely complex—food webs, spectra of hierarchical connectedness. . . . Screw up any one level, and the whole thing can collapse—unless you've evolved the system into some kind of Gaian self-stabilizing regime, which is hard enough when you're not trying to re-create an alien ecology, where there might be all sorts of unexpected emergent phenomena."

"Maybe that's the point, though? A game of dexterity, like balancing spinning plates?"

Risa made the noise that told she was half acknowledging the probable truthfulness of my statement. "They must constrain it in some way. Strip it down to the essentials, and then build in some mechanism whereby players can influence things."

I nodded. I'd been unwilling to probe the creature too deeply until now, perhaps still suspicious of a trap—but I knew that if I didn't, the little arthropod would drive me quietly insane. At the very least, I had to know whether it had anything resembling a brain—and if I got that far, I could begin to guess at the kinds of behavioral routines scripted into its synapses, especially if I could trace pathways to sensory organs. Maybe I was being optimistic, though. The thing didn't even have recognizable eyes, so it was anyone's guess as to how it assembled a mental model of its surroundings. And of course that told me something, though it wasn't particularly useful.

The creature had evolved somewhere dark.

A month later, Icehammer began a teaser campaign for *Stroboscopic*. The premiere was to take place two months later in Tycho, but a handful of selected players would be invited to an exclusive preview a few weeks earlier, me among them.

I began to warm up to competition fitness.

Even with insider knowledge, no game was ever a walkover, and my contacts in the resistance movement would be disappointed if I didn't turn in a tidy profit. The trouble was I didn't know enough about the game to finesse the required skills; whether they were mental or physical or some combination of the two. Hedging my bets, I played as many different types of game as possible in the time frame, culminating in a race through the atmosphere of Jupiter piloting frail cloudjammers. The game was one that demanded an acute grasp of aerodynamic physics, coupled with sharp reflexes and a willingness to indulge in extreme personal risk.

It was during the last of the races that Angela Valdez misjudged a thermal and collapsed her foil. Valdez had been a friend of mine years ago, and though we'd since fallen into rivalry, we'd never lost our mutual respect. I attended her funeral on Europa with an acute sense of my own mortality. There, I met most of the other gamers in the system, including a youngish man called Zubek whose star was in the ascendant. He and Valdez had been lovers, I knew—just as I'd loved her years before I met Risa.

"I suppose you've heard of *Stroboscopic?*" he asked, sidling up to me after Valdez's ashes had been scattered on Europa's ice.

"Of course."

"I presume you won't be playing, in that case." Zubek smiled. "I gather the game's going to be more than slightly challenging."

"You think I'm not up to it?"

"Oh, you were good once, Nozomi—nobody'd dispute that." He nodded to the smear of ash on the frost. "But so was Angela. She was good enough to beat the hardest of games—until the day when she wasn't."

I wanted to punch him. What stopped me was the thought that maybe he was right.

I was on my way back from the funeral when White called, using the secure channel to the yacht.

"What have you learnt about the package, Nozomi? I'm curious."

"Not much," I said, nibbling a fingernail. With my other hand I was toying with Risa's dreadlocks, her head resting on my chest. "Other than the fact that the animal responds to light. The mottled patches on its carapace are a matrix of light-sensitive organs; silicon and quartz deposits. Silicon and silicon oxides, doped with a few other metals. I think they work as organic semiconductors, converting light into electrical nerve impulses."

I couldn't see White's face—it was obscured by a golden blur that more or less approximated the visor of his suit—but he tapped a finger against the blur, knowingly. "That's all? A response to light? That's hardly going to give you a winning edge."

"There's nothing about it. The light has to reach a certain threshold intensity before there's any activity at all."

"And then it wakes up?"

"No. It moves for a few seconds, like a clockwork toy given a few turns of the key. Then it freezes up again, even if the light level remains constant. It needs a period of darkness before it shows another response to light."

"How long?"

"Seventy seconds, more or less. I think it gets all the energy it needs during that one burst of light, then goes into hibernation until the next burst. Its chemistry must be optimized so highly that it simply can't process more rapid bursts."

The gold ovoid of his face nodded. "Maybe that ties in with the title of the game," he said. "*Stroboscopic*."

"You wouldn't care to hazard a guess as to what kind of evolutionary adaptation this might be?"

"I wish there was time for it, Nozomi. But I'm afraid that isn't why I called. There's trouble."

"What sort?" Though I didn't really need to ask.

He paused, looking to one side, as if nervous of being interrupted. "Black's vanished. My guess is the goons got to him. They'll have unpicked his memory by now."

"I'm sorry."

"It may be hazardous for you to risk competition now that you're implicated."

I let the words sink in, then shook my head. "It's too late," I said. "I've already given them my word that I'll be there."

Risa stirred. "Too pigheaded to back down?"

"No," I said. "But on the other hand, I do have a reputation to uphold."

As the premiere approached we learned what we could of the creature. It was happier in vacuum than air, although the latter did not seem to harm it provided it was kept cold. Maybe that had something to do with its silicon biochemistry. Silicon had never seemed like a likely rival to carbon as a basis for life, largely because silicon's higher valency denied its compounds the same long-term stability. But under extreme cold, silicon biochemistry might have the edge, or at least be an equally probable pathway for evolution. And with silicon came the possibility of exploit light itself as an energy source, with no clumsy intermediate molecular machinery like the rhodopsin molecule in the human retina.

But the creature lived in darkness.

I couldn't resolve this paradox. It needed light to energize itself—a flash of intense blue light, shading into the UV—and yet it hadn't evolved an organ as simple as the eye. The eye, I knew, had been invented at least 40 times during the evolution of life on Earth. Nature came up with the eye whenever there was the slightest use for it.

It got stranger.

There was something I called the secondary response—also triggered by exposure to light. Normally, shown a flash every 70-odd seconds, the animal would execute a few seemingly purposeful movements, each burst of locomotion coordinated with the previous one, implying that the creature kept some record of what it had been doing previously. But if we allowed it to settle into a stable pattern of movement bursts, the creature began to show richer behavior. The probability of eliciting the secondary response rose to a maximum midway through the gap between normal bursts, roughly half a minute after the last, before smoothly diminishing. But at its peak, the creature was hypersensitized to any kind of ambient light at all, even if it was well below the threshold energy of the normal flash. If no light appeared during the time of hypersensitivity, nothing happened; the creature simply waited out the remaining half a minute until the next scheduled flash. But if even a few hundred photons fell on its carapace, it would always do the same thing; thrashing its limbs violently for a few seconds, evidently drawing on some final reserve of energy that it saved for just this response.

I didn't have a clue why.

And I wasn't going to get one, either—at least not by studying the creature. One day we'd set it up in the autodoc analysis chamber as usual, and we'd locked it into the burst cycle, working in complete darkness apart from the regular pulses of light every minute and ten seconds. But we forgot to lash the animal down properly. A status light flashed on the autodoc console, signifying some routine health-monitoring function. It wasn't bright at all, but it happened just when the creature was hypersensitized. It thrashed its limbs wildly, making a noise like a box of chopsticks.

And hurled itself from the chamber, falling to the floor.

Even though it was dark, I saw something of its shattering, as it cleaved into a million pieces. It sparkled as it died.

"Oops," Risa said.

The premiere soon arrived. Games took place all over the system, but the real epicenter was Tycho. The lunar crater had been domed, pressurized, and infused with a luminous mass of habitats and biomes, all dedicated to the pursuit of pleasure through game. I'd visited the place dozens of times, of course—but even then, I'd experienced only a tiny fraction of what it had to offer. Now all I wanted to do was get in and out—and if Stroboscopic was the last game I ever played there, I didn't mind.

"Something's bothering you, Noz," Risa said, as we took a monorail over the Icehammer zone. "Ever since you came back from Valdez's funeral."

"I spoke to Zubek."

"Him?" She laughed. "You've got more talent in your dick."

"He suggested I should consider giving this one a miss."

"He's just trying to rile you. Means you still scare him."
Then she leaned toward the window of our private cabin.
"There. The Arena."

It was a matt-black geodesic ball about half a kilometer
wide, carbuncled by ancillary buildings. Searchlights scis-
sored the air above it, neon letters spelling out the name of
the game, running around the ball's circumference.

Stroboscopic.

Thirty years ago the eponymous CEO of Icehammer
Games had been a top-class player in his own right—until
neutral feedback incinerated most of his higher motor
functions. Now Icehammer's frame was cradled within a
powered exoskeleton, stenciled with luminous Chinese
dragons. He greeted myself, the players, and assorted
hangers-on as we assembled in an atrium adjoining the
Arena. After a short preliminary speech a huge screen was
unveiled behind him. He stood aside and let the presenta-
tion roll.

A drab, wrinkled planet hove into view on the screen,
lightly sprinkled with craters; one ice cap poking into
view.

"PSR-J2034+454A," Icehammer said. "The decidedly
unpoetic name for a planet nearly 500 light-years from
here. Utterly airless and barely larger than our moon, it
shouldn't really be there at all. Less than ten million years
ago its sun reached the end of its nuclear-burning life cycle
and went supernova." He clapped his hands together in
emphasis; some trick of acoustics magnifying the clap
concussively. "Apart from a few comets, nothing else remains. The planet moves in total darkness, even starlight
attenuated by the nebula of dust that embeds the system.
Even the star it once drew life from has become a corpse."

The star rose above one limb of the planet: a searing
point of light, pulsing on and off like a beacon.

"A pulsar," Icehammer said. "A 15-kilometer ball of
nuclear matter, sending out an intense beam of light as it

rotates, four flashes a second; each no more than 13 hundredths of a second long. The pulsar has a wobble in its rotational axis, however, which means that the beam only crosses our line of sight once every 72 seconds, and then only for a few seconds at a time." Then he showed us how the pulsar beam swept across the surface of the planet, dousing it in intense, flickering light for a few instants, outlining every nuance of the planet's topography in eye-wrenching violet. Followed by utter darkness on the face of the world, for another 72 seconds.

"Now the really astonishing thing," Icehammer said, "is that something evolved to live on the planet, although only on the one face, which it always turns to the star. A whole order of creatures, in fact, their biology tuned to exploit that regular flash of light. Now we believe that life on Earth originated in self-replicating structures in pyritic minerals, or certain kinds of clay. Eventually, this mineralogic life formed the scaffolding for the first form of carbon-based life, which—being more efficient and flexible—quickly usurped its predecessor. But perhaps that genetic takeover never happened here, stymied by the cold and the vacuum and the radiative effects of the star." Now he showed us holo-images of the creatures themselves, rendered in the style of watercolors from a naturalist's fieldbook, annotated in handwritten Latin. Dozens of forms—including several radically different bodyplans and modes of locomotion—but everything was hard-shelled and a clear cousin to the animal we'd examined on the yacht. Some of the more obvious predators looked incredibly fearsome. "They do all their living in bursts lasting a dozen seconds, punctuated by nearly a minute of total inactivity. Evidently some selection mechanism determined that a concentrated burst of activity is more useful than long, drawn-out mobility."

Jumping, I thought. You couldn't jump in slow motion. Predators must have been the first creatures to evolve toward the burst strategy—and then grazers had been forced to follow suit.

"We've given them the collective term Strobelife—and their planet we've called Strobeworld, for obvious reasons." Icehammer rubbed his palms together with a whine of actuating motors. "Which, ladies and gentlemen, brings us rather neatly to the game itself. Shall we continue?"

"Get on with it, you bastard," I murmured. Next to me, Risa squeezed my hand and whispered something calming.

We were escorted up a sapphire staircase into a busy room packed with consoles and viewing stands. There was no direct view of the Arena itself, but screens hanging from the ceiling showed angles in various wavebands.

The Arena was a mockup of part of the surface of Strobeworld, simulated with astonishing precision: the correct rocky terrain alleviated only by tufts of colorless vacuum-tolerant "vegetation," gravity that was only a few percent from Strobeworld's own, and a magnetic field that simulated in strength and vector the ambient field at the point on Strobeworld from which the animals had been snatched. The roof of the dome was studded with lamps that would blaze for less than 13 hundredths of a second, once every 72 seconds, precisely mimicking the passage of the star's mercilessly bright beam.

The game itself—Level One, at least—would be played in rounds: single player against single player, or team against team. Each competitor would be allocated a fraction of the thousand-odd individual animals released into the Arena at the start—fifty/fifty in the absence of any handicapping. The sample would include animals from every ecological level, from grazers that fed on the flora, right up to the relatively scarce top predators, of which there were only a dozen basic variants. They had to eat, of course: light could provide their daily energy needs, but they'd still need to consume each other for growth and replication. Each competitor's animals would be labeled with infrared markers, capable of being picked up by Arena cams. It was the competitor's goal to ensure that their population of Strobeworld creatures outperformed the rival's, simply by staying alive longest. Computers would assess the fitness of each population after a round and the winner would be announced.

I watched a few initial heats before my turn.

Most of the animals were sufficiently far from each other—or huddled in herds—that during each movement burst they did little except shuffle around or move slightly more in one direction than another. But the animals that were near each other exhibited more interesting behavior. Prey creatures—small, flat-bodied grazers or midlevel predators—would try and get away from the higher-level predators, which in turn would advance toward the grazers and subordinate predators. But then they'd come to a stop, perfectly motionless, their locations revealed only by the cams, since it was completely dark in the Arena.

Waiting.

It was harder than it looked—the dynamics of the ecosystem far subtler than I'd expected. Interfering at any level could have wildly unexpected consequences.

Risa would have loved it.

Soon it was my turn. I took my console after nodding briefly at my opponent; a rising player of moderate renown, but no real match for myself, even though neither of us had played *Stroboscopic* before.

We commenced play.

The Arena—initially empty—was populated by Strobe-life via robot drones that dashed out from concealed hatches. The Strobelife was in stasis; no light flashes from the dome to trigger the life cycle; as stiff and sculptural as the animal we'd studied in the yacht. My console displayed a schematic overlay of the Arena, with "my" animals designated by marker symbols. The screens showed the same relationships from different angles. Initial placement was pseudo-random; animals placed in lifelike groupings, but with distances between predator and prey, determined by algorithms compiled from real Strobeworld populations.

We were given five minutes to study the grouping and evolve a strategy before the first flash. Thereafter, the flashes would follow at 72-second intervals until the game's conclusion.

The five minutes slammed past before I'd examined less than a dozen possible opening gambits.

For a few flash cycles nothing much happened; too much distance between potential enemies. But after the fifth cycle some of the animals were within striking range of each other. Little local hot spots of carnage began to ensue; animals being dismembered or eaten in episodic bursts.

We began to influence the game. After each movement burst—during the minute or so of near-immobility—we were able to selectively reposition or withdraw our own or our opponent's animals from the Arena, according to a complex shifting value scheme. The immobile animals would be spirited away, or relocated, by the same robots that had placed them initially. When the next flash came, play would continue seamlessly.

All sorts of unanticipated things could happen.

Wipe out one predator and you might think that the animals it was preying on would thrive, or at least not be decimated so rapidly. But what often happened was that a second rival predator—until then contained in number—would invade the now unoccupied niche and become *more successful* than the animal that had been wiped out. If that new predator also pursued the prey animals of the other, then they might actually be worse off.

I began to grasp some of *Stroboscopic*'s latent complexity. Maybe it was going to be a challenge after all.

I played and won four rounds out of five. No point deluding myself: at least two of my victories had been sheer luck, or had evolved from dynamics of the ecology that were just too labyrinthine to guess at. But I was impressed, and for the first time in years, I didn't feel as if I'd already exhausted every aspect of a game.

I was enjoying myself.

I waited for the other heats to cycle through, my own name only displaced from the top of the leader board when the last player had completed his series.

Zubek had beaten me.

"Bad luck," he said, in the immediate aftermath, after we'd delivered our sound bites. He slung an arm around my shoulder, matishly. "I'm sorry what I said about you before, Nozomi."

"Would you be apologizing now if I'd won?"

"But you didn't, did you? Put up a good fight, I'll admit. Were you playing to your limit?" Zubek stopped a passing waiter and snatched two drinks from his tray, something fizzy, passing one to me. "Listen, Nozomi. Either way, we won in style and trashed the rest."

"Good. Can I go now? I'd like to speak to my wife." And get the hell away from Tycho, I thought.

"Not so fast. I've got a proposition. Will you hear me out?"

I listened to what Zubek had to say. Then caught up with Risa a few minutes later and told her what he had outlined.

"You're not serious," she said. "He's playing a game with you, don't you realize?"

"Isn't that the point?"

Risa shook her head exasperatedly. "Angela Valdez is dead. She died a good death, doing what she loved. Nothing the two of you can do now can make the slightest difference."

"Zubek will make the challenge whether I like it or not."

"But you don't have to agree." Her voice was calm but her eyes promised tears. "You know what the rumors said. That the next level was more dangerous than the first."

"That'll make it all the more interesting, then."

But she wasn't really listening to me, perhaps knowing that I'd already made my mind up.

Zubek and I arranged a press conference an hour later, sharing the same podium, microphones radiating out from our faces like the rifles of a firing squad; stroboscopic flashes of cameras prefiguring the game ahead. We explained our proposition: how we'd agreed between ourselves to another game; one that would be dedicated to the memory of Angela Valdez.

But that we'd be playing Level Two.

Icehammer took the podium during the wild applause and cheering that followed our announcement.

"This is extremely unwise," he said, still stiffly clad in his mobility frame. "Level Two is hardly tested yet; there are bound to be bugs in the system. It could be exceedingly dangerous." Then he smiled and a palpable aura of relief swept through the spectators. "On the other hand, my shareholders would never forgive me if I forewent an opportunity for publicity like this."

The cheers rose to a deafening crescendo.

Shortly afterward I was strapped into the console, with neuro-effectors crowning my skull, ready to light up my pain center. The computer overseeing the game would allocate jolts of pain according to the losses suffered by my population of Strobelife. All in the mind, of course. But that wouldn't make the pain any less agonizing, and it wouldn't reduce the chances of my heart simply stopping at the shock of it all.

Zubek leant in and shook my hand.

"For Angela," I said, and then watched as they strapped Zubek in the adjacent console, applying the neuro-effector.

It was hard. It wasn't just the pain. The game was made more difficult by deliberately limiting our overview of the Arena. I no longer saw my population in its entirety—the best I could do was hop my point of view from creature to creature, my visual field offering a simulation of the electrical-field environment sensed by each Strobelife animal; a snapshot only updated during Strobetime. When there was no movement, there was no electrical-field generation. Most of the time I was blind.

Most of the time I was screaming.

Yet somehow—when the computer assessed the fitness of the two populations—I was declared the winner over Zubek.

Lying in the couch, my body quivered, saliva waterfalling from my slack jaw. A moan filled the air, which it took me long moments to realize was my own attempt at vocalization. And then I saw something odd; something that shouldn't have happened at all.

Zubek hauled himself from his couch, not even sweating.

He didn't look like a man who'd just been through agony.

An unfamiliar face blocked my view of him. I knew who it was, just from his posture and the cadences of his speech.

"Yes, you're right. Zubek was never wired into the neuro-effector. He was working for us—persuading you to play Level Two."

"White," I slurred. "You, isn't it?"

"The very man. Now how would you like to see your wife alive?"

I reached for his collar, fingers grasping ineffectually at the fabric. "Where's Risa?"

"In our care, I assure you. Now kindly follow me."

He waited while I heaved myself from the enclosure of the couch, my legs threatening to turn to jelly beneath me.

"Oh, dear," White said, wrinkling his nose. "You've emptied your bladder, haven't you?"

"I'll empty your face if you don't shut up."

My nervous system had just about recovered by the time we reached Icehammer's quarters, elsewhere in the building. But my belief system was still in ruins.

White was working for the IWP.

Icehammer was lounging on a maroon settee, divested of his exoskeletal support system. Just as I was marveling at how pitiable he looked, he jumped up and strode to me, extending a hand.

"Good to meet you, Nozomi."

I nodded at the frame, racked on one wall next to an elaborate suit of armor. "You don't need that thing?"

"Hell, no. Not in years. Good for publicity, though—neural burnout and all that."

"It's a setup, isn't it?"

"How do you think it played?" Icehammer said.

"Black really was working for the movement," I said, aware that I was compromising myself with each word, but also that it didn't matter. "White wasn't. You were in hock to the IWP all along. You were the reason Black vanished."

"Nothing persona, Nozomi," White said. "They got to my family, just as we've got to Risa."

Icehammer took over: "She's in our care now, Nozomi—quite unharmed, I assure you. But if you want to see her alive, I advise that you pay meticulous attention to my words." While he talked he brushed a hand over the tabard of the hanging suit of armor, leaving a greasy imprint on the black metal. "You disappointed me. That a man of your talents should be reduced to cheating."

"I didn't do it for myself."

"You don't seriously imagine that the movement could possibly pose a threat to the IWP? Most of its cells have been infiltrated. Face it, man, it was always an empty gesture."

"Then where was the harm?"

Icehammer tried a smile but it looked fake. "Obviously I'm not happy at your exploiting company secrets, even if you were good enough to keep them largely to yourself."

"It's not as if I sold them on."

"No, I'll credit you with discretion, if nothing else. But even if I thought killing you might be justified, there'd be grave difficulties with such a course of action. You're too well known; I can't just make you disappear without attracting a lot of attention. And I can't expose you as a cheat without revealing the degree to which my organization's security was breached. So I'm forced to another option—one that, on reflection, will serve the both of us rather well."

"Which is?"

"I'll let Risa go, provided you agree to play the next level of the game."

I thought about that for a few moments before answering. "That's all? Why the blackmail?"

"Because no one in their right minds would play Level Three if they knew what was involved." Icehammer toyed with the elegantly flared cuff of his bottle-green smoking jacket. "The third level is exponentially more hazardous than the second. Of course, it will eventually draw competitors—but no one would consent to playing it until they'd attained total mastery of the lower levels. We don't expect that to happen for at least a year. You, on the other hand, flushed with success at beating Zubek, will rashly declare your desire to play Level Three. And in the process of doing so you will probably die, or at the very least be severely maimed."

"I thought you said it would serve me well."

"I meant your posthumous reputation." Icehammer raised a finger. "But don't imagine that the game will be rigged, either. It will be completely fair, by the rules."

Feeling sick to my stomach, I still managed a smile. "I'll just have to cheat, then, won't I?"

A few minutes later I stood at the podium again, a full audience before me, and read a short prepared statement. There wasn't much to it, and as I hadn't written a word of it, I can't say that I injected any great enthusiasm into proceedings.

"I'm retiring," I said, to the hushed silence in the atrium. "This will be my last competition."

Muted cheers. But they quickly died away.

"But I'm not finished yet. Today I played the first two levels of what I believe will be one of the most challenging and successful games in Tycho, for many years to come. I now intend to play the final level."

Cheers followed again—but they were still a little fearful. I didn't blame them. What I was doing was insane.

Icehammer came out—back in his frame again—and made some halfhearted protestations, but the charade was even more theatrical than last time. Nothing could be better for publicity than my failing to complete the level—except possibly my death.

I tried not to think about that part.

"I admire your courage," he said, turning to the audience. "Give it up for Nozomi—he's a brave man!" Then he whispered in my ear: "Maybe we'll auction your body parts."

But I kept on smiling my best shit-eating smile, even as

they wheeled in the same suit of armor that I'd seen hanging on Icehammer's wall.

I walked into the Arena, the armor's servo-assisted joints whirring with each step. The suit was heated and pressurized, of course—but the tiny air-circulator was almost silent, and the ease of walking meant that my own exertions were slight.

The Arena was empty of Strobelife now, brightly lit; dusty topsoil like lunar regolith, apart from the patches of flora. I walked to the spot that had been randomly assigned me, designated by a livid red circle.

Icehammer's words still rang in my ears. "You don't even know what happens in Level Three, do you?"

"I'm sure you're going to enjoy telling me."

"Level One is abstracted—the Arena is observed, but it might as well be taking place in a computer. Level Two's a little more visceral, as you're now well aware—but there's still no actual physical risk to the competitor. And, of course, even Level Two could be simulated. You must have asked yourself that question, Nozomi? Why create a real ecology of Strobelife creatures at all, if you're never going to enter it?"

That was when he had drawn my attention to the suit of armor. "You'll wear this. It'll offer protection against the vacuum and the effects of the pulse, but don't delude yourself that the armor itself is much more than cosmetic."

"I'm going into the Arena?"

"Where else? It's the logical progression. Now your viewpoint will be entirely limited to one participant in the game—yourself."

"Get it over with."

"You'll still have the ability to intervene in the ecology, just as before—the commands will be interpreted by your suit and transmitted to the controlling computer. The added complexity, of course, is that you'll have to structure your game around your own survival at each step."

"And if—when—I win?"

"You'll be reunited with Risa, I promise. Free to go. All the rest. You can even sell your story, if you can find anyone who'll believe you."

"Know a good ghostwriter?"

He'd winked at me then. "Enjoy the game, Nozomi. I know I will."

Now I stood on my designated spot and waited.

The lights went out.

I had a sense of rapid subliminal motion all around me. The drones were whisking out and positioning the inert Strobelife creatures in their initial formations. The process lasted a few seconds, performed in total silence. I could move, but only within the confines of the suit, which had now become rigid apart from my fingers.

Unguessable minutes passed.

Then the first stammering pulse came, bright as a nuclear explosion, even with the visor's shielding. My suit lost its rigidity, but for a moment I didn't dare move. On the faceplate's head-up display I could see that I was surrounded by Strobelife creatures, rendered according to their electrical field properties. There were grazers and predators and all the intermediates, and they all seemed to be moving in my direction.

And something was dreadfully wrong. *They were too big*.

I'd never asked myself whether the creature we'd examined on the yacht was an adult. Now I knew it wasn't.

The afterflash of the flash died from my vision, and as the seconds crawled by, the creatures' movements became steadily more sluggish, until only the smallest of them were moving at all.

Then they, too, locked into immobility.

As did my suit, its own motors deactivating until triggered by the next flash.

I tried to hold the scene in my memory, recalling the large predator whose foreclaw might scythe within range of my suit, if he was able to lurch three or four steps closer to me during the next pulse. I'd have to move fast, when it came—and on the pulse after that, I'd have another two to contend with, nearing me on my left flank.

The flash came—intense and eye-hurting.

No shadows; almost everything washed out in the brilliance. Maybe that was why Strobelife had never evolved the eye: it was too bright for contrast, offering no advantage over electrical field sensitivity.

The big predator—a cross among a tank, armadillo, and lobster—came three steps closer and slammed his foreclaw into a wide arc that grazed my chest. The impact hit me like a bullet.

I fell backward, into the dirt, knowing that I'd broken a rib or two.

The electrical field overlay dwindled to darkness. My suit seized into rigidity.

Think, Noz. Think.

My hand grasped something. I could still move my fingers, if nothing else. The gloves were the only articulated parts of the suit that weren't slaved to the pulse cycle.

I was holding something hard, rocklike. But it wasn't a rock. My fingers traced the line of a carapace; the pielike fluting around the legs. It was a small grazer.

An idea formed in my mind. I thought of what Icehammer had said about the Strobeworld system; how there was nothing apart from the planet, the pulsar, and a few comets.

Sooner or later, one of those comets would crash into the star.It might not happen very often, maybe only once every few years, but when it did it would be very bad indeed: a massive flare of X rays as the comet was shredded by the gravitational field of the pulsar. It would be a pulse of energy far more intense than the normal flash of light; too energetic for the creatures to absorb.

Strobelife must have evolved a protection mechanism.

The onset of a major flare would be signaled by visible light, as the comet began to break up. A tiny glint at first, but harbinger of far worse to come. The creatures would be sensitized to burrow into the topdirt at the first sign of light, which did not come at the expected time. . . .

I'd already seen the reaction in action. It was what had driven the thrashing behavior of our specimen before it dropped to its death on the cabin floor. It had been trying to burrow; to bury itself in topdirt before the storm came.

The Arena wasn't Strobeworld, just a clever facsimile of it—and there was no longer any threat from an X-ray burst. But the evolved reflex would remain, hardwired into every animal in the ecology.

All I had to do was trigger it.

The next flash came, like the brightest, quickest dawn imaginable. Ignoring the pain in my chest, I stood up—still holding the little grazer in my gloved hand.

But how could I trigger it? I'd need a source of light, albeit small, but I'd need to have it go off when I was completely immobile.

There was a way.

The predator lashed at me again, gouging into my leg. I began to topple, but forced myself to stay upright, if nothing else. Another gouge, painful this time, as if the leg armor was almost lost.

The electrical overlay faded again, and my suit froze into immobility. I began to count aloud in my head.

I'd remembered something. It had seemed completely insignificant at the time; a detail so trivial that I was barely conscious of committing it to memory. When the specimen had shattered, it had done so in complete darkness. And yet I'd seen it happen. I'd seen glints of light as it smashed into a million fragments.

And now I understood. The creature's quartz deposits were highly crystalline. And sometimes—when crystals are stressed—they release light; something called piezoluminescene. Not much; only the amount corresponding to the energy levels of electrons trapped deep within lattices—but I didn't need much, either. Not if I waited until the proper time, when the animals would be hypersensitized to that warning glint. I counted to 35, what I judged to be halfway between the flash intervals. And then let my fingers relax.

The grazer dropped in silence toward the floor.

I didn't hear it shatter, not in vacuum. But in the total darkness in which I was immersed, I couldn't miss the sparkle of light.

I felt the ground rumble all around me. Half a minute later, when the next flash came from the ceiling, I looked around.

I was alone.

No creatures remained, apart from the corpses of those that had already died. Instead, there were a lot of rocky mounds, where even the largest of them had buried themselves under topdirt. Nothing moved, except for a few pathetic avalanches of disturbed dirt. And there they'd wait, I knew—for however long it was evolution had programmed them to sit out the X-ray flare.

Thanks to the specimens on the yacht, I happened to know exactly how long that time was. Slightly more than four and a half hours.

Grinning to myself, knowing that Nozomi had done it again—cheated and made it look like winner's luck—I began to stroll to safety, and to Risa.

VANILLA DUNK

Jonathan Lethem

One of the most acclaimed of all the talented new writers who emerged in the 1990s, Jonathan Lethem has worked at an antiquarian bookstore, written slogans for buttons and lyrics for several rock bands (including Two Fettered Apes, EDO, Jolley Ramey, and Feet Wet), and is also the creator of the "Dr. Sphincter" character on MTV. In addition to all these Certifiably Cool credentials, Lethem also has made short fiction sales to Asimov's Science Fiction, Interzone, New Pathways, Pulphouse, Universe, Journal Wired, Marion Zimmer Bradley's Fantasy Magazine, Aboriginal SF, Crank!, Full Spectrum, The Magazine of Fantasy and Science Fiction, *and elsewhere. His first novel,* Gun, with Occasional Music, *won the Locus Award for the Best First Novel as well as the Crawford Award for Best Fantasy Novel, and was one of the most talked-about books of the year. His other books include the novels* Amnesia Moon, As She Climbed Across the Table, *and* Girl in Landscape, *and a collection of his short fiction,* The Wall of the Sky, the Wall of the Eye. *His most recent novel,* Motherless Brooklyn, *won the National Book Critics Circle Award in 2000.*

In the compelling story that follows, he shows us that even in a future where skills *can be bought and sold, what matters most is what's in the* heart. . . .

Elwood Fossett and I were in a hotel room in Portland, after dropping a meaningless game to the Sony Trail Blazers—we'd already made the playoffs—when the lottery came on the television, the one where they gave away the Michael Jordan subroutines.

The lottery, ironically, was happening back in our home arena, the Garden, while we were on the road. It was an absurd spectacle, the place full of partisan fans rooting for their team's rookie to draw the Jordan skills, the rookies all sitting sheepishly with their families and agents, waiting. The press scurried around like wingless mosquitoes.

"Yo, Lassner, check it out," said Elwood, tapping the screen with his long black club of a finger. "We gonna get you and McFront some company."

He meant the white kid in the Gulf + Western Knicks jersey, stranded with his parents in that sea of black faces. Michael Front—"McFront" to the black players—and I were the two white players on the Knicks.

"Not too likely," I said. "He won't make the team unless he draws the Jordan."

Elwood sat back down on the end of the bed. "Nobody else we'd take?"

"Nope." There were, of course, six other sets of skills available that night—Tim Hardaway, if I remember correctly, and Karl Malone—but none with the potential impact of Jordan's. In a league where everyone played with the skills of one star or another, it took a Jordan to get people's attention. As for the little white rookie, he could have been anyone. It didn't matter who you drafted anymore. What mattered was what skills they picked up in the lottery. Which star's moves would be lifted out of the archives and plugged into the rookie's exosuit. More specifically, what mattered tonight was that the Michael Jordan skills were up for grabs. It was fifteen years since Jordan's retirement, so the required waiting period was over.

The Jordan skills were just about the last, too. The supply of old NBA stars was pretty much depleted. It was only a couple of years after Jordan retired that the exosuits took over, and basketball stopped growing, started feeding on itself instead, becoming a kind of live 3-D highlights film, a chance to see all the dream teams and matchups that had never actually happened; Bird feeding passes to Earl the Pearl, Wilt Chamberlin going one on one with Ewing, Bill Walton and Marques Johnson playing out their careers instead of being felled by injuries, Earl Maginault and Connie Hawkins bringing their legendary schoolyard games to the pros, seeing if they could make it against the best.

Only a few of the genuine stars had retired later than Jordan; after that they'd have to think up something new. Start playing real basketball again, maybe. Or just go back to the beginning of the list of stars and start over.

"Nobody for real this year?" asked Elwood. He counted on me to read the sports papers.

"I don't think so. I heard the kid for the Sixers can play, actually. But not good enough to go without skills." Mixed in among us sampled stars were a handful of players making it on their own, without exosuits: Willard Daynight, Barry Porush, Tony Smerks, Marvin Franklin. These were the guys who would have been the Magic Johnsons, Walt Fraziers, and Charles Barkleys of our era, and in a way they were the guys I felt sorriest for. Instead of playing in a league full of average guys and being big stars, the way they would have in the past, they were forced to go up against the sampled skills of the Basketball Hall of Fame every night. Younger fans probably got mixed up and credited *their* great plays to some sampled program, instead of realizing they were seeing the real thing.

The lottery started with the tall black kid with the Pan Am Nuggets drawing the David Robinson skills package. It was a formality, a foregone conclusion, since he was the only rookie tall enough to make use of a center's skills. The kid stepped up to the mike and thanked his management and his representation and, almost as an afterthought,

his mom and dad, and everyone smiled and flashed bulbs
for a minute or two. You could see that the Nuggets' general manager had his mind on other things. The Pan Am
team was one of the worst in the league at that point, and
as a result they had another lottery spot out of the seven, a
lean, well-muscled kid who could play with the Jordan
skills if he drew them. If they came up with Robinson and
Jordan the Nuggets could be a force in the league
overnight.

Personally, I always winced when a talented seven-
footer like Robinson was reincarnated into the league.
Center was my position, and I already spent most games
riding the bench. Sal Pharoah, the Knicks' regular center,
played with the skills of Moses Malone, one of the best
ever, and a workhorse who didn't like to sit.

Elwood read me like a book. "You're sweatin', Lassner.
You afraid the Nuggets gonna trade their center now they
got Robinson?"

"Fuck you, Elwood." The Nuggets' old center played
with the skills of a guy named Wes Unseld. Not a superstar, not in this league, but better than me.

I played with Ralph Sampson's skills—sort of. Sampson was briefly a star in his time, mostly because of his
height, and as centers go he was pretty passive, not all that
dominant in the paint. He was too gentle, and up against
the sampled skills of Abdul-Jabbar, Ewing, Walton, Olajuwon, Chamberlain, and all the other great centers we faced
every night, he and I were pretty damned ineffective.

The reason I say I only sort of played with the Sampson
skills is that, lacking the ability to dominate inside, when I
actually got on the floor—usually in the junk minutes toward the end of a game—I leaned pretty heavily on an outside jump shot. It's a ridiculous shot for a center, but hey,
it was what I had to offer. And my dirty little secret was
that Bo Lassner's own jump shot was just a little better
than Ralph Sampson's. So when I took it I switched my

exosuit off. The sportswriters didn't know, and neither did
Coach Van.

"Relax, fool," said Elwood. "You ain't never gonna get
traded. You got skin insurance." He reached over and
pinched my thigh.

"Ouch!"

They gave away the Hardaway subroutines, to a skinny
little guy with the Coors Suns. His smile showed his disappointment. It was down to four rookies now, and the Jordan skills were still unclaimed. Our kid—they flashed his
name, Alan Gornan, under the picture—was still in the
running.

"Shit," said Elwood. "Jordan's moves are too funky for
a white cat, man. They program his suit it's gonna break
his hips."

"You were pretty into Michael Jordan growing up,
weren't you?" I asked. Elwood grew up in a Chicago slum.

"You got that," he said. His eyes were fixed on the
screen.

"He won't get it," I said. "There's three other teams."
What I meant, though I didn't say it, was that there were
three other black guys still in the draw. I had a funny feeling
Elwood didn't want our rookie to pick up the Jordan moves.
I could think of a couple of different reasons for that.

The Karl Malone skills went to the kid from the I. G.
Farben 76ers. Down to three. Then they took a break for
commercials. Elwood was suddenly pacing the room. I
called the desk and had them bring us up a couple of beers,
out of mercy.

The Nuggets' second man picked up Adrian Dantley,
leaving it down to two rookies, for two teams: us and the
Beatrice Jazz. I was suddenly caught up in the excitement,
my contempt for the media circus put aside for the moment.

We watched the commissioner punch up the number on
his terminal, look up, and sigh. His mouth hung open and

the crowd fell silent, so that for a second I thought the sound on the hotel television had died.

"Jazz, second pick."

That was it. Alan Gornan, and the Knicks, had the rights to the Jordan skills. The poor kid from the Jazz, who looked like a panther, had just landed the skills of Chris Mullin, undeniably a great shooter, a top-rank star, but just as undeniably slow, flat-footed, and white. It was a silly twist, but hey—it's a silly game.

The media swarmed around Gornan and his parents. Martin Fishall, the Knicks GM, thrust himself between the rookie and the newsmen and began answering questions, a huge grin on his face. I thought to look over at Elwood. He hated Fishall. He had his head tossed back, and he was chugging his beer.

The camera closed in on a head shot of Alan Gornan. He looked pretty self-possessed. He wore a little diamond earring and his eyes already knew how to find the camera and play to it.

They shoved a microphone in his face. "Got anything you want to say, kid?"

"Yeah." He grinned, and brushed the hair out of his eyes. Charisma.

"Go ahead. You're live."

"Look out, New York," said Alan Gornan. "Clear the runway. Vanilla Dunk is due for takeoff." The line started out a little underplayed, almost shy, but by the time he had the whole thing out he had a sneer on his face that reminded me of nothing, I swear, so much as pictures I've seen of the young Elvis Presley.

"Vanilla Dunk?" I said aloud, involuntarily.

"Turn that shit off," said Elwood, and I did.

That was the last of Alan Gornan for the moment. The new players weren't eligible until next season. All bravado aside, it would take Gornan a few months of working with the Knicks' programming experts to get control of the Jordan skills. In the meantime, we were knocked out of the playoffs in the semifinal round by the Hyundai Celtics. It should have been a great series—and we should have won it, I think—but Otis Pettingale, our star guard, who carried Nate Archibald's skills, twisted his ankle in the first game and had to sit, and the series was just a bummer.

I spent that off-season mostly brooding, as I remember. Ringing my ex-wife's answering machine, watching TV, fun stuff like that, mostly. Plus practicing my jump shot. Silly me. If I'd only been six inches shorter I could have been a big star . . . that's a joke, son.

Training camp was a media zoo. Was Otis Pettingale too old to carry the load for another season? What about the Sal Pharoah trade rumors? And how were they going to fit Alan Gornan in, anyway? Who would sit to make room for the kid with the Jordan skills—Michael Front, who played with Kevin McHale's skills, or Elwood Fossett, who played with Maurice Lucas's? The reporters circled the camp like hungry wolves, putting everyone in a bad mood. They kept trying to bait us into second-guessing Coach Van on the makeup of the starting five, kept wanting to know what we thought of Gornan, who we'd barely even met.

And they all wanted a piece of Gornan. Martin Fishall and Coach Van kept him insulated at first, but it became clear pretty fast that he knew how to handle himself, and that he actually liked talking to the press. He had a knack for playing the bad boy, and with no effort at all he had them eating his "Vanilla Dunk" bullshit for breakfast, lunch, and dinner.

At practices he more or less behaved himself. The Jordan skills were pretty dynamic, and Gornan was smart enough to know how to work them into the style of the rest of the team. It was a little scary, actually, seeing how fast

something new and different was coming into being. The
Knicks' core had been solid for a couple of years—but of
course the Jordan skills weren't going to sit on the bench.

Gornan was initially polite with me, which was fine.
But nothing more developed, and by the third week of
camp what had passed for politeness was seeming a little
more like arrogance. I got the feeling it was the same way
with Otis and McFront. He seemed to have won a friend in
Sal Pharoah, though, for no apparent reason. We played a
lot of split-squad games, which meant I got to start at center for the B-team. As such it was my job to clog up the
middle and keep Gornan from driving, and I got a quick
taste of what the other teams were going to be facing this
year, with Pharoah playing the muscle, setting picks, clearing the lanes for the kid's drives. It was a bruising experience, to put it mildly.

One afternoon after one of those split-squad events I
found myself in the dressing room with Pharoah and
Elwood.

"You like protecting that fucker," said Elwood. "Why
don't you let him take his licks?"

Pharoah smirked. He and Elwood were the two intim-
idators on our team, and when they went head to head neither had any edge. "It's not about that, Elwood," he said.

"He thinks he's fucking Michael Jordan," said Elwood.

"As far as the team's concerned, he is Michael Jordan,"
said Pharoah. "Just like I'm Moses Malone, and your stupid ass is Maurice Lucas."

"That white boy's gonna ruin this team, Sal."

Pharoah shook his head. "Different team now, man.
Figure it out, Elwood. Stop looking back." He wadded up
his sweaty shorts and tossed them into the bottom of a
locker, then headed for the showers.

"What was that shit?" Elwood snapped at me, the
minute Pharoah was out of earshot. " 'Figure it out.' Is he
trying to tell me I'm not making the cut?"

"Don't be stupid," I said. "You're in. McFront'll sit."

"White boys don't sit. 'Less they suck as bad as you."

"I think you're wrong. Don't you see? With Gornan they've got their token white starter. You're a better player than McFront." What I was saying, of course, was that the Maurice Lucas skills were more valuable than the Kevin McHale skills. Which was true, but it didn't take team chemistry into account.

"Two white forwards," he said. "They won't be able to fucking resist."

"Wrong. You and Pharoah both in there to protect Gornan. All that muscle to surround the Jordan skills. That's what they won't be able to resist."

"Huh." He considered my logic. "Shit, Lassner."

"What?"

"Shit," he said. "I smell shit around here."

At the start of the season Coach Van played Gornan very conservatively, off the bench. He was a rookie, and we were a very solid team, so it was justifiable. But not for long. When he got in he was averaging more points per minute than Elwood or McFront, and they were points that counted, that won games. He was a little shaky on defense, but the offensive impact of the Jordan subroutines was astonishing, and Gornan was meshing well with Sal Pharoah, just like in the practices. Otis Pettingale's offense at guard was fading a bit, but we had plenty of other weapons. Our other guard was Derrick Flash, who with Maurice Cheeks's skills was just coming into his own. We reeled off six wins in a row at the start of the season before taking a loss, to the Hyundai Celtics, on a night where Gornan didn't see many minutes. That was the night the chanting started, midway through the third quarter: "Vanilla Dunk! Vanilla Dunk! Vanilla Dunk . . ."

The next night he started, and scored forty-three points,

in a game we won easily. He was a starter after that. McFront was benched, which broke the heart of his fan club, but the sports pages agreed that Elwood belonged on the floor, and most of them thought we were the team to beat. We should have been.

The trouble started one night when we were beating— no, make that thrashing—the Disney Heat, 65 to 44, at the start of the third quarter. I was in, actually. I guess Gornan had been working overtime with the programming guys, and he hauled out a slam-dunk move all of a sudden, one where he floated up over three of the Disney players, switched the ball from his right to his left hand, and flipped it in as he fell away. It was a nice move—make that an astonishing move—but it wasn't strictly necessary, given the situation.

No big deal. But a minute later, he did it again. Actually this time he soared under the basket and dropped it in backward. As we jogged back on defense I heard Elwood muttering to himself. The Disney player tossed up a brick and I came up with the rebound, and when I looked up-court there was Gornan again, all alone, signaling for the pass.

I ignored him—we were up more than twenty points— and fed it in slow to Otis. Otis dribbled up a few feet, let the Disney defender catch up with Gornan, and we put a different play together.

Next time the ball got into Gornan's hands he broke loose with it, and went up to dunk. The crowd there in Miami, having nothing better to do, started cheering for us to pass it to him. Elwood's mood darkened. He began trying to run the team in Otis's place, trying to set up plays that locked Gornan out of the action. I could feel the resistance—like being part of a machine where the gears suddenly start grinding.

Coach Van pulled me out of the game. From the bench I had a clearer sense of how much Gornan was milking this crowd, and of how much they were begging to be milked. He was giving them Michael Jordan, the legend they'd never seen themselves, the instant replay man, the one who stood out even in a field of stars. And the awful thing about Gornan's theatrics was that they worked, as basketball. We were up almost thirty points now. He'd reduced the Disney team to spectators.

A minute later Elwood joined me on the bench, and McFront went in. Elwood put a towel over his head and then lowered his head almost below his big knees. The bench got real quiet, which meant the noise from the crowd stood out even better.

Elwood toweled off his head and stood up suddenly, like he was putting himself back in. He turned and looked at me and over at Coach Van. Then he spat, just over the line and onto the court, and turned and walked toward the locker room.

Coach Van jerked his thumb at me, meaning I should go play therapist. I guess my contribution wasn't sorely needed on the court. Sometimes I wondered if they kept me around because I knew how to talk to Elwood.

I found him dressing up in his street clothes, without having showered. When he looked up at me I almost turned and ran back to the bench. I held up my hands, pleading not guilty. But of course the skin on those hands was white.

"You see that shit out there," he said. It was a command that I nod, not a question. "That's poor taste, man."

"Poor taste?"

"That dunk is from the third game of the '91 finals, Lassner. That's sacrilege, hauling it out for no reason, against these Disney chumps."

"You *recognize* the dunk?"

"'Course I recognize the dunk. You never watch any Jordan tapes, man? That dunk is a *prayer*. He can't just—"

"Whoa, Elwood. Hold on a minute. You're sampling,

I'm sampling. This isn't some purist thing here, man. Get some perspective."

"Michael Jordan, Lassner. You ever see the tape of Michael crying after winning in '91?"

"At least he's on our team. Jeez, what would happen if you had to play *against* the almighty Jordan, or somebody with his skills—you'd probably fold up completely!"

"It's not just the dunks, Lassner. He won't play defense. He's always up the court cherry-picking, waiting for the easy pass. Michael was a great defensive player!"

"C'mon, Elwood. This is a showtime league and you know it. You're one of about five guys playing serious defense. *Everybody* goes for the fancy moves. That's what the sampling is all about. He's just better than most, because he's got the hot skills package. *Somebody* had to get the Jordan skills."

"It didn't have to be some little white jerk."

Once it was out it was kind of a relief. Black and white was the issue. Of course. As much as that was supposed to be a thing of the past. I'd known all along, but in some stupid way I guess I'd thought not saying anything might make it better.

"I'm a white guy with a black guy's skills," I pointed out.

He waved it aside. "Not important. It's not Jordan. You play white, anyway."

What was it about basketball that made it all seem so stark? As though it were designed as a metaphor—the white style of play so plodding and corporate and reliable, the black style so individual and expressive and so often self-destructive, so "me against the world." When a black guy couldn't jump they said he had "white legs," or if he was slow it was "white man's disease." Basketball was a white sport that blacks had taken over, and yet the audience was still pretty much white. And that white audience adored the black players for their brilliant moves—thanks

to sampling, that adoration would probably kill the sport—
and yet was still thought to require the token white face,
for purposes of "identification."

Solve basketball, I sometimes thought, and you'd solve
everything.

"Okay," I said. "He's a jerk. But '*white* jerk' shouldn't
matter. Jordan wasn't a black separatist, as I remember. I
mean, call me naive, but scrambling the racial stuff up was
supposed to be one of the few good things about this sampling deal, right?"

"Michael's career meant something," Elwood mumbled. "Should be treated with respect."

"Look who turns out to be Mr. Historical," I said. "You
gotta get hip, Elwood. Basketball is Postmodern now."

"What's that supposed to mean?"

"Means Michael's career might have meant something,
but yours doesn't, and neither does 'Vanilla Dunk's'—so
relax."

Once Gornan started hauling out the real-time poster shots,
the media wouldn't let it go. He was all over the sports
channels, dunking in slow mo, grinning and pumping his
fists. He made the cover of Rolling Stone, diamond earring
flashing, spinning a basketball with one hand, groping a
babe with the other. Then his agent started connecting with
the endorsement people, and you couldn't turn on the tube
without seeing Vanilla Dunk downing vitaburgers at Mc-
Donald's, Vanilla Dunk slurping on a Pepsi or a Fazz,
Vanilla Dunk checking out the synthetic upholstery inside
a new Chrysler SunFrame.

With Gornan playing the exuberant Michael Jordan
game and Elwood playing angry, we kept on winning. In
fact, we opened up a sizable lead over the Celtics in the
division, and it wasn't necessarily a good thing. Being too
far ahead was almost as bad as floundering in the basement

of the division. Without the tension of a tight race to bind us together as a team all the egos came rushing to the forefront. Otis was struggling with accepting his fading powers and diminished role, and we all missed the way his easy confidence had been at the heart of the team. McFront was sulking on the bench. Pharoah was playing hard, trying to make the new team work, trying to show by force that Gornan fit in. Meanwhile, Gornan's theatrics got more and more outrageous, and every slam dunk was another blow to the dam holding back Elwood's rage.

One afternoon in Oakland before a game with the IBM Warriors someone made the mistake of leaving the TV on in the visitors' clubhouse. Elwood and Otis and I were sitting playing cards when a pretaped interview with Gornan turned up on the sports channel.

Somewhat surprisingly, the interviewer seemed to be trying to work around to the subject of race. "How'd you choose your nickname, Dunk? Why Vanilla, in particular? What point are you trying to make?"

Gornan shrugged. "Hey, don't get heavy," he said. "They call me Vanilla 'cause I'm completely smooth and completely sweet. It's simple."

"Why not something else, then?" said the interviewer. "Chocolate, say."

Gornan laughed, and for a minute I thought he was going to grant the man his point. Instead he realigned his sneer and said: "Chocolate don't go down smooth."

"What are you saying, Dunk?"

"Nothing, man. Just that I'm not chocolate. That's why I'm like a breath of fresh air—I go down smooth. People are ready for that, ready to lighten up. Chocolate's sweet, but it's always got that bitter edge, y'know?"

And then, God help me, he turned to the camera and gave it a big wink.

I got up and shut the TV off, but it was too late. Elwood had already slammed his cards down on the table and stalked out. Otis looked sick. I prayed that Gornan wasn't in the locker room. I went through and found Elwood out on the edge of the floor, watching the Warriors take their warm-ups.

At game time we managed to get out on the floor without any explosions. But from the opening tip-off I knew it was going to be a bad night. When the ball got into Elwood's hands he drove like a steamroller up the middle and went up for a vicious dunk. Then he stole an inbound pass and did it again, only this time he fouled his man on the drive. Everyone on the floor looked nervous, even the Warriors—even, for once, Gornan, who was usually oblivious.

The Warrior hit his free throws and the game resumed. The pattern came clear soon enough: Elwood was calling for every pass, and when he got it he was going up for the dunk, every time. He was trying to play Gornan's game, but he was too big and strong, too angry to pull it off. He was stuffing a lot of shots but he'd accumulated four fouls before the second quarter. When Coach Van finally pulled him he had twice as many points as Gornan or anyone else, but the Warriors were ahead.

He sat until halftime, and with McFront in we got the game tied. During the break Coach Van called Elwood into an office and closed the door. Meanwhile Gornan was off in his usual corner of the locker room smoking a cigarette, but he had a hollow, haunted expression on him, one I'd never seen before.

Elwood was back in for the start of the third quarter, and whatever Coach Van had said to him in his office hadn't worked: he picked up right where he'd left off, breaking for insane inside moves at every opportunity, going up for ill-fated dunks and making some of them, smearing a lot of guys with his sweat. The Oakland crowd, which had been abuzz with expectations of seeing the Vanilla Dunk Revue, fell to a low, ugly murmur. When Elwood got called

for another foul I was almost relieved; that made five,
and with six he'd foul out of the game, and it would be
over

But he wasn't quite done. On the next play he pulled
down a rebound and dribbled the length of the court, flat-
tening a Warrior on his way up. I waited for the ref's whistle, but no whistle came. The Warrior center braced himself
between Elwood and the net. Elwood ran straight at him,
tossed off a perfunctory head fake, and then went up with
a spinning move, his bulk barely clearing a tremendous
head-on collision with the jumping center. He jammed the
ball down with both hands and hit the glass so hard it
shattered.

Suddenly the arena was dead silent, as Elwood and the
Warrior center fell in a tangle amid a rain of Plexiglas fragments. When the two men got up unhurt, the roar started.
The referees called the game a Warrior victory by forfeit,
and Elwood took them on single-handedly; we had to drag
him off the floor.

When we got him into the clubhouse we found Gornan
already showered and in his street clothes, giving his version of events to the press.

I looked up the details on Maurice Lucas's career once. I
was working on a theory that the basketball skills you sampled contained an element of the previous player's person-
ality, some kind of style or attitude that was intrinsic to the
way they played, something that could be imparted, gradually, to the later player, along with the actual basketball
skills.

Well, bingo, as far as Maurice Lucas and Elwood
Fossett were concerned. Lucas, it turned out, spent a considerable part of his career feeling misunderstood and
underpaid. Specifically underpaid in comparison to the
white players on his team. As a result he spent a lot of time

playing *angry*. I mean apart from the forcefulness that came with him (and Elwood) being so big and strong; his game was specifically fueled by rage.

Another result of the conflicts in his career was that he was widely understood to have dogged it, to have played intentionally poorly, as a kind of protest, during some of the key years of his career. Which got me thinking: the skills that Elwood inherited might also contain an element of this struggle that Lucas was waging against himself, to suppress his skills, to not give the best of what he had to the company men he hated.

Elwood wouldn't have known, either. Maurice Lucas's career was before his time. Elwood's interest in basketball history went as far back as Michael Jordan's rookie year.

McFront started in Elwood's place the next night, and Elwood went back to the lockers, got dressed, and walked out. Gornan had a great two quarters, undeniable as basketball, unsurpassable as spectacle, and in the locker room at the half he was more exuberant than usual, clowning with Pharoah and McFront, turning the charm he'd previously saved for the media on his teammates. It was a fun scene, but it made me a little sick to see Elwood being drummed out so easily, even if he'd opened the door to it himself, with his walkout.

On the bench during the second half I scooted up next to Coach Van.

"You're letting this team fall apart," I said.

"Come on, Lassner."

"What?"

"You're not gonna start this in the middle of a game." He sounded tired of the conversation before it had even started. "Nobody's letting the team fall apart. This could be a championship team."

"This could have *been* a championship team. Now it's a championship Vanilla Dunk and his Dunkettes."

He made a face.

"What does ownership say?" I asked.

"What do you think? Fishall wants Gornan starting every game. The fans want it, too. As long as we're winning I'm gonna have a tough time arguing for anything else."

"Yeah."

"I want Elwood out there, too, Bo, but if he doesn't even suit up—"

"I know, I know."

"Look, I can't make everybody like Gornan. *I* don't particularly like him. But if you get Elwood back in here, he'll see playing time. The backboard—that's no big deal. Just more headlines, is the way Fishall sees it. But this walkout deal—"

He didn't finish his sentence. Something happened out on the floor, something that, as it turned out, would change everything. There was a crash, and a loud sigh, and the crowd fell to silence. It was so quiet you could make out the squeak of the team doctor's sneakers as he crossed the floor, rushing toward the fallen player.

I got up and peered over the top of the cluster of players, but couldn't see anything. So I counted heads. It was a Knick on the floor, and height—or rather, lack of it—told me it was Sal Pharoah.

In a minute they had him on his feet, and the crowd starting buzzing again, which made things feel more normal. Pharoah walked with his head bowed, while the doctor peeled the exosuit away from his damaged wrist. They hurried him off toward the trainer's room, and a couple of kids with towels rushed over and wiped the sweat off the floor where he'd fallen.

Coach Van slapped me on the ass. "Wake up, Lassner. Get in there."

I stumbled out onto the floor and we restarted the game. We'd built up a good lead, and even without Pharoah or Elwood available we cruised to victory—mostly on the strength of Gornan's play, I have to admit. He was the only one on the floor who didn't seem a little stunned by Pharoah's going down. I did my best to fill the role of Gornan's protector, though I must admit I felt a renegade urge to do what Elwood would have wanted, and leave him out there naked.

At the start of the fourth quarter, before Coach Van pulled the starters out, it hit me that with me, McFront, and Vanilla Dunk our entire frontcourt was white—the first time the Knicks had had more whites than blacks on the floor since I'd joined the team.

Sal Pharoah had broken his right wrist in the fall, and he'd be out for at least six weeks, probably more—I learned that from the television in our hotel room that night. Elwood burst in half an hour later, and he learned it from me.

What it meant, of course, was that I was the starting center for the time being. It also meant good things for Elwood, if he behaved himself. With Pharoah out he was our only enforcer, so he'd probably get the nod over McFront. With me in instead of Pharoah we also lost a lot of defense and rebounding, and Elwood was a better defender and rebounder than McFront.

On the other hand, Pharoah had served as a buffer between Gornan and Elwood—also between Gornan and the rest of the league, all those teams frustrated by being beaten by a white hot dog who was getting more endorsements in his rookie year than they'd see for their whole careers. I wasn't going to be able to serve that role. I wasn't strong enough, or black enough. That role fell to Elwood. The two of them had to play together or the team was in trouble.

Two nights later, in L.A., against the Time Warner Lakers, I saw that the team was in trouble.

The Lakers were a team that would have tested us with Pharoah on the floor. It was bad timing that we hit them on the first night without him, and the first night since Elwood's walkout. We should have had a patsy, a fall guy, to give us confidence, to give Elwood and Gornan a chance to have some fun together. No such luck.

In the first quarter Gornan was playing his usual game, to the delight of the crowd. He was scoring a lot of the time but we weren't coming up with any rebounds, and our defense had nothing, and very quickly the Lakers were up by ten points. I got all passive, starting leaning on my jump shot, and left the inside open, waiting for Elwood to take over. But Elwood was invisible. He was playing man-to-man defense so stubbornly that he had nothing left for the fast break. He was putting on a clinic, demonstrating what Gornan was doing wrong, but Gornan wasn't paying any attention, and the crowd didn't have the faintest idea what was going on.

At halftime the Lakers were fifteen points up, and in the second half things really started breaking down. Gornan tried to compensate the only way he knew how, by diving for ridiculous steals, hogging the ball even more, putting on an air show. He got fouled so hard I actually started to get a little worried about him, but each time he jumped back up with a grin. I tried to play a little post-up but the Lakers' center, who had Artis Gilmore's skills, was making me look stupid. Our guards were working the margins, trying to get us into the game from the perimeter, but the Lakers were picking up every rebound, so missed shots from the outside were very costly.

Elwood lost his patience, started falling off the defense and trying to mount a show of his own. As usual he strung together some impressive slams, and for a minute the momentum seemed ours, but another minute later he racked up two fouls in a row and the Lakers beefed up their score at the free-throw line. There isn't any way to defend against free throws—not that anyone was playing defense.

Gornan responded as only he could, by taking up increasingly improbable moves. They had two or three guys on him every time he touched the ball, and he was turning it over a lot. He was airborne, but a lot of balls were being stripped away on the way up.

By the fourth quarter I was exhausted and humiliated. Coach Van called a time-out and I jogged reflexively toward the bench, but he wasn't taking me out. He subbed McFront in for Elwood and sent in another rookie for Gornan. We lost the game by twenty-three points, our worst margin of the season so far.

We lost in a similar fashion the next night, and at the end Coach Van called me and Elwood and Gornan into his office. I assumed the idea was to mediate between the two of them, and that I was there more or less as Elwood's official interpreter.

"What's happening, guys?" said Coach Van.

Gornan jumped right in. "We need a center who can play, Coach."

"What?" I blurted.

"Sorry, man," said Gornan. "But let's face facts."

"I was starting for this team before you—"

"Whoa," said Coach Van. "Relax, Bo. Alan, that wasn't exactly what I had in mind. Seems to me the team is suffering from what I'd call, for want of a better word, a feud."

"Feud?" Gornan played completely dumb. Elwood just sulked in his chair.

"I don't care about the personal stuff," said Coach Van. "It's a matter of how you play. You have to play like you like each other. You have to be able to pretend on the court. You guys don't seem to be managing it, and it shows in your game."

"Hey, me and Bo get along fine," said Gornan. "Far as I know. But he's just not as strong as Pharoah under the net. If me and Elwood's games are hurting, that's the reason why."

"This is ridiculous," I said. Gornan's strategy began to dawn on me. He was going to pretend he hadn't even noticed Elwood's hostility. It was instinctively brilliant, and vicious. He'd avoid the appearance of a black-white conflict by cutting me down instead.

I looked over at Elwood, but he wasn't offering me any help.

"Look," said Gornan. "Me and Elwood are playing the same as when the team was winning. Lassner here is the difference."

"Are you gonna take this?" I said to Elwood. "He's saying that the way you've been playing in the last few games is your normal game. Can't you see what a veiled insult that is? You can play a hell of a lot better—"

"You getting down on my game, Lassner?" growled Elwood. "You a fine one to fucking talk, man."

"No, no, I mean, I'm just trying to say, look at what *he's* saying—"

"Enough, Bo. Be quiet for a minute. Maybe I've misunderstood the situation—"

"Coach," I protested, "Gornan is twisting this—"

"Let me talk! As I was saying, I don't know the details, I don't want to know the details. What matters is the chemistry sucks right now. All three of you are playing below your capabilities. That's my opinion, and I've told ownership as much, and I'll tell the press the same when we get home. That's all for now."

End of meeting.

We lost the last two games of the road trip and flew back to New York. On the plane I slept and dreamed of missed shots. The cabbie who took me back to my Brooklyn apartment asked me how I felt about the trade.

"What trade?" I asked, and the cabbie just said: "I'm sorry."

The Disney Heat were a mediocre team with one big star: Gerald Flynnan, their center. He played with the skills of Akeem Olajuwon, and he carried their team to the lower rounds of the playoffs each year, but no farther. The rest of the team was talented but young, disorganized, and possibly stupid.

Knicks management had offered me, Elwood, and a first-round lottery pick to the Heat in exchange for Flynnan, and the Disney team had taken the bait. The Knicks picked up a dominant center to replace the injured Pharoah, and to fill his shoes in protecting Vanilla Dunk. And they'd gotten rid of the tension in their frontcourt by unloading Elwood; McFront and Dunk would start.

What the Heat got was a midseason mess: an angry, talented star and a tall white guy with a jump shot. The lottery spot wouldn't help the team until next year. Elwood and I were flown down and in the Disney uniforms before we knew what hit us, and the coach tossed us into a game before we'd even had a chance to introduce ourselves to the other players.

The result was an ugly loss, but then the players there seemed pretty used to that.

The crowd, too. The Disney fans were a jaded, abusive bunch, mostly concerned with heckling Coach Wilder for not playing local favorite Earlharm "Early" Natt, a talented eccentric who carried the skills of Marvin Barnes. At the start of the game they cheered Elwood and greeted me with shouts of "Where's Gerald?," but by halftime they were drinking beer and shouting for Early Natt, a request that Coach Wilder ignored except in the final, hopeless moments of each game. Natt looked pretty dynamic when he got in, which explained the crowd's affection. He also paid zero attention to defense or team play, which explained the coach's resistance.

The same pattern held in the two losses that followed.

That brought us to the all-star break. Elwood and I were 0–3 with our new team, and nobody was particularly happy. I couldn't figure Elwood—he was playing quiet, walking quiet, and, I suspected, mixing a little thinking in with his brooding. For my part, I was just trying to keep my head above water—to my embarrassment, I was exhausted by starting every night. Plus management and media caught on that I was the communicative one of the new pair, which meant I was answering questions for me and Elwood both.

The all-star break gave us most of a week before we played again, and Elwood surprised me by suggesting we get out of town. He'd located a beach hotel on Key West with a nearby high school gym we could rent. I agreed. Without having to say so, we were both avoiding paying any attention to the all-star game, which was sure to be yet another installment of the Vanilla Dunk show.

Elwood shocked me again by getting up first that morning, to rouse me out of bed. He called up a breakfast on room service; I swear in all our years rooming together I'd never seen him pick up a phone before.

At the gym he said: "Okay, Lassner. I'm gonna teach your tall white ass how to play a trapping defense."

"What?"

"You heard."

"What is this punishment for, Elwood? What did I do? Just tell me."

"Here—" He threw me the ball.

And proceeded to do exactly what he'd promised.

The next day word had gotten around—possibly with Elwood's help, I never found out—that a couple of pros were working out in the local gym. Six guys showed up: confident, tall kids out to impress, all lean and strong from boating on the island, a couple of them with real talent. Elwood worked them into the clinic he was giving me, and they and he spent the next four days busting my ass.

I went back to Miami exhausted, and Elwood still wouldn't tell me what he was getting at.

It quickly became clear, however, that he'd been looking at the schedule. The first team we played after the break was the Knicks. That afternoon in practice, while the rest of the team was drilling, he took Coach Wilder aside.

"Let me call the plays tonight," he said, as if it were the most natural thing in the world.

"What?"

"Let me call the plays." He actually smiled.

"We're playing the Knicks."

"Exactly."

"What are you saying, Elwood?"

"You traded for me, man. Give me a night to run the show. One night. If you don't like the results we go back to your way tomorrow. Nobody will ever know."

I walked over to show my support—for what, I didn't exactly know. "Give him a half, at least," I said.

"He did this in New York?" asked Coach Wilder.

"Yes," I lied.

Elwood pulled Early Natt off the bench as we took the floor at the start of the game, saying to him only, "Go crazy."

I got Elwood aside. "Okay," I said. "I've waited long enough. What's the deal here, Elwood?"

"We're gonna defend these mothers," he said. "That's the deal. Our guards can play a zone defense if they hang back. You and me are boxing out Dunk, taking the rebounds, stripping the ball. Don't hold anything back."

"What's Early doing?"

"Cherry-picking. Outdunking the Dunk."

"I never saw Marvin Barnes play," I said, "but I didn't think he could hang with Michael Jordan. Early is stupid, Elwood."

"We're not playing against Michael Jordan," said Elwood. "We're playing against Vanilla Dunk. Jordan had an integrated game. The best there ever was. Dunk's just a show. I've played a little one-on-one with Early. He can put on a show, if he doesn't have to think about defense or passing, and if the coach isn't breathing down his neck. That's our job, Lassner. Keep Early from having to think about anything. He'll put on a show. Trust me."

Gerald Flynnan, the Knicks' new center, beat me on the tip-off, so the Knicks came up with the ball. I followed Elwood's lead—after the week of drills, it was second nature. We charged the ball, my hands up wide and high to block the pass, Elwood's hands low for the steal off the dribble. Our guards scurried behind us on the zone defense, picking up the slack.

Otis Pettingale beat us on a head fake and went up. Score: Gulf + Western 2, Disney 0.

One of our guards fed it in to me, and Elwood hissed, "Up to Early!" I did what I was told. Early Natt was halfway up the court. He twisted through three Knicks, not looking back to see if he had any support, and scored. Tie game.

The second time up the court the ball was in Vanilla Dunk's hands, and Elwood seemed to go into another time signature. He was all over him. Dunk dribbled back and circled and came up again. I put up my hands and cut off a pass opportunity. Dunk hesitated, and Elwood stripped the ball away. A flip pass upcourt into Early's hands and we were ahead.

The crowd went wild. Not because they had any idea of what Elwood and me were up to, but because Early was in the game, showing off, doing the only thing he knew how to do: score. The Knicks brought the ball back to us, and this time Elwood took it away from McFront, tipping it into my waiting hands. Not waiting to be told this time, I tossed it to Early. Score.

The strategy was working, at least for the moment. No team in the league played this kind of defense, and it had the Knicks confused. High on the novelty of it, and the crowd's response, we roared to a fifteen-point lead by half-time. Elwood ran back to the bench and spread his hands in a mute appeal to Coach Wilder.

"This one's yours," said the coach.

In the second half the Knicks adjusted somewhat, and I got tired and had to sit for a few minutes. Flynnan bulled his way through Elwood for six straight points, and Otis added a couple of outside shots, and they nearly tied it. But Vanilla Dunk looked all flummoxed, and he never got into the game. A few minutes later we opened up the lead again and we ended up winning by five points.

I took Elwood aside in the locker room. The media all wanted Early Natt anyway. "When I was sitting in the third period I checked my suit," I said. "It wasn't working."

Elwood just smiled, and made a little pair of imaginary scissors with his fingers.

"You fucked with my suit?"

"I just noticed you play better without it, man. You think I didn't see you were turning it off?"

"That's just for my jump shot!"

"I saw you in practice in Key West, white boy. You play better without it. Notice I ain't saying you play *good*. Just better."

"Fuck you, Elwood."

It was a nice night, but it was just a night. A fluke loss by the almighty Knicks—it happens sometimes. The Vanilla Dunk Revue went back to cakewalking its way to a championship, while we struggled on, treading water in the middle of our division, barely clinging to our playoff hopes. Surprisingly, Elwood didn't seem that interested in applying the defensive techniques we'd developed together against any of the other teams. Oh, we trapped here and there, but Elwood didn't ever take command the way he had. He seemed to go back into a trance, like he'd done when we were first traded. We won our share of games, but nobody was particularly impressed. As for Early Natt, he saw more minutes, but they only seemed to give him more opportunities to blow it, and soon enough he was in the doghouse. Elwood had abandoned him. I guess Elwood liked that one-dimensional game a little better on a hapless black man than he liked it on an arrogant white one, but not so much that he wanted to encourage Early to make it a regular habit.

Elwood and I were shooting alone in the gym when I asked, "Why don't we go back to that trapping game?"

He didn't even turn around, just sank a shot as he answered. "Element of surprise the only thing makes it work, Bo. Teams'd see through that shit if we hauled it out two nights in a row."

"Some great teams won with defense, back—"

"Shut up, Bo. You don't know what you're talkin' about."

"What have we got to lose?"

"Shut up."

Elwood's playing got more and more distracted, and we went on a losing streak, but I didn't catch on until two weeks before the end of the season, when the Knicks came to town again. I waited for Elwood to rouse us again, to make a big demonstration, and instead he played in what was becoming his usual trance. He almost seemed to be taking a masochistic thrill in letting Vanilla Dunk run wild.

The next day I glanced at the papers, and I realized that, for once, Elwood was watching the standings.

We had to lose three games in the standings to drop out of a regular playoff spot and into the wild-card spot. The wild-card team played the team with the conference's best record in the first round of the playoffs, in a quick best-of-five series, a sort of warm-up for the real playoffs.

The Knicks, thanks to their win over us the night before, were now the team with the best record, by one game over the Pistons.

In other words, the victory over the Knicks earlier in the season wasn't the main point; that was just Elwood finding out if he could do it.

Elwood and Coach Wilder yelled at each other for a straight half hour in the visiting coach's office in the bowels of the Garden. In the meantime I was left to play diplomat with the press and the rest of the team. I'd never been in the visitors' locker rooms of the Garden before, and it frankly got me a little depressed. I'd never dared mention it to Elwood, but I missed the Knicks.

When they came out it was Coach Wilder who looked beaten. Elwood didn't say anything to me, but his eyes said he'd won his point. When we got out on the floor he flipped the practice ball to Early Natt, then crooked a finger and beckoned Early over to him.

"Remember when I told you to go crazy?" he said.

Early just nodded, smiling defensively. He looked a little intimidated by the roar of the Garden crowd.

"We gonna do that again. Remember how?"

Early nodded.

"Just stay uptown, look for the pass. Stay open, that's all." Elwood turned to me but didn't say anything, just stretched his arms up in the air. I mirrored them with my own—albeit six inches higher.

Our moment was swallowed in a roar, as the Knicks came out of the lockers and were greeted by the crowd in the Garden. I looked out and then back down at the Heat uniform on my chest. I felt about as small as a seven-foot guy can feel, at that moment.

This time I somehow beat Flynnan on the tip-off, flipping the ball to one of our guards. We went up the court and scored, Elwood sinking a jumper from midway out. The Knicks inbounded and I realized I was frozen, that I wasn't following Elwood into the trap defense. The Knicks got the ball to Vanilla Dunk. Dunk flew upcourt, Elwood dogging his steps, and broke loose for a fabulous midair hook shot. I cursed myself.

Elwood grabbed the ball and hurled it upcourt to Early, who ran into a crowd and had the ball stripped away. Defense again. This time I rushed the ball—it was in Otis's hands—and forced a weak pass to Flynnan, who was too far out for his shot. I jumped on Flynnan, my hands in his face, and heard a whistle. I'd fouled him.

Flynnan went to the line and hit both shots. 4–2, Knicks.

Elwood rushed the ball to Early again, passing into a thicket of Knicks, and Early was immediately fouled. Early went to the line and missed one.

The Knicks came up and Flynnan rolled over me for an easy layup. God, he's a big mother, I wanted to whisper to Elwood, but Elwood wasn't meeting my eye.

Elwood went up, got caught in traffic, and bailed out to one of our guards, who threw up a brick from outside. Flynnan and I fought for the rebound, and Flynnan won. He dumped it out to Vanilla Dunk, who immediately had Elwood all over him. I rushed up from behind and stabbed at the ball.

Dunk twisted out from between us, head-faked, made a move. The move didn't come off. He and Elwood tangled up and fell together. A whistle. The ref signaled: offensive foul, Knicks. Number double zero, Alan Gornan. Vanilla Dunk.

Dunk got up screaming. Elwood shook himself out and turned his back. The ref rushed up between them while a kid wiped the sweat off the floor.

Then Dunk yelled one word too many.

"What?" Elwood turned fast and got in his face, real close, without touching. The ref squirted out of the way.

"I said nigger," repeated Dunk.

They both drew back a fist. I grabbed Elwood from behind, so he couldn't get his shot off. Don't ask me why I grabbed Elwood instead of Dunk.

Vanilla Dunk's punch was off-line. It slammed into Elwood's shoulder. That was his only shot. The other Knicks were all over him.

The refs threw them both out of the game, and soon, all too soon, it was restarted. With Elwood gone it was too much a matter of me against Flynnan, and it was Flynnan's night. I couldn't hang with him. For help on offense all I had was Early, who seemed completely cowed by the Garden and baffled with Elwood gone. I tried to dump it off to him, but he'd lost sight of the basket, kept trying dumb passes instead. Whereas Flynnan had McFront, who'd found his midrange shot, and was pouring in pull-up jumpers.

They blew us out. An hour later I was sitting on the edge of my hotel bed, watching it on television. Early Natt and one of our guards were there with me, but the room was silent except for the tube. Elwood had disappeared, so we didn't have to be ashamed to watch the sportscast.

It was Vanilla Dunk all the way. He'd run straight to the press, as usual, and the tape of his interview was replayed every fifteen minutes. The commissioner had already decided: both players were available to their teams for the rest of the series. Elwood would be fined five thousand. Dunk, who'd thrown a punch, would pay fifteen thou. I'd saved Elwood ten grand by grabbing him. And probably saved Dunk a broken jaw.

They barely even mentioned the fact that we'd lost. I guess the New York press considered that pretty much a foregone conclusion.

. I flipped to MTV just in time to catch Vanilla Dunk's new video "(Dunkin') in Yo Face."

Elwood showed up just in time for the second game. I never did find out where he spent that night. For a minute I was afraid he was stoned on something—I'd seen him stoned, and gotten stoned with him, but never before a game—because he looked too happy, too loose. I even wondered for a second if he somehow thought we'd won last night.

There wasn't time to confer. He flipped a thumbs-up signal to Coach Wilder, and called Early over to him. The coach just shook his head. A minute later the refs started the game.

I put my head down and vowed to get physical with Flynnan. I wanted rebounds, I wanted blocked shots, I wanted steals. I wanted Elwood not to hate me, primarily. He still wasn't meeting my eye.

Otis missed a shot and Elwood came down with the rebound, and passed it to Early with nearly the same motion. Early ducked underneath Flynnan and jumped up to the height of the basket. Slam.

The Knicks came upcourt and put the ball in Dunk's hands. Elwood and I swarmed him. He faked a move, pivoted, then faked a pass, which shook Elwood for half a second. Half a second was all Dunk needed: he went up.

But I got my hand around the ball and stuffed his shot backward, out of his hands. It bounced upcourt, to Early, who was alone.

Slam.

The Knicks came back up, and McFront hit from outside. We took it back up and this time Elwood faked to Early and twisted inside himself for a pretty backward layup. 6–2, Visitors.

Otis brought it up for the Knicks, and flipped it to Flynnan, inside. I went up and matched his jump, forced him to dump it off or be stuffed. He looked for help, didn't find any, and Elwood took the ball away from him. Early was waiting upcourt, like a puppy dog. 8–2.

So it went for the first half. We kept Dunk frustrated with our hectoring defense, and I took my game straight to Flynnan, however bruising. McFront's hand wasn't as hot as the night before. Elwood was hyperkinetic on defense.

And on offense, we were making Early look like the star the fans back in Florida had always hoped he would be. All he had was a handful of one-on-one moves, but if you kept him from having to think about anything but the basket, he was sensational.

We ended the half with a twenty-two-point lead. The Knicks nibbled away in the second half, Otis shining like the Otis of old for a few minutes, but it was our night. We dug in on defense and finished fourteen points up. The crowd drained out of the Garden in silence. We were taking the series back to Florida tied at a game apiece. There were two games on our home court, then back to New York.

Unless somebody won two in a row.

For the third game the Knicks just looked tired. They weren't adjusting to our defensive pressure. Vanilla Dunk was wearing his cynical sneer, but you could see it drove him crazy not to be able to cut loose. The Miami crowd gave Flynnan, their ex-hero, a hard time, and he responded by getting sheepish—for the first time I felt I could actually push him around a little.

This one was Early's game. He played to the crowd, and the slams just kept getting showier. Elwood poured in a few himself, but Early was the star that night. We led all the way, and the game was over by the third quarter. Both teams pulled their regulars and started thinking about the next game.

Elwood was glowing on the bench. We all were. We had a chance to take it from them. They had to beat us tomorrow to even stay alive. This was supposed to be their year of destiny, the Vanilla Dunk Victory Tour, and we had them down, 2–1. The wild-card team.

Flynnan woke up. Dunk was still moribund, but Flynnan woke up; I knew because he started punishing me. I was taking down some rebounds, but I was paying in flesh. I looked for help, but who was going to help me? That's the horror of the center: there's just two of you seven-foot monsters out there, and you're enemies. If the other guy's a little bigger and meaner, who's going to tell him to leave you alone? Some shrimpy 6-5 guard? The Tokyo army? The ref? Your mother?

This one wasn't a game. It was a trench battle. Elwood and I were working together, stripping balls away, bottling up the middle, but there was no communication between us. Just sweat and grunts. We had to keep our eyes peeled or we'd be flattened. McFront and Dunk were both fighting to open the lanes, throwing elbows, double-faking to make sure we got our faces in the way. Where were the whistles? I'm sure the Knicks were asking the same question at their end. The refs were letting us duke it out.

It was Knicks 34, Heat 30 late in the second quarter: a defensive struggle. We'd forced the Knicks into our game, and they were playing it. Every time Early touched the ball he was mobbed. He'd dump it back out and our guards would chuck it up from the outside and hope for the best.

Most of our points belonged to Elwood, who was scoring by grabbing rebounds and muscling back up for the layup.

We were holding on until two minutes before the half, when Dunk broke loose for a couple in a row, and we went to the lockers down eight points.

Elwood stood to one side, a wild look in his eyes. He wasn't playing coach anymore; he was too far inside himself. He and Dunk had been in each other's faces every minute of the first half, and I could feel the hate burning off Elwood's skin, like gasoline vapor. I could almost imagine that Elwood would rather lose this one and take it back to New York, just to maximize his crazed masochistic war with Dunk, just to push it to the very edge.

I personally had a strong preference for ending it here.

Coach Wilder, seeing that Elwood wasn't receiving, looked over at me. I shrugged. The rest of the team milled nervously, waiting for someone to break the silence.

"Okay, boys," said Coach Wilder courageously. "Let this get away and it's just another tied series going back to New York. That's handing it to them."

No one spoke. Elwood's foot was tapping out accompaniment to some internal rhythm.

"You're only eight points back," said the coach. "Just keep tying them up on defense. They'll turn it over when they get tired."

With his voice trailing away, he sounded like he didn't believe himself. I felt like patting him on the head and sending him to the showers. The fact was it was Elwood's team now, and Elwood didn't give halftime pep talks. We would all have to feed off his energy on the floor; it would happen there or it wouldn't happen at all.

We drifted apart, and what seemed like seconds later we were back on the court. The ball was ours; Elwood hit from midway out and we fell back on defense. We stuck to our one plan, of course: I caged Vanilla Dunk with my long arms, and Elwood harassed the ball from underneath. This time the gamble worked, and we forced a bad pass, which one of our guards picked up. He found Early, and Early found the net. We'd closed the gap to four points.

And that's where it stayed. We all gritted our teeth and went back to the trenches; even Vanilla Dunk and Early were playing defense. Both sides would have fouled out if the refs hadn't been squelching the whistle. We forced turnovers, then turned it over ourselves, rolled our eyes, and fell back for defense again. Elwood was a maniac on rebounds, but he'd pass it up to Early, and Early would disappear in a cloud of Knick uniforms. Otis stripped the ball from him with two seconds left in the third quarter and chucked up an improbable three-point shot from midcourt which only hit net, putting them up seven points as the buzzer for the fourth sounded.

At the start of the fourth Elwood began trying to do it all, to outrebound everybody at *both* ends of the court, to steal the ball, pass it to Early, then run up and set a pick for Early and rebound Early's shot if he missed. I watched in amazement, near total exhaustion myself just from our frantic play on the defensive end. In frustration with the Knicks' defensive adjustments he started going up himself, with his usual too-powerful stuff moves, scoring some points but committing fouls the refs couldn't ignore. Still, he bulled us to three points back, then doubled over with a leg cramp.

Coach Wilder called a time-out. Elwood limped back to the bench.

"Okay, Elwood, you got us close. Now you better sit."

"Uh-uh," said Elwood. "I'm stayin' in. Listen, Early—"

Early leaned in, his eyes wide.

"You gotta figure out one new trick, 'cause they're bumping you off, man."

"What?" said Early in his high, frightened voice.

"Pass off when you go up now. Don't shoot. Find the big man here." Elwood jerked his thumb at me. "He's big and white, you can't miss him, man. Just throw it up to him every time you get a clean line."

"Elwood," I began to complain, "I'm not like you. I can't go back and forth. I won't make it back on defense if I'm up fighting with Flynnan under their basket."

"Don't go up under their basket," he said. "Shoot from wherever you are when you get the ball, man."

"What?"

"I seen your jump shot, Lassner. Just shoot."

The time-out was over. Elwood hobbled out, massaging his own thigh, and we took the ball up. We fed it in to Early and he drew three men. He spun out and five hands went up between him and the basket.

He didn't try and shoot over the hands. Instead he turned and lobbed a clumsy pass high in the air to me, halfway back to our end of the court.

"Shoot!" hissed Elwood.

I tossed it up, not even noticing which side of the three-point line I was on. It went in.

I panted a thank-you prayer and zeroed in on the ball, which was in Flynnan's hands. I threw myself in his path and forced him to give it up, miraculously avoiding destruction in the process. Elwood followed the ball out to Vanilla Dunk, who pumped, pivoted, pumped, head-faked, shrugged, anything to try to get out of Elwood's cage. He lifted the ball up and I batted it out of bounds.

Elwood stole the inbound pass and scored on a solo drive for a layup.

The Knicks brought it up and Otis, looking frustrated with Dunk, shot from outside. He missed. Elwood directed the ball to Early, who drove to the basket and was surrounded there. He threw it out to me where I stood at the top of the key. "Shoot!" said Elwood again. The ball floated up out of my hands and hit.

Tie game, four minutes left.

Elwood got too excited and fouled McFront on the next

possession. McFront, ever solid, hit both from the line, putting the Knicks up two. Elwood brought the ball up to midcourt, then passed it directly to me and nodded.

Swish. My jump shot was on. Practice, I guess.

We traded turnovers again, and then the Knicks called a time-out with just over two minutes left. Their season was getting very, very small. We only went halfway to the bench and then just hovered there, waiting for the Knicks to come back out. There wasn't anything to say. We were too pumped up to huddle and trade homilies. Too much in the zone.

The Knicks brought it up and Flynnan staked out prime real estate under the net. I sighed and went in to try and box him out. He got the ball and I went up with him, tipped the shot away. Elwood took it and charged upcourt, slamming it home at the other end.

Since he was all the way up there anyway he decided to steal the inbound pass and do it again, and we suddenly had a four-point lead.

But Elwood was tired, and at the wrong end of the floor. They sent Vanilla Dunk up. I tried to stop him alone; we both jumped. I landed what seemed like a couple of seconds before he did. His jam was a poster shot, I heard later. I sure didn't see it.

We came up again and sent Early in to try and answer. He got caught in traffic and bailed it out to me, and I shot from where I stood all alone, in three-point territory.

That made four in a row for me and a five-point lead for the team.

They answered with a quick basket. So quick that I glanced at the clock; we were in a position to run the clock out. I brought it up slow, dribbling with my big body curled protectively around the ball.

"Nobody foul!" I heard Coach Wilder yell from the sidelines. Thanks, coach. I passed it to Elwood. He passed it to one of our guards, who passed it back to me. Flynnan lunged for the ball, and I passed it away again. It got passed around the circuit, everybody touching it except Early, who wouldn't have known what to do with it. He only existed in two dimensions, up and down. Time was beyond him.

The ball came back to me with two seconds on the shot clock. What the hell, I thought, and chucked it up.

Swish.

We'd won. Five points up with 16 seconds. No way for them to come back. The Knicks milked it, of course, using two time-outs, scoring once, but two commercials later we got official confirmation. When the final buzzer sounded we had a nice, healthy three-point edge.

The locker room was mayhem. All the Disney executive people I'd managed never to meet wanted to shake my hand. The media swarmed, medialike. Some beer company exec gave Early Natt an award for series MVP and they stuck a mike in his face and Early just grinned and made this sort of bubbling sound with his lips, ignoring the questions. Another bunch of TV people isolated me and Elwood by our lockers, and I readied myself to do the talking once again.

"Well, Elwood, care to break your media silence for once?"

Elwood paused, then grinned. "Sure, asshole, let's break some silence. What you wanna know?"

The reporter clung to his pasted-on smile. "Uh, you were a real leader out there, Elwood. Some would say the MVP belongs to you. You took an unconventional mix of talents and made them work together—"

Elwood stuck his big finger against the reporter's chest. "You wanna know who the star of this team is?"

"Uh—"

"This dude here, man. He's taught himself to play without sampling, man, 'cause the skills they gave him sucked, and he didn't even tell anybody. Me, Early, Vanilla Fucking Dunk, all them other dudes are playing with exosuits, but not my man Lassner, man. He's a defensive star. He can hang with the exosuits, man, and that's a rare thing." He laughed. "He's also got this funny jump shot ain't too bad. Big white elbows stickin' out all over the place, but it ain't too bad. No suit for that either."

They turned to me. I nodded and shrugged and looked back to Elwood.

"How does it feel beating Michael Jordan?" The question was directed at either one of us, but Elwood picked it up again.

"Didn't beat Michael Jordan," he said angrily. "Beat Vanilla Dunk. If that was Jordan we wouldn't have beat him."

"What's going to become of your feud?"

Elwood's face went through a quick series of expressions; first angry, then sarcastic, then sealed up, like he wasn't going to talk any more. Then he went past that, smiling at himself for a minute before answering the question.

What came out was a strangely heartfelt jumble of sports clichés. I don't mean to be insulting when I say that I don't think I ever saw Elwood speak from a deeper place within himself than at that moment. I really do think he was the last modernist in a sport gone completely post-modern.

"There ain't no feud. Alan Gornan is a rookie, man, and you got to give him time to put it together. I was honored to play alongside the man in New York and I'm honored to face him now. I hope we meet many times again—after the Heat wins this championship, that is. I'm sure he'll grow into the suit. Ain't no feud. I plan to beat the man every time I can, but when he beats me it ain't gonna be Michael Jordan then, neither, man. It's gonna be Gornan, or Dunk, or whatever he wants to call his ass, and when he does I'll

shake the dude's hand. Here, you oughta ask the big white
dufus some questions now."

That should be the end of the story, but it isn't. Elwood and
I were in a bar two hours later when the sports channel
switched to a live broadcast of Vanilla Dunk's press conference, his last with the big Knicks logo on the wall behind him.

His agent spoke first. "Mr. Gornan has reached an
agreement with United Artists Tokyo, regarding his motion
picture and recording career—"

"What about the Knicks?"

"UA Tokyo has purchased Mr. Gornan's contract from
Gulf + Western. This is a binding, five-year agreement that
guarantees Mr. Gornan eight million a year before box-of-
fice—"

"I wanted to wait till the end of the season to make this
announcement," said Dunk. "Didn't think it would come
this quick, but hey"—he paused to sneer—"that's the way
it goes. Look out, America, we're gonna make some
movies!"

"Dunk—what about basketball?"

He smirked. "That's a little rough for me, y'know?
Gotta stay pretty." He rubbed his face exaggeratedly.
"You'll see plenty of action on the screen, anyway. Might
even dunk a few." He winked.

Elwood and I sat watching, silently transfixed. The implications sank in gradually. The Jordan skills were gone;
league rules stated that they were retired with the player.
The occasion that Elwood had so slowly and painfully
risen to had vanished, been whisked away, in an instant.

"Tell us about the films," said a reporter.

"Ahh, we're still working out my character. Called
Vanilla Dunk, of course. Gonna do some fightin', some

rappin', some other stuff. Not like anything you've ever seen before, so you'll just have to wait."

"The contract includes album and video production," added the agent. "You'll be seeing Vanilla Dunk on the charts as well as on the screen."

"Your whole sports career is over, then? No championships?"

He snorted. "This is bigger than a sports career, my friend. *I'm* bigger. Besides, sports is just entertainment, anyway. I'm still in the *entertainment* business."

"Your decision anything to do with Elwood Fossett?"

He cocked his head. "Who?"

I turned away from the television. I started to speak, but stopped when I saw Elwood's expression, which was completely hollow.

And that *is* the end of the story.

I'd like to say we went on to win the championship, but life doesn't work that way. The Hyundai Celtics beat us in the next round of the playoffs. They seemed completely ready for our defense, and we were lucky to win one game. Elwood faded in and out, tantalizingly brilliant and then god-awful in the space of five minutes. The Celtics went on to lose to the Coors Suns in the final.

I myself did win a ring, later, after I was traded to the Lakers. That led indirectly to a fancy Hollywood party where I got to drunkenly tell Alan Gornan what I thought of him. I garbled my lines, but it was still pretty satisfying.

Elwood I mostly lost touch with after my trade. We partied when the Lakers went to Miami, and when the Heat came to L.A. I had him over for dinner with my second wife—an awkward scene, but we played it a few times.

When I think about what happened with him and Vanilla Dunk, I always come around to the same question. Assuming that it's right to view the whole episode as a personal battle between the two of them—who won? Sometimes I drive myself crazy with it. I mean, who came out on top, really?

Other times I conclude that there's something really pretty fundamentally stupid about the question.